THE EARTH ANGEL AWAKENING

Also by Michelle Gordon:

Earth Angel Series:

The Earth Angel Training Academy

The Earth Angel Awakening

The Other Side

The Twin Flame Reunion

The Twin Flame Retreat

The Twin Flame Resurrection

The Twin Flame Reality

The Twin Flame Rebellion

Visionary Collection:

Heaven Dot Com

The Doorway to PAM

The Elphite

I'm Here

THE EARTH ANGEL AWAKENING

MICHELLE GORDON

The Amethyst Angel

First published in Great Britain in 2012 by The Amethyst Angel
Second Edition published in 2013 by The Amethyst Angel
Third Edition published in 2017 by The Amethyst Angel

Cover Design by madappledesigns, The Amethyst Angel & Soulscape Design

ISBN: 978-1-912257-02-7

Third Edition

ACKNOWLEDGEMENTS

A massive thank you to my wonderful Angel friend, editor, colleague and life coach – Elizabeth Lockwood. She has not only made this book possible, but she has also been my supporter and cheerleader through all the tough times in the last year, and I love her dearly for all that she has done for me.

Thank you to my Earth Angel friend, Mim. Her wisdom and insight has saved me on so many occasions, and she has been a bright light in darker times. Without her guidance I would surely have been lost by now. Thank you, Mim, for your friendship. And thank you also for the lovely Angel poem.

Thank you, Kelly, my amazing Spiritual Sister. You are a beautiful Angel, and I am so very proud to be your friend.

Thank you, Liz, for your motivational talks, your networking help and for your belief and investment in me! Your encouragement, love and support means a lot to me.

Thank you, Mum, for putting up with me while I finished this book, and for all of your love and encouragement. You're an Angel.

Thank you to all my Spiritual Sisters, Kelly, Anne, Lisa and Buckso, for inspiring me and being such wonderful friends. I miss our weekly meetings!

Thank you, Annette, Dad, and Helen, for your belief in me.

Thank you to Laura at Luminous Editing, for your editorial help, it has been very much appreciated.

Thank you, Alex, for the logo designs, much appreciated!

Thank you, John C. Parkin, for your fantastic book, and your permission to mention it. Without it, I may never have got started on writing this one!

Thanks to Doreen Virtue, for her books on Earth Angels. They have been instrumental in my own Awakening. And thank you to Hay House for the permission to mention Realms of the Earth Angels by Doreen Virtue.

Thank you, DreamMoods for the dream interpretation information I needed for this book. www.dreammoods.com

Thank you, Jack Shalatain, for your incredible illustrations of Velvet, Amethyst and Aria, and for your encouragement and belief in my books.

Jason Mordecai, what can I say? You are an artistic genius. Working with you has been fantastic.

Thank you to HelpX, for their amazing website that provides people with the means to travel the world on a very small budget! And thank you to hosts Debbie and Daniel in Vimoutiers, for allowing their Vegetarian Hotel and restaurant to feature in the book:
www.helpx.net www.maisonduvert.com

And finally, Jon, thank you for sharing your life, your soul and your love with me over the last two years. They have been the best of my existence, I love you.

This book is dedicated to my Twin Flame.
Without him, this book wouldn't have been possible.

CHAPTER ONE

"Fuck it!"

"Fuck it!"

"Fuck it!"

As the cacophony of voices rose and fell around her, Violet couldn't stop herself from laughing. She never thought in a million years that she would ever find herself in a roomful of women shouting profanities.

Before long the others were also giggling, and in the end, they were gasping for breath, tears rolling down their cheeks.

Once they'd all calmed down, Violet went out into the kitchen to boil the kettle, leaving the others to talk about all the things they'd said 'fuck it' to that week. As Violet got the mismatched, chipped cups out, and made the hot drinks, she wondered if she should suggest a new theme tonight to her Spiritual Sisters. For a few nights now, Violet had been haunted by recurring dreams about a certain person, a person who Violet thought she had put out of her mind. Obviously her subconscious mind was holding on, the question was, why?

After Amy had helped Violet carry the drinks into the living room, and everyone was settled and munching on

Violet's homemade chocolate chip cookies, Violet brought the subject up.

"Now that we have thoroughly embraced the 'fuck it' way, I thought it might be time to start a new topic. I know we've dabbled a little with dream interpretation, but I thought it would be a good idea if, for a whole week, we write down our dreams, in as much detail as possible. Then next week, we could take it in turns to read them out, and everyone could try to interpret them. I've got a few books on the subject, of course, but I think it would be fun to see if any of us can decipher the meanings ourselves. So, what do you think?"

Amy, though the shyest of the group, was the first to respond. "I think it's a great idea, I've been having some pretty crazy dreams lately."

"I think it sounds like a great idea, but my biggest problem will be remembering to write them down quick enough," Leila said.

"Put a notebook next to your bed," Violet suggested. "That way, you can write them down as soon as you wake up."

"I'll give it a try," Keeley said. "Though I'm not sure if I want to delve too deeply into what my subconscious is doing... my waking thoughts are dodgy enough!"

"Yes, we know, darling. Half of those dodgy thoughts make up your daily conversation," Beattie remarked dryly, reaching for another cookie.

"Hey!" Keeley exclaimed. "I'm not *that* bad!"

"Oh yes, you are!" the rest of the group chimed in together, bursting into laughter at the expression of mock hurt on Keeley's face.

"Oh, come on, Keel," Leila said, "You've always had a dirty mind."

Keeley sighed and gave up on trying to protest. "Okay, okay, so I'm no angel, I admit it."

"So, a dream diary this week then?" Fay confirmed, tucking a red curl behind her ear as she took a sip of tea.

"Yes, I think it would be a good exercise for all of us," Violet said, her mind already running through the few details she could remember of the previous night's dream.

"I don't know about anyone else, but I have to get up early for work tomorrow, so I'd better make a move."

Violet glanced at the clock then nodded at Amy, slightly surprised. Their weekly meetings always went far too fast. Violet walked Amy to the door and gave her a hug before she left. "Call me tomorrow!" she called after her friend, slightly worried by the conversation they'd had earlier about Amy's boyfriend. She hoped everything would turn out okay; Amy was one of the nicest people she'd ever met.

One by one, the Sisters trickled out the door, heading out into the mild summer's evening. Once alone in her little house, Violet began to clear away the debris, but then decided to say 'fuck it' and leave it until the next day. She locked up, switched off the lights and went upstairs. She got into her cosiest pair of pyjamas and settled down into her bed to watch a movie. Less than halfway through, Violet felt her eyelids sliding shut, and before she could fall asleep completely, she switched off the TV and her bedside lamp. Within seconds, she was asleep.

* * *

With the fading remnants of her dream set precariously on the edge of her consciousness, Violet reached out blindly for something to write the details in, but when her search lasted for more than a minute, the dream faded and she was left with just one word to write down: Lyle. Why was she dreaming about him all the time? It made no sense. Yes, she had liked him when they were younger. Yes, she'd even had a crush on him. But she'd given up on the notion of them being together a long time ago. Hadn't she? Shaking her head, Violet tucked her notebook away in her bedside table, threw the covers aside and got up.

The rest of the day passed in a blur as she went through the motions of her normal working day as a data entry clerk in a busy council office. The work was undemanding and boring, but at least it meant she could daydream, and of course, pay the bills. Stepping off the bus at the end of the day, Violet made her way home, and wondered what she could possibly do about Lyle. There must be a reason why he was haunting her dreams now. She hadn't thought of him in quite some time. The problem was that she had lost touch with him years ago. She wasn't quite sure how to go about contacting him. Reaching her front door, still lost in thought, Violet jumped when she heard a voice call her name. She turned to see her neighbour waving at her from next door. She crossed the lawn, heading towards Kendrick.

"Hey, Kend, what's up?"

"I've got a parcel here for you," Kendrick replied, disappearing into the house for a moment, and returning with a large box. "Didn't think you'd have time to get to the post office so I offered to take it for you."

Violet smiled at her neighbour. "Thanks for that," she said, taking the box, which despite its size was quite light. "I wouldn't have had time until the weekend. Even then it would have been a little tricky."

Kendrick smiled, her lined face wrinkling even more. "Don't mention it, dear. Good day at work?"

Violet shrugged. "Same as usual, nothing terribly exciting."

Kendrick tutted. "You need to find something that does excite you. Don't just get by like I did, only to get to old age and find that you haven't achieved all that you set out to."

"I know, there's so much I would love to do, I just don't

know how to-"

"Ah ah," Kendrick interrupted, holding her hand out. "Forget the *how*, focus on the *what*. The how is for God to figure out."

Violet chuckled. "I guess so."

Kendrick winked. "I know so. I better go, dear Violet. Don't you forget what I said now, it's important."

"I won't, and thanks again for the parcel."

Kendrick nodded and closed the door, leaving Violet feeling slightly perplexed on the doorstep. Though she'd exchanged pleasantries with her neighbour before, she'd never had such a philosophical discussion with her. Shrugging her shoulders slightly, Violet shifted the box in her arms and headed back to her own front door.

Once she had tidied the carnage from the previous night, done the washing up, got her dinner in the oven and made a cup of tea, Violet sat on the sofa and finally got round to opening the parcel. She'd been racking her brains for what it might be, having no recollection of ordering anything, but she couldn't think of what it might contain. There was no return address either, which was odd, as usually the post office insisted on such things. After wrestling with the string for a few seconds, Violet gave up and went to get the kitchen scissors, which made short work of the neat packaging. After pulling out all the screwed up newspaper and bubble wrap, Violet finally saw the contents. She frowned as she lifted out the small, ornately carved jewellery box. The outer packaging was far too big for such a tiny box. She wondered why the person had spent so much on postage by over-packaging it. Pushing the now-empty cardboard box off the coffee table, Violet set the jewellery box down. She looked at the carvings more closely, and could make out mermaids and tiny seashells on it.

Taking a deep breath, and unsure as to why she felt such a huge sense of expectation, Violet gently undid the metal clasp and opened the lid. Inside was a small leather pouch. Hesitantly, Violet reached in and pulled the pouch out, feeling a little silly for being afraid of a jewellery box and a pouch, but at the same time, inexplicably feeling as though everything was about to change.

Slowly, she pulled the cords of the pouch and shook the contents into her left hand. A leather cord with a small wooden pendant fell onto her palm. She turned over the simple pebble of smooth wood to see a rune on the other side. Unsure as to which rune it was, or what it meant, Violet jumped up from the sofa and crossed the room to her bookcase, which was bulging with books on every spiritual subject under the sun.

Years ago, she had bought a handbook on runes, intending to study them and use them as a form of divination, but as with most other things, it was something she had yet to do.

After searching the spines for several minutes, Violet finally found the small pink handbook, and settled back onto the sofa with it. She sipped her cold cup of tea and started flicking through the pages, until she managed to locate the rune symbol in the book; it was called Laguz. She scanned the meaning of the rune, but found nothing that particularly fitted her life at the moment. The only interesting connection was that its meaning was to do with the God of the Ocean, and the box it came in had mermaids carved on it.

But Violet wasn't entirely sure what that meant. What was she supposed do with it? Who had sent it? Surely it must mean something. Violet didn't believe in randomness - everything happened for a reason. But she usually found that the reason didn't always surface straight away. Violet closed the book and set it on the coffee table. She studied the pendant carefully. Its smooth, worn edges and slightly frayed leather cord suggested it had been well-worn, it certainly wasn't new. Violet sighed. She really wished that some signs from the Universe came with an instruction manual.

Deciding to see what would happen, Violet lifted the pendant up to her neck and tied it firmly. The rune felt warm when it settled on her chest. She felt a little deflated by the rush of expectation and the pure confusion that followed. The oven timer rang then, making her jump. She shook herself and went to get her dinner.

* * *

The week passed uneventfully. The only change was that Violet's dreams had become more vivid, and she had managed to record a few more details, ready for her Spiritual Sisters to decipher in their meeting. Despite having a few more details, and trying to interpret them using the books she had on the subject, Violet was no closer to the meaning of them. She continued to wear the rune pendant, but so far nothing unusual had happened; no one had even noticed it. On Saturday morning Violet was just hovering on the edges of consciousness, having just had her most vivid dream yet, when she was jolted fully awake by the doorbell. Groaning, she hauled herself out of bed. She groaned even louder when she saw it was only eight. Far too early to be up on a weekend.

Tugging her dressing gown on as she went, Violet made it to her front door and scrabbled around in her coat pocket for her keys. When she opened the door, her vivid dreams and her mumblings about being woken early flew out of her head.

"Oh, Amy, what's wrong?"

Without a word, her friend just shrugged, her tear-stained face speaking volumes. Violet stepped back a little and gestured for her to come in. Once inside, Amy collapsed onto the sofa and more tears rolled down her cheeks. Violet gave her a box of tissues then went to put the kettle on.

How many times would they go through this routine before Amy finally left her boyfriend, Violet wondered. She wished Amy could see just how amazing she was, so that she would finally understand that she deserved so much better than her lying, cheating boyfriend who obviously didn't respect her. A few minutes later, two mugs of tea in hand, Violet returned to the lounge where Amy had already gone through several tissues, but at least seemed to have calmed down slightly. She handed Amy her tea, then settled into the chair and waited for Amy to speak.

"He didn't come home last night," Amy began. "He says he stayed at a friend's house, but he absolutely stank of beer when he came in this morning. Beer, and, and, perfume." Amy's voice broke on the last word.

Violet reached over to squeeze her friend's hand.

"He was supposed to be doing a shift at work today. Overtime. Because we need to pay for the car repairs, but he was so out of it this morning, he just went to bed. I had to call his manager and lie about him being ill." Amy looked up from the tissue she was shredding. "I just don't know what to do, Violet. He swears he's not seeing anyone else, but this is the third time that he's stayed out all night and not told me."

"Amy," Violet began gently. "You know how I feel about him. I've been telling you for a while now that you deserve so much better. He's not treating you the way you should be treated. You need to stand up for yourself."

Amy nodded, her lip quivering. "I know, and I know that you're right, I just don't know how to do that."

Violet smiled a little, remembering Kendrick's words from earlier in the week. She repeated them now for Amy. "Forget the *how*, focus on the *what*. The how is for God to figure out."

Amy looked at her, a little puzzled. "God? I didn't think you believed in him?"

"Okay then, the how is for the Goddess to figure out," Violet corrected, a smile playing on her lips. "Or even, for the Universe to figure out. Basically, the how is not something you need to worry about. Just figure out what it is you want, and it will happen."

Amy frowned. "That's the problem, I think. I don't even know what it is that I do want."

"You want to be happy, right?"

Amy nodded, and took a sip of her tea.

"Then focus on that. Focus on feeling happy. The more you focus on the feeling of happiness, the more things will come along that make you feel happy."

"I can do that."

"Good, it's a good start. Then hopefully you'll believe me when I say you need to ditch that lying good-for-nothing idiot and get yourself a man who not only loves and adores you, but treats you like the amazing person you are."

Amy smiled at her friend. "Thank you, Violet. I'm sorry I ruined your lie-in."

Violet rolled her eyes. "Don't worry about that, you know you are welcome here any time you want. What's mine is yours, okay? We're Sisters after all." She got up and sat next to Amy, pulling her into a hug.

A few moments later, Violet pulled back and jumped up, pulling Amy with her. "Right, that's enough wallowing, we're going shopping."

Amy laughed. "Okay, can I just use the bathroom first?"

Violet gestured at her dressing gown. "Please do, I've got to get some clothes on anyway. I don't think I should go out looking like this, do you?"

"Oh, I don't know, I think you could start a new trend."

"Uh huh, sure." Violet headed for the stairs. "Please promise me you will never become a fashion designer."
"Promise!" Amy called after her.

* * *

After a ridiculously giant hot chocolate each with marshmallows, cream and a chocolate flake on top, Violet and Amy set off for the book shop, planning on sitting in the Mind, Body, Spirit section and looking through the extensive selection on offer. By the time they'd settled themselves into the comfortable chairs, Violet noticed that Amy was much more relaxed.

They both chose several titles, then set about flicking through, seeing if they were worth purchasing. Sometimes they just read the relevant parts, then put the books back. But Violet could never resist buying another new book. This time, she had pretty much cleaned out the dream section, but after half an hour, she was no closer to deciphering her dream.

"Anything good?" she asked Amy, who seemed to be reading a small book very intently.

"Actually, yeah, I think I might get this one." She held it up so Violet could read the cover.

"*Realms of the Earth Angels*, Doreen Virtue," she read aloud. "What's it about?"

"It's basically describing different categories of people who have been born on Earth in this lifetime, but in past lives are from different realms."

"Different realms?"

"You know, from the Angelic Realm, the Elemental Realm or even another planet."

"Sounds quite interesting. So which planet are you from?" Violet teased.

Amy stuck her tongue out at her friend. "I don't think

I'm an alien. Actually, there is a category I fit into."

"Yeah? Which one?"

"The Angelic one."

Violet smiled. "Well, I could have told you that, Amy. You're one of the sweetest people I've ever met. I've no doubt that you could have been an Angel in a former life."

"Regardless, I think I might buy this one."

"Not much point now is there? You've nearly read the whole thing already," Violet teased.

"Have you found anything interesting?"

Violet stacked the dream books neatly and sighed. "No, not really."

"You've really got into dream interpretation, haven't you? Why are you so interested all of a sudden?"

"I keep having these really vivid dreams about someone I knew a long time ago. And to be honest, I just have no idea what they mean." She stood and replaced the books on the shelf. "And these books don't seem to be able to tell me either."

Amy set her book down. "Are they good dreams or bad ones?"

Violet thought for a moment. "Good ones. I think."

"And what do you feel when you wake up from them?"

Longing, Violet wanted to say. But didn't. "I don't know, I guess I feel a little empty. And a little lonely. But strangely happy at the same time. Do you think it's just because I've been single for so long? My subconscious is trying to tell me to get out there and meet someone?"

"Hmm, it could be. Though surely if that were it, then you'd be dreaming about all different guys. But you said it was just one specific guy?"

Violet nodded. "Yeah, just one in particular. Thing is, until the dreams, I hadn't thought of him in years. We went to school together for a few years, I had a bit of a crush on him, but then I moved away and I haven't seen him since."

Amy sat back, deep in thought. "What happens in the dreams?"

"In some of them we're swimming in the ocean, and he disappears. I wake up wondering where he went. But we were having a great time up until that point. In others we're walking on the beach, in another, we're in a garden."

"Are they places that you know?"

Violet shook her head. "No, they're not real places. I mean, they feel familiar, but then everything is always slightly odd in dreams, isn't it? In your dream you think it's your house, but when you wake up and remember, the house is nothing like yours."

"Yeah, I know what you mean. Aside from the guy, is there anything else that's constant throughout the dreams?"

Violet searched her now-vague memories of the dreams then shook her head. "I don't think so. I've been trying to write the details down as soon as I wake up, but for some reason by the time I grab the pen and open the notebook, they've pretty much faded away already." Violet glanced down at Amy's watch. "Guess we'd better get going, I promised myself I would get on with the washing today. If I leave it any longer I'll have no clean pants left."

Amy laughed and also checked the time. "I'd better get back, anyway. Danny might be awake by now."

"Just promise me you won't take any more crap from him, okay? And I'm serious about my place being yours. If you need to get away for a while, come and stay with me. He needs to understand that the way he's behaving is unacceptable."

Amy sighed, her spirit deflating a little. "I know." She put all of the books back apart from the one she was reading. "I'm going to get this one. You getting any?"

Violet shook her head. "Nah, haven't found one that

appeals today, bizarrely enough. Though I wouldn't mind reading yours when you're done. I'd love to know if I'm from another planet."

Amy grinned, and headed for the checkout. "Well, I could tell you that, I don't need a book to confirm that you're an alien."

* * *

By the third load of washing, Violet was getting bored. Even listening to her favourite CD wasn't making the chore any more interesting. She wished Amy hadn't gone home. They could have watched movies and done Angel Oracle readings for each other. As much as she liked her own space, living on her own could get quite lonely and boring at times. It wasn't that she wanted to be single, she just hadn't met anyone that she really liked yet.

In fact, she sometimes wondered if she ever would. Perhaps she was just too fussy. Years of watching romantic movies and reading romance novels had left her with somewhat unrealistic expectations when it came to relationships. That was probably why she just didn't understand Amy at times. Why on Earth would anyone choose to be with someone who was so unhealthy for them? Someone so incompatible and disrespectful? There were millions of people in the world, why settle for someone who made you feel like shit on a daily basis? It certainly was a mystery to Violet. But then, maybe that was why she was still single at the age of twenty five; she was waiting for the perfect person, and he just didn't exist.

Feeling quite depressed, Violet dug some ice cream out of the freezer and abandoned the washing. She settled on the sofa in front of her favourite film, *Practical Magic*, and proceeded to eat an entire tub of mint chocolate chip.

It had just reached Violet's favourite part, (when the

cop said that he had wished for Sally, too), when the phone rang, making Violet jump. She put down the empty tub, paused the movie and crossed the room to where the cordless phone sat in its holder.

"Hello?" she said, after pressing the green button. "Oh hey, Mum, how's it going? Yes, yes, I'm looking after myself," Violet said, looking guiltily at the empty ice cream tub on the coffee table. "I've spent most of the day doing the housework." Violet sighed as she listened to her mother ramble on.

"Yes, Mum, I know I need to get myself a nice young man, and I know I need to get out more. But most of my friends are in their thirties or forties and are either attached or have kids. They're not exactly up for going out on the pull, you know? Yes, I know that there's always the internet, but you know I haven't exactly had much luck finding anyone on there. I mean seriously, remember that guy with the awful accent and bad skin? I had to pretend to be ill just to get rid of him. It was a nightmare."

Violet settled back on the sofa and closed her eyes as her mother continued to lecture her. "Look, Mum, I have to go, I promised Amy I'd give her a ring tonight, she was having rather a bad day. Yes, she is still with him. No, I don't know why she hasn't left him yet. Okay, great, speak to you soon, love you, bye." Violet pressed the red button and put the phone on the table. She sat and stared at the screen for a while, at Sandra Bullock's frozen, anguished expression.

Feeling a little restless, Violet switched off the TV and retrieved her laptop from the bag by the door. Within minutes she was logging on to the internet. She figured it couldn't hurt to just take a quick look at some of the more popular dating sites. Just for a laugh of course.

Two hours later, Violet blinked tiredly at the hundredth profile she'd looked at. Maybe she was just destined to be single forever. Were there any normal guys out there? Ones that didn't love football or enjoy dressing up as women on the weekends? Violet was seriously beginning to doubt that she would ever find someone she liked. Maybe she should just make someone up so that her mother would get off her back. Violet sighed, it would never work; her mum knew her too well. She would see through the lies instantly.

Closing down the laptop in defeat, Violet took the ice cream tub out to the kitchen and placed it in the sink. As she turned away, something moving outside caught her attention. Unsure if it was just part of her own reflection she had seen in the window, Violet switched off the fluorescent light and moved slowly back towards the window, her eyes adjusting to the darkness. There it was again. Violet blinked, wondering if she was so tired that she was seeing things. She inched closer still, but her movement must have made it aware of her presence, because in a second, it was gone. Violet rubbed her eyes. It must have been a moth or a dragonfly or something. Though dragonflies didn't normally come out at night, did they? Violet shook her head. She needed to get some sleep. All these books and films about the spiritual and occult were beginning to make her a little crazy.

Because there was absolutely no possible way that she could have just seen a tiny green faerie flying around just outside her window. No way at all.

CHAPTER TWO

"She saw me! She actually saw me! Can you believe it?"

Linen blinked rapidly as he tried to focus on Aria, who was flying around him in dizzying circles.

"Wasn't that kind of the point?" he asked, closing his eyes before he felt the need to throw up.

Aria came to a sudden halt. "Yeah, I guess it was, but to be honest, I didn't expect her to actually see me. I mean, it's supposed to be quite hard for old humans, isn't it? To see us?"

Linen opened his eyes and smiled at Aria. "Well yes, but Velvet isn't that old yet, she's only in her twenties. She must be more Awake than we thought. Having Gold's friend step in and open her eyes two years ago really did help though. He definitely set her on the spiritual path. The Angels had been trying to get through to her for years before that, but she'd closed off from them completely. She didn't even see Faeries when she was younger, so it's amazing that she saw you really."

"Hmm, well, I guess it won't be long now before she totally wakes up and sorts herself out. We need her for the Golden Age! Without her, the Rainbows might not be able to leave."

"I know, Aria, but we must be patient. We can't just expect Velvet to suddenly remember everything and begin the Awakening process in the rest of the humans. I mean, it's a lot to expect from just one person."

"But she ran this place while she was here," Aria said, opening her arms wide as if to encompass the whole Academy. "I'm sure she can do it there too."

Linen smiled patiently. "You've never experienced being human, so I guess I can't really expect you to fully understand. It's not like here, Aria. Or like the Elemental Realm. It's dense and full of negativity and problems. Things aren't manifested instantly; it takes time for things to develop. And it's all too easy for humans to find ways to escape their purpose and bury themselves in meaningless things, or worse, in harmful things that numb them to what's truly real."

Aria sighed. "I guess maybe I should have given the human thing a go, but it all just sounds too depressing! Why on Earth the Rainbows want to go there, I have no idea."

"For the same reason all the Earth Angels, Indigos and Crystal Children wanted to go - to help the humans experience the Golden Age."

"If the Golden Age doesn't happen though, what happens to the humans?"

"Without the Awakening, the humans will eventually kill all resources on the planet, kill each other and then die out completely."

"So that's the worst thing? That all humans would die?"

"Yes it is."

"That's not so bad then. I mean, there's nothing wrong with dying. The Fifth Dimension is pretty cool, if you ask me."

Linen laughed. "You're right, there is nothing wrong with dying, the Angels are great company. But it would be a tragedy if the human race ceased to exist."

"Why?"

"Because for starters, it would mean that the entire Faerie race would be extinguished. I mean, if there is no Earth, then there's no Elemental Realm, either. The Angels would be out of work too, because there would be no one to guide, or to save. The Starpeople would just stick to their own planets I guess, but the Merpeople wouldn't have a home either, so they'd all die too."

Aria's face fell further and further as Linen detailed the drastic consequences of losing the human race. "So if the humans are all on the Other Side, then everyone else is too? What does that mean? That no one or nothing really exists? What about other planets though? Aliens would still exist, and some of them are pretty human-like, Amethyst told me. She said that Earth wasn't the only place with humans on it."

"And she was right. But just because there are other planets out there with humans on, doesn't mean it's not worth saving Earth. That would be like saying that there are plenty of other Faeries out there, why save you? Why keep you alive?"

"Because I'm special! I'm unique! And besides, you'd be really sad without me!"

"All valid points. Don't you think that Earth is also special and unique?"

"Hmm, you could be right. Though I do think humans could be just a little more cheerful. Why do they have to be so serious all the time?"

"I agree with you there. They could do with laughing more and worrying less. Hopefully the Earth Angel Faeries will all wake up and bring more light and laughter and fun to the human race."

"I'm sure they will! We Faeries certainly know how to have fun! Speaking of which," Aria said, hovering closer to where Linen was sat at his desk. "Are we done for the day? Because I can think of much more fun things to do right now than work."

Linen put down the papers he had in his hand and flew up to join Aria. "Me too."

* * *

"Right then," Violet said, looking around at her fellow Spiritual Sisters. "To make this a little less embarrassing, I've decided that we should each write down a dream that we've had this week that we want to interpret. I will read each of them out in turn, and we will try to decipher them as a group. That way, no one will know whose dream it is. I think, also, it will make the interpretation less biased, as we all know each other quite well, so it'll stop us from making guesses based on what we know about each other. Sound fair?"

Everyone nodded, and Violet handed out a sheet of paper and a pen to each woman. While they were busy scribbling, Violet went out to the kitchen to make the drinks. After a few minutes, Amy joined her.

"I really think you need to read this," Amy said, handing Violet the small purple book she'd bought on the weekend. "I read it in a couple of hours, it's brilliant. I think it may even surprise you a little."

Violet took the book and smiled. "Thanks, Amy, I could do with some new reading material. Sorry we haven't had a chance to chat since Saturday. How are things going with Danny?"

Amy shrugged. "The same as usual. I haven't mentioned Friday night and neither has he. We've just fallen back into our normal routine."

Violet shook her head. "I just don't know how you manage to do that. I would have been dying to say something by now. I mean surely it would be healthier to have a blazing row and get it all out into the open, than to just let it simmer under the surface?"

"You're probably right, but I just know that somehow he'd turn it all around so it would end up being my fault. You know what he's like."

"Yeah, I do, and that's why I can't stand him. I'm sorry, Amy, but I really can't."

Amy nodded, but didn't say any more. All of her family felt the same way, but she couldn't help it, she still loved Danny, despite everything he had done, despite the way he treated her.

They re-joined the rest of the group, who were having a noisy conversation about men. It took a few minutes, but Violet eventually managed to collect in their papers and quiet them down so she could read out the first dream.

"Okay then," she said, squinting at the almost illegible scrawl on the paper. "I'm in school again, I'm in the middle of an exam, and my pencil keeps breaking. I keep asking for a new one, but every one of them breaks until I run out of time and all I've written is my name." Violet looked up at the group. "Any ideas?"

"Hmm, being back in school usually signifies some kind of innocence? A regression to childhood, the feeling of not being in control of your own life?" Fay mused.

"Exams are stressful, so maybe there's a particularly stressful event or time that the person doesn't feel in control of, or maybe feels too ill-equipped to deal with?" Keeley added.

Violet looked down at the paper again, recognising the handwriting as Amy's. "Or maybe it's the Universe's way of telling this person that she's taking the wrong exam. The broken pencil represents all the problems, the obstacles. If she walked out of the exam, then she would ultimately be happier."

"Or maybe she hasn't learnt what she needs to yet, to pass the exam. Maybe she needs to do a little more studying before she is able to do it," Amy said.

Violet shook her head. "I don't think so. If it was a case of needing to learn more, then she'd be failing the exam not because her pencil kept breaking, but because she couldn't remember what she was supposed to write. I really think it's just the wrong exam."

"How do you know? What do the dream books say?" Amy asked, pointing to the books on the table.

Leila, who had been listening to the exchange with interest, was the first to reach over for one of the dream books. "Let me see," she said, flicking through. "What should I look for, exams? Broken pencils? Failing?"

"Try exams first," Violet decided, setting down the papers for a moment, while she sipped her tea and bit into a piece of sponge cake.

"Okay then. Ah, exams," Leila said, finding the right page. "Dreams that involve taking and failing an exam are an indication of a lack of self-esteem and believing the worst about yourself. Feelings of being unworthy or undeserving are linked with such dreams. You are worried about failing to meet others' expectations of you."

Throughout the interpretation, Amy's frown got deeper. Violet caught her friend's eye and raised her eyebrows. Amy nodded slightly.

"Right, well we haven't got all night, so let's move onto the next one," Violet said, picking up the next sheet of paper, and recognising the handwriting as her own. She took a deep breath. "I've had several dreams about a guy that I went to school with. We are together in different places, always as a couple, always happy."

Violet looked up from the paper to see the rest of the group waiting expectantly.

"That's it?" Keeley asked. "What are we supposed to

interpret from that?"

"The person whose dream it is could give us more information if they wanted to," Fay said, looking around the room.

Violet sighed. "Okay, it's mine. I'm sorry I haven't added much detail. Truth is, I just can't remember the details when I wake up. Which is weird, because the dreams are so vivid at the time. They feel so real. But as soon as I open my eyes and grab the pen, there are very few details left. Other than it's always the same guy, in different places. Though the beach has always featured more than the other places."

Leila immediately started flicking through the dream book again. Keeley looked thoughtful for a minute.

"Who was the guy? A friend?"

"He was a friend, yes. I had a bit of a crush on him, I suppose. But I haven't seen him in years, and I haven't even really thought about him, either. Until these dreams."

"According to this book, the beach signifies the two different states of mind: the sand is the material and the sea is the emotional and spiritual. Umm, were you looking at the sea or towards the land?"

Violet frowned, trying to picture the scene. "Mostly towards the sea, I think."

"Looking out towards the sea indicates that unknown and major changes are going to happen in your life."

"Maybe you're going to hook up with this old friend?" Keeley suggested.

Violet shook her head. "I doubt that, he's probably forgotten that I even exist by now."

"Maybe you are supposed to contact him though," Beattie said. "I mean, there must be a reason why it's always him you dream about. Have you thought about looking him up?"

"How would I do that? I didn't really keep in touch with anyone from school. To be honest, I never really got on with any of them much."

"You could try Googling him."

Violet raised an eyebrow. "I'm not so sure that would be of any use."

"You won't know if you don't try it," Amy said. "Shall we move onto the next dream?"

Violet sighed. She was a little frustrated that the group hadn't managed to come up with any more ideas on the meanings of her dreams. She put the piece of paper aside and moved onto the next dream.

"Okay, 'I'm with my husband, I'm completely naked…'" Violet quickly scanned the rest of the dream to see where it was going. "Aww, Keeley, that's gross!"

* * *

"My goodness, she really can be a little dense sometimes, can't she?" Aria commented, reaching for the popcorn.

"You're really enjoying this, aren't you?" Linen asked, grabbing a handful for himself. He and Aria were sat on the edge of the Angelic Lake, watching Violet struggling with the interpretation of her dreams.

"What do you mean?" Aria asked innocently.

"Watching Velvet struggle with these things. You know, it's easier for us up here, we can see the bigger picture," he said, gesturing across the still lake where the lives of the other Earth Angels could be seen. "On Earth it's not so easy to see-"

"Yeah, yeah," Aria cut in. "On Earth it's so much harder and more difficult, la la la. Actually, I'm not really enjoying this. I just want Velvet to wake up already. I mean, she's already wasted so much time that it's going to be nearly impossible for her and Laguz to be together again. She's been having these dreams for weeks now, and they're so obvious, yet she hasn't figured it out. I mean, the answer was just given to her, and she's ignored it! Why is she so resistant to being with her Twin Flame?"

"Maybe because a subconscious part of her knows that once she is with her Twin Flame again, it will be the end of the world as they know it. Or, even more likely - she has no idea that he is her Twin Flame, or anything close. After all, she did go to Earth thinking that her Twin Flame was already on Earth and that there was a twenty year age gap between them."

"Hmm, I guess you could be right. But I still wish she would just go and find him already! Do you think she'll make it?"

"I don't know," Linen said, grabbing another handful of popcorn. "It's possible, just like anything is possible, but I have a gut feeling that maybe she won't."

Aria frowned, her tiny Faerie face sad. "That would be awful. I mean, Laguz came back to the Academy, missed her, then begged Gold to go back so he could be with her, and yet they might miss each other again? Being on Earth really does suck."

"It's all just part of the process. There's something to be learnt from this for both of them. Maybe they're going to miss each other this time, because the body that Laguz's soul went into wasn't the body he should have been in. Maybe they're going to miss each other again because Gold shouldn't have sent Laguz back when he did. Who knows?"

"The Seers know! Why did they all have to go back to Earth? Would have been handy to have kept a couple up here to give us some kind of warning of what was about to happen. I mean, we haven't even heard from Gold in ages."

"I guess he's got better things to do." Linen waved his hand across the clear surface of the lake, clearing the image of Violet having yet another dream about Lyle, and flew upwards. Aria clicked her fingers and the popcorn vanished. She flew up to meet Linen.

"Time to go?" she asked.

"Yep," Linen replied, holding his hand out. She grasped it firmly and with a click of Linen's fingers they left the Angelic Realm.

* * *

Violet was walking along in a world of her own when she vaguely heard someone calling her name. She stopped and turned round to see her hairdresser running across the busy high street towards her.

"Violet! I'm so glad I bumped into you! Haven't seen you in a while. When are you going to have your hair cut again?"

Violet self-consciously ran her hand through her hair. "I was trying to grow it out long, so I decided not to cut it for a while."

"Fair enough, you should still get the ends trimmed regularly though. Anyway, the reason I wanted to see you is because I have a number for you, it's a lady whose hair I cut, she and I were chatting and she's really into all that stuff you were telling me about, and I told her you had a spiritual group. She said she'd love to come along if that was possible, so she gave me her number to pass on for you to call her."

Violet blinked at all the run-on sentences. She remembered the other reason for not going to have her hair cut at Celia's Salon. She took the piece of paper that Celia now held out to her, and nodded.

"Okay, that's great. I'll give her a ring. I'm sure we can make room for one more."

"Excellent! Well, gotta run, I'm already late for my next appointment!"

"Yeah I better go too. I'll be late back from my lunch otherwise."

"See you soon! I'll book you in for a trim!"

"Uh, well," Violet started, but was too late, as she watched Celia dash back across the road to her hair salon.

Violet sighed and stuffed the piece of paper into her handbag before walking back to the office.

* * *

Lyle stared at his reflection in the mirror and couldn't believe what he saw. How was it possible that he had got himself into this state again? He rubbed his stubbly cheek and sighed. He wished he had the energy or the motivation to change things, but it just seemed so pointless. In twenty-five years he still hadn't figured out why he was here. Why he had been born. He had the vague feeling that there had been a purpose to his existence once, but that purpose was beyond him now. He felt like he had missed something earlier on in his life, and now it was too late.

Shaking his head at his own internal ramblings, he turned away from the mirror and headed for the kitchen. A quick look in the fridge confirmed what he'd already thought - he was completely out of beer. Time to get some more, it seemed. He headed for the door, grabbing his jacket and wallet on the way. He always seemed to be broke when it came to paying the rent, but there was always money for beer.

Walking down the dark street towards the garage shop, Lyle was so out of it, he didn't even hear the screech of the tyres, and by the time he registered the sound of the squealing brakes and turned around, it was too late.

CHAPTER THREE

"Hi, Maggie, is it? Violet here. I believe you gave Celia your number for me to contact you about the spiritual group?" Violet put the phone between her ear and shoulder and started folding the towels from the airer. "Yes, we've been meeting up for a few months now. We all met through rather unusual circumstances. We were originally meeting up in a rented room in the local community centre, but it just seemed cheaper and easier to meet at my house, so that's where we meet every week on a Monday night."

Violet listened for a while, and continued to fold her washing.

"We tend to change the topic every few weeks. We haven't really covered the afterlife and mediumship much, so it would be cool to do that... Tarot as well? No, we haven't done much on Tarot, we usually stick to Oracle cards, they're a bit easier. But we'd be open to learning. Why don't you join us next week, and see what you think? Yeah, I can text you my address if that's easier. Okay, great, see you next Monday then. Okay, bye."

Violet pressed the red button and put the phone down, continuing to fold the washing, deep in thought. She'd had yet another dream about Lyle. This time she'd managed to remember some of what they'd said to one another, and the words had bothered her. As much as she hated to admit it, she was beginning to think that maybe Keeley and Beattie were right. Maybe she was supposed to find him and get in touch. Abandoning the washing yet again, Violet went to her laptop and logged in. Within minutes, she was online and Googling Lyle's name, feeling slightly ridiculous. Just for good measure, she added the name of the town they'd both lived in, then hit the search button.

She nearly fell out of her chair in shock when the first hit contained a photograph of Lyle. Older, paler and thinner than she remembered, it was Lyle nevertheless. She read the headline that accompanied it, and closed her eyes, tears seeping out from underneath her eyelids.

"Oh, Lyle," she whispered.

* * *

Feeling a little out of place, yet recognising many of the faces, Violet sat through the funeral service with tears streaming down her face. She wondered if it would have made a difference if she had tried to contact him earlier. Would she have been able to prevent his death? Struggling to follow the hymn in her hymn book, Violet bowed her head, letting her tears hit the worn pages.

"And now we would like to play Lyle's favourite piece of music."

As the first notes filled the church, Violet's ragged breath caught in her throat. The familiarity of the music filled her with that feeling of longing again, and she found herself transported back to the first dream she'd had of Lyle.

The waves were lapping gently on the shore as they walked along hand in hand. Violet found herself stopping then, and looking up at Lyle, smiling at his green eyes and long tangled blond hair.

"I can't believe it's taken so long for us to be together," he said, reaching his hand out to touch her cheek.

Violet frowned. "I'm sorry it took me so long to remember."

He put his finger to her lips. "Shhh. It wasn't your fault. Besides, it doesn't matter, we're together now."

"But all that time that we lost, all that time we could have been together."

Lyle shook his head. "Are we or are we not together right now?"

Violet smiled. "We are."

"Then we have lost nothing." He leant down and kissed her. She reached up and held him close, determined not to let him go again.

He pulled back slightly and gazed into her deep brown eyes.

"I'll love you for eternity," he said, his voice filled with unwavering certainty.

She blinked, and a distant memory resurfaced in her mind. She smiled up at him and whispered back,

"Our love will outlast eternity itself."

"And so we commit the body and spirit of our dear friend, Lyle, to God everlasting, for eternity."

Violet's head snapped up at the vicar's words as her daydream faded away. One last detail stuck in her mind this time, and her hand flew up to the rune pendant around her neck. It had been the same as the one Lyle was wearing in her dream. Confusion swirled around her head as she tried to figure out what it all meant. Why did that song mean so much to her? Why did it trigger the memory of her dream about Lyle? How had she received a rune pendant in the post that was identical to the one Lyle was wearing in her dream?

Before Violet could work out the meaning of any of it, the service was over and people were filing quietly out of the church. Violet stood and followed, making her way to the cemetery in a daze, where the hole waited, ready to consume Lyle's body.

Violet stood on the fringes of the crowd, wishing she could just slip away from the funeral and go home unnoticed. She wanted to sit quietly somewhere and try to work out what was happening. She felt strange, like the very fabric of the Universe was reshaping, restructuring; weaving itself into an entirely new form. Life really wasn't the way that Violet thought it was. Dreams weren't merely the subconscious trying to work out the mysteries of daily reality; dreams were actually a form of communication between souls, between humans, between the divine and the mundane. Had Lyle's soul being calling out to her? Were they supposed to have met again, to have been together and in doing so, discover their purpose in this life?

Violet barely followed the short ceremony by the graveside, and so was a little surprised when she realised that everyone had gone, except for Lyle's mother, who stood beside her.

Violet looked up at her drawn, tear-stained face. "I'm so sorry, Mrs Evans. I wish there was something I could do."

Lyle's mother turned and looked her in the eye for a moment, then her gaze dropped down to the rune around Violet's neck. She reached out and traced the symbol etched into the smooth surface.

"There is something you can do. Next time, don't wait. Listen to your intuition. Follow your heart. Don't miss him again." With a small nod, Mrs Evans left.

Violet watched her go, her earlier confusion now exploding into complete chaos in her mind. Even Lyle's mother seemed to know that they were supposed to have met again. She walked forwards to the edge of the grave and stared down at the coffin six feet below, covered in roses and etched with Lyle's name.

"Oh, Lyle, I'm so sorry I didn't find you earlier. Please know that I wish things had been different. I wish that I had listened. I won't make that mistake again. I just hope that somehow it's not too late."

Violet took a deep breath, and dropped a single red rose onto the coffin. Her shoulders slumped, and several more tears fell, joining the rose. After a few moments, she turned and walked away.

* * *

Violet was back in her house, curled up on the sofa and staring blankly at the wall when the doorbell rang. Hardly able to get up, Violet struggled to the front door to find Amy on the doorstep. Suddenly she remembered that it was Monday. She glanced at the clock in the hallway; Amy was always a little early.

"Violet? What's happened? Are you okay?" Amy stepped in and gathered Violet into a hug.

After a moment Violet pulled away and wiped her eyes with her hand.

"I'd totally forgotten about the group tonight, I don't know if I'll be very good company."

"Do you want me to call everyone quickly and tell them it's cancelled?" Amy asked, pulling out her mobile phone.

Violet shook her head. "No, it's a bit late for that. Let me just get changed and get myself together, and I'll be fine. This might be exactly what I need right now."

"Do you want to tell me what's happened?"

"Not right now," Violet whispered.

Amy nodded and pushed her gently towards the stairs. "Go sort yourself out. I'll sort things out down here."

Violet trudged slowly up the stairs, trying to pick up her spirits and ready herself for an evening with her Sisters. It was probably just what she needed, though she wasn't sure she would be able to get through the evening without crying, and if there was one thing Violet hated, it was crying in front of people. Even her closest friends.

In slow motion, Violet pulled her black top and black trousers off, and picked out a pair of jeans and a cream t-shirt. Feeling slightly cheered by the brighter, more comfortable clothing, Violet went into the bathroom to try and cover up her splotchy face with makeup. She heard the doorbell ring several more times, and by the time she arrived downstairs her lounge was filled with the chattering voices of Fay, Keeley, Beattie, Leila, Amy and the new lady Violet had spoken to - Maggie.

They all looked up when she entered the room, but no one mentioned her bloodshot eyes. They must have been warned by Amy not to say anything. Bless her, Violet thought; she really was a brilliant friend.

"Evening, everyone, I see you've met our newest Sister. Hello, Maggie, I'm Violet, we spoke on the phone." Violet walked over to where Maggie sat and held her hand out. When Maggie shook it, she gave Violet the strangest look, but Violet ignored it and released her hand. She took her usual spot on the sofa and took the cup of tea Amy offered her.

"So, anything unusual anyone would like to report this week?" she asked, slipping into her usual host mode. "Maggie here is very interested in mediumship and Tarot, so I've said that we would be interested in learning about that."

Everyone in the room nodded except for Amy, who looked a little apprehensive.

"Amy, are you okay?" Fay asked.

"I'm just not sure about the Tarot part. They've always scared me a little."

"Is it because of the Death card?" Maggie asked.

Amy nodded.

"I can understand that, but please believe me when I say there is absolutely no reason to be afraid of the Tarot, or the Death card. The card doesn't necessarily mean the death of a person, but the death of one stage before moving onto the next. It could be the death of a relationship, a job or even just the place in life that you are currently in. Of course, death isn't something to be afraid of anyway, it's a part of life, a part of us. Without death there would be no life."

Violet listened to her words silently, praying that she wouldn't begin to cry again. Death may be nothing to be scared of, but that didn't stop you from wishing it didn't happen. She thought of Lyle, and she wished she hadn't taken the rune necklace off while she was upstairs. Somehow, it made her feel closer to him.

"Would anyone like me to read their cards for them?"

No one jumped in immediately, and then Amy spoke up. "I think Violet could do with a reading."

Violet looked up at her friend, wondering why she was volunteering her. Amy shrugged slightly, smiling encouragingly.

Violet shrugged too. "Okay, sure, I'll have mine read."

"Do you mind if I add my own interpretation and any messages I get from the Other Side, too?"

"Sure, go ahead."

"Excellent." Maggie reached into her handbag and pulled out a deck of Tarot cards wrapped in a deep pink cloth. She laid the cloth out on the coffee table, and handed the cards to Violet. "First of all, knock your knuckles on the deck three times, to dispel any energy left over from the last person."

Violet knocked on the cards three times, feeling a little bit silly as she did so.

"Now if you could shuffle the cards, then cut them into three piles with your left hand. Then put the deck back together however you choose."

Violet nodded and clumsily shuffled the cards. She set them down on the cloth, cut them into three uneven piles, and then put them back together before handing them back to Maggie. Fay, Keeley, Leila, Amy and Beattie all watched silently.

Maggie took the first five cards from the top of the deck and fanned them out in her hand as though she were playing a game of poker.

She looked at them for a few seconds then nodded.

"I know it's quite ironic that I just said that the Death card had nothing to do with a person dying, but I get the feeling that in this case, that's not true." She took the first card and laid it down on the cloth. The dark depiction of the hooded figure with a scythe made Amy shiver. "There's been a death recently, and it's turned your entire world into turmoil," Maggie said, setting the next card, The Tower, next to Death.

Violet couldn't bring herself to nod. Maggie continued anyway.

"I feel as though there were signs, there were symbols, but they were misunderstood or misread, and that the delays meant that an opportunity was missed." She laid the next card down, the Five of Cups. "You are focusing too much on what is lost, and not on what you have." She stared at the next card for a minute before continuing. "The Lovers reversed," she said, a frown on her face. "This person that you missed was the one you were meant to be with." Maggie looked up at Violet, who was struggling to remain composed. "Death wasn't just signifying the actual death, but also the death of the relationship you should have had."

Violet bit her lip, unable to look up at her Sisters. She nodded mutely.

Maggie looked back at the last card in her hand, her

frown smoothing out. "But this isn't the end. There will be another chance; there will be a reunion, a redemption." She laid the last card down, the Three of Cups. "There will be a celebration, and you will be together again."

Violet frowned. "How is that even possible? He's dead, I went to his funeral today; he's not coming back." Despite her best intentions, a tear escaped, and Violet brushed it away. She felt Amy's hand on her shoulder.

Maggie looked at Violet, then looked over Violet's left shoulder, her gaze glazing over slightly. Violet felt a sense of déjà vu. Her thoughts flicked back to the beach, only this time she wasn't with Lyle, but with Maggie, and they were sat on a sofa, just like they were now.

Maggie's gaze snapped back to Violet's. "I was trying to See if the spirits had any messages for you, but all I got was a rune."

"What rune was it?" Violet asked, hardly daring to believe that she might know about the wooden rune she had received.

"Laguz. The rune of the God of the Ocean."

Violet stopped breathing. Her hand went up to her neck, but the necklace was on her dressing table upstairs. There was no way that Maggie could have seen it.

"Wait here a second," Violet said, getting up. She ran lightly up the stairs to her room and grabbed the leather cord. Back downstairs, slightly out of breath, she handed the necklace to Maggie. She heard Fay gasp when Maggie turned the pendant over to see the rune.

"Isn't that strange?" Maggie mused. "My brother, my twin brother, had the exact same necklace, but it went missing just after he died. I never did find it."

There was silence, and Violet wondered again who had sent her the necklace. "Hang on another minute." She ran back upstairs, this time, to grab the small wooden jewellery box that the rune had arrived in.

This time, Maggie wasn't quite so calm. "Where did you get this from?" she whispered, her face white.

"Someone sent me the rune necklace inside a small leather pouch, which was inside this jewellery box."

"Who sent it to you?"

"I don't know. There was no note, no return postal address, no identifying clues on the outer box at all. So you recognise the box?"

There was hushed silence as everyone seemed to be holding their breath for Maggie's answer.

"Yes," she whispered. "It's mine. It went missing along with the rune after my brother died." She turned it over in her hands, running her fingers over the tiny carved mermaids.

"Are you sure it's yours?" Keeley asked.

"Yes, I am. Because you see, my brother, Adrian, he made it himself. As part of a woodworking class at school. He made the simple box in class, then spent hours at home carving all the figures on it. He told me all their names once, but I don't remember them now." She turned the box over again, then traced the figure carved in the centre. It was the only one with legs. "Except this one, I remember the name of this one because of her beautiful flowing dress. Her name was Velvet."

Everyone leaned forwards for a closer look at the figure, who seemed to be staring straight out, a wistful look on her face.

"He told me that if he could colour it in, her dress would be purple, because that was her first name. He always had such a vivid imagination, I teased him about being psychic, but he always brushed it off. He dreamt of her though, this Velvet. He said that in his dreams, they were together again, and that one day they would be together for real. But then he died, so I guess that didn't happen."

"How did he die?" Keeley asked. Violet shot her a look.

Keeley wasn't the most tactful of people. But Maggie didn't seem to mind.

"He had cancer. It was really aggressive. By the time they'd found it and diagnosed him, it was already too late. He died two weeks later."

Violet felt tears pricking at her eyelids again, feeling pain for this Adrian whom she had never met, who longed to be with Velvet. Her gaze travelled down to the carved figure on the box. Even as a wooden carving, she was beautiful. Her heart ached to think that they wouldn't be together, just like she would never be with Lyle.

Maggie sighed and wiped her eyes with a tissue she'd dug out of her pocket. She handed the box back to Violet.

"Don't you want to keep it?" Violet asked. "It was yours."

"No, I think you should have it. Someone, somewhere in the world felt that you should have it, so there must be a reason why it came to you. You might need it yet."

Violet smiled, and reached over to put her hand on Maggie's.

"Thank you, I'll take good care of it, I promise."

"I know you will."

CHAPTER FOUR

"I've fucked up again haven't I?" Laguz looked at Gold, sorrow squeezing his ethereal heart.

"Come on now, Laguz. I know God doesn't judge, but such language isn't exactly appropriate considering where we are," Gold said, gesturing at their otherworldly surroundings.

"I'm sorry, Gold, I just can't believe that I missed her. That I went back to be with her one last time, and I totally messed it up. I didn't Awaken at all, did I? I didn't see it. I mean, for years, all through school, there she was, right in front of me! And I didn't see her! How could I have been so blind?"

"It was not blindness, my dear Laguz, but a lack of awareness. You knew the risks when you left to be with her. There was always the possibility that you wouldn't be together, even though I did place you in bodies as close to one another as I could. The rest was up to both of you to Awaken and find each other. Of course, it probably didn't help that Violet left this dimension with the thought in her soul that she would never be with you. It's probably why she missed all of the signs and ignored all of the clues in her dreams. I am sorry for you both, but as you well know, everything happens for a reason. Perhaps it was not time for you two to be together."

Laguz frowned at Gold. "Are you saying that the world isn't ending? That the Flames no longer need to hurry because there will be more lifetimes?"

Gold shifted uncomfortably, his right eye beginning its tell-tale twitch. "Not exactly, no, that's not what I'm saying."

"Then what are you saying, Gold? Because as far as I can see, the world isn't waking up. The humans are still sleepwalking through life, totally unaware of the shift that is happening. So if you ask me, the Flames need each other now more than ever. Without the reunion of the Flames, the Crystals and Rainbows may never be able to pull us into the Golden Age."

"That may indeed be true. But perhaps you and Velvet are just not meant to be together this time."

Laguz was incredulous. "Why on Earth would that be the case? Why shouldn't we be together this time?"

"Perhaps it would be more of a distraction than it would be of help in the Awakening," Gold said mildly.

"So you think that if we were together, we would be so focused on each other that we would forget the bigger picture? Forget our purpose of Awakening the humans and other Earth Angels?"

"Yes, that is what I'm saying."

"How do you know? What if we need to be together to help each other Awaken? To help others to do the same? Our combined strength and passion is surely what the world needs?" Laguz moved closer to Gold, his raised voice dropping nearly to a whisper. "Look, Gold, I know I messed up, I know that I probably don't deserve yet another chance, but I am begging you, I need to go back. I need a way to be with her. To help her. Please, Gold."

Gold sighed. "I'm afraid it's out of my hands now,

Laguz. You will have to stay here until you hear the call again, if it is indeed your time to return. If not, you are more than welcome to go to the School for the Children of the Golden Age and see if they need any assistance at all. If neither of those things appeal to you, then you are free to move onto the Angelic Realm, to progress your soul to the next level."

Laguz's spirit deflated at Gold's words. A tiny spark of hope still glimmered though. "I guess I'll go to the School, it would be good to see Linen and Aria anyway, if they're still there?"

"Yes, they are still there, and doing a fine job, too. When they can concentrate, that is," Gold added, his eyebrow raised.

Laguz nodded and was about to say goodbye when he heard Gold's fingers click.

* * *

"Laguz! Oh dear! She didn't find you in time?"

Laguz shook his head at the tiny green Faerie who'd greeted him as he entered the School.

"No, I missed her again. I just didn't wake up. I messed up, Aria."

Aria frowned, then flew over to Laguz and patted him awkwardly on the shoulder. "Oh, Laguz, maybe it just wasn't meant to happen this time."

"Then when is it supposed to happen?" Laguz asked, his tone bitter. "If the humans don't Awaken soon, it'll be the end of the bloody world! Then there will be no time left because nothing will exist anyway!"

"You'll be together in this dimension then," Aria said timidly, a little scared by his raised voice.

"And what good is that?" Laguz asked, pacing up and down the small office. "Yes, it was good to be with her here, but it's completely different on Earth. Here, well, it's just not real, is it?"

Aria frowned again. "Isn't it? What's real anyway? Most humans would say that Faeries aren't real, but hey, here I am. Here is as real as anywhere else in the Universe."

Laguz suddenly stopped his pacing. "So that's it, is it? Gold thinks I'd be too much of a distraction to Velvet, so we're not supposed to be together on Earth? I've got to just wait here, until the end of the world, or Velvet's death, whichever comes first, before we can be together again?"

Aria bit her lip. "I don't know," she said quietly, wishing that Linen were there; he always knew the right things to say. "I keep telling Linen that one of the Seers should have stayed behind, so that we would know what was going to happen."

Laguz nodded, thinking of Magenta, his Earthly sister for a short while, who, having been a Seer on the Other Side, had always provided great insights, and had saved his life on a few occasions. He wished he could speak to her now and ask her if she knew what was supposed to happen. He remembered her words to him in that life.

"Once you find her, Adrian, don't let her go. Go to the ends of the Earth if you have to, you need to be with her."

Surely she was right? In their lifetime as twin siblings, she'd never been wrong. He felt more inclined to believe her than Gold, even though Gold was an Elder on the Other Side and she was merely a human at the time. Laguz became aware of Aria then, who had stopped flying around in circles, which she tended to do when trying to think of a solution, and was now staring at Laguz intently.

"What?"

"I think you should stay here a while. Perhaps there's something you need to learn before you move on."

Laguz sighed. "I don't think I have much choice in the

matter, to be honest. Can you tell Linen I'm here? I think I'll go to the gardens for a while."

"Sure, I will. I hope you find some answers."

"Me too."

* * *

"May I join you?"

Without moving his gaze from the statue in front of him, Laguz nodded at Linen, who sat next to him on the crystal bench in the Atlantis Garden. They sat quietly for several minutes before Laguz spoke.

"I was so sure, when I was here last and I heard the call, that I would be with her again. That we would share another Earthly life together, finally, after so long. My memories of Atlantis are crystal clear, but they were so long ago. How could I have been so close to her and not realise she was the one?"

"Believe me, it's easy to do. We can become so focused on things that don't matter, that we completely miss the things that do."

Laguz smiled slightly. "That sounds just like something Velvet would say."

"I did spend an awful lot of time with her here before she left. I think her wise Old Soul-ness must have rubbed off on me. What I don't understand, is why you're giving up on being with her now. I mean, surely there must be a way?"

Laguz shook his head. "Gold and Aria both seem to think that I'll have to wait until she comes here, to the Other Side, to be with her again. So it'll either be her death or the end of the world, whichever comes first. I don't know how I'm going to be able to wait that long."

"You won't have to wait too long. After all, for every day that passes here, a whole year passes on Earth."

Laguz sighed. "I'd forgotten that. So by tonight, months will have passed, and by then, she'll have probably forgotten all about me."

"Oh, I doubt that, Laguz. After all, she went to your funeral."

Laguz wrenched his gaze from Velvet's statue to look at Linen. "Really? How do you know?"

"Because I was watching from the Angelic Realm. She went to your funeral and she was a complete wreck. I think she finally realised that you two were supposed to meet again and be with each other."

"But how did she know that I'd died? I mean, we hadn't spoken for years."

"She Googled you," Linen replied with a slight smile. "She Googled your name and the newspaper article came up about your accident."

"Unbelievable. If only she'd tried to find me just a few days earlier."

"Yes, but we cannot live in the world of 'if only'. We must live in the present moment."

"You did spend far too much time with Velvet."

"I know."

"So she went to my funeral, anything else?"

"Yes, but I'm not sure how much I should be telling you."

"Oh, come on, Linen, I need to know everything if I'm going to figure out how to get back to her."

Linen smiled at Laguz's renewed determination. "She's found Magenta."

Laguz's eyes widened. "What? Magenta? Maggie? My sister from my other life? How on Earth did they meet?"

"Magenta was telling her hairdresser about her mediumship work and the hairdresser mentioned Velvet, who has her own spiritual group. Magenta went along to the group on the evening of your funeral, and she gave

Velvet a reading. The rune, Laguz, came up in the reading, which prompted Velvet to show Magenta a rune necklace she'd received. Your rune necklace."

Laguz looked up at Velvet's statue at the rune necklace around her neck then turned back to Linen. "What do you mean, my rune necklace?"

"The rune necklace you wore in your life as Adrian has found its way to Velvet now. Magenta recognised it, along with the carved wooden box that you had given her in that life. Both items came into Velvet's possession, and because of those two items, the two women now realise they have a link between them. It should mean that they will become quite close, which of course is excellent news on the Awakening front."

Laguz blinked at all of the information. "How did it come to her?"

"Ah, remember, Laguz, the *how* is not important. The fact that she has it is what's important. It's a link to you and a link to her life as head of the Earth Angel Training Academy. It should just be a matter of time now before we are able to communicate with her more accurately and clearly through her dreams."

"You're going to talk to her through her dreams? Can I do that?"

Linen smiled. "It's not a clear line yet, but we're working on it. That is, the Angels are working on it. We've managed to get through sporadically when she's awake, but talking to her in her dreams is so much easier. The main problem is getting her to remember her dreams on awakening in the morning."

Laguz's gaze returned to Velvet's statue. "Why does it all have to be so complicated, Linen? Why can't we just choose to go back to Earth but remember everything from our previous lives so that we can make the right choices, be with the right people and live our purpose in life?"

"Because it would be impossible for a human to retain all that information. It's easy here; we are linked to the whole Universe, all thoughts and emotions and ideas are within easy reach. And yes, the same is partially true for humans, but for them to be able to link to the Universe takes a lot of strength, and a lot of faith. Most humans just don't believe enough."

"Why is that, Linen? Why don't they believe?" Laguz sounded tired and lost. "After experiencing all these lifetimes in so many civilisations, there are still so many things that I cannot even begin to fathom when it comes to human nature."

"That is why we need to keep the world from ending. There are still so many more mysteries yet to be solved."

Laguz closed his eyes and leant back. "There's just one mystery I would like to solve right now," he muttered.

"Which is?"

"Will I get to be with Velvet now? As she is on Earth, as Violet?" Laguz kept his eyes closed, and listened to Linen's breathing, vaguely aware of the distant sound of laughter and running water.

After a few moments, Linen replied.

"I think only the Rainbows could possibly answer that."

* * *

A month passed by uneventfully, though Violet found her weekly meetings with her Sisters had become very interesting since Maggie had joined the group. They'd even had a go at mediumship, and tried to receive messages from the Other Side. Violet had been trying every night since that meeting to contact Lyle, but hadn't been successful. The biggest change in her otherwise mundane life of working in the council offices, was that her dreams about Lyle had stopped. Instead, she now dreamt of strange places, and weird conversations that she couldn't quite remember when she woke up. She missed the dreams of Lyle. Every day, she felt as though he was slipping away from her completely.

Violet was busy washing up ready for another Spiritual Sisters meeting, staring out at the deep red roses growing in her back garden, when the doorbell rang. She checked the time, and knew that Amy had arrived early again.

Drying her hands on her way to the door, Violet greeted her friend warmly, but her heart sank when she noted the bloodshot eyes and pale face.

Without saying a word, Amy followed Violet into the house, to the kitchen, where Violet made them both a cup of tea before settling in the lounge.

"He didn't come home again last night," Amy began, her voice quivering slightly. "Haven't seen him all day and I know he didn't go to work, because they called the house, looking for him." Amy took a sip of the scalding hot tea. "Part of me is so furious that he's done this yet again, but another part of me is wondering if he's okay. I mean, what if something's happened to him? I tried his mobile, but it's going straight to voicemail. What if he's been hurt, or worse? Do you think I should ring the hospital?"

"Amy," Violet said quietly, putting her hand on her friend's. "I'm sure that wherever he is, he's okay. I'm more concerned about whether *you're* okay right now."

Amy shrugged. "I just don't know anymore. I don't know how to feel. I don't know what to think. And I really don't know what to do." Her eyes welled up with tears and she sucked in a jagged breath.

Violet set her cup down and took Amy's from her and put it down too. Then she reached over and pulled Amy into a hug.

"Listen, you are an amazing woman. You are a beautiful human being, and, according to your book, an Angel, too.

So please, please, start looking after yourself. The world needs you. And you do not need Danny."

Violet felt Amy's shoulders shake as she tried to suppress her sobs. "I can't bear to see you like this, Amy, you deserve so much more. You deserve to be happy."

Before Amy could respond, the doorbell rang, signalling the arrival of the other Sisters. In a complete role reversal to a month before, this time it was Violet who was pushing Amy gently towards the stairs.

"Go sort yourself out and come down when you're ready."

Violet watched her friend go up the stairs for a second before composing herself and answering the door. Fay and Beattie came in. They were in the middle of a heated discussion on the proper use of the horn when driving.

Not long later, Keeley, Leila and Maggie arrived, and once they all had a hot drink in hand, Violet decided to begin the evening, knowing that Amy would come down and join in when she was ready. She'd already warned the others that Amy was in a bit of a state and to not say anything.

"Right, this week, I thought we could perhaps try and contact the spirits again, but instead of each of us trying individually, I thought it would be a better idea to join forces and try to contact one particular individual. I've been reading some books on the subject, and one of them suggested using an Angel Board, so," Violet said, reaching behind the sofa. "I made this one for us to use." She set the Angel Board on the coffee table.

"Isn't that just a Ouija Board?" Keeley asked.

"Not exactly. It's the same concept, but with an Angel Board, you ask the Angels to only let in the spirits you wish to speak to. With a Ouija Board, the doors are open to anyone and everyone."

"Even a Ouija Board can be used safely if you use the proper protection techniques," Maggie added. "I haven't used one myself, but I do know some mediums who do."

"Exactly," Violet said, before getting a glass from the kitchen and setting it in the middle of the board. "I've put pictures of the Archangels on the board to protect us, but we also have to mentally ask the Angels to protect us from any lower energies."

Beattie nodded. "So, shall we get started?"

Violet smiled at her enthusiasm. "Yes, let me just get something from upstairs. We'll dim the lights and then begin."

She ran up the stairs and frowned when she saw the bathroom light was off. She pushed open the door to her bedroom slightly and smiled when she saw Amy lying on her bed, fast asleep, her face peaceful. Deciding that she probably needed some rest, Violet crept in, grabbed the piece of paper from the bedside table, then crept out again, closing the door quietly behind her.

Back downstairs, the Sisters had arranged themselves in a circle around the board, so that each of them could reach the glass. Violet dimmed the lights and joined them, then straightened the piece of paper.

"I wrote down a short invocation to ask the Angels for their help. So, here goes:

'With the love of God and the Goddess, we ask our personal guardian spirits to act as a gateway to the spirit realms. We ask for protection from the highest source and we wish to contact only those specified for the highest good. Thanks be to the Goddess and the God for blessing us with their presence tonight. Thanks be to the Angels for helping us with our plight. Thanks be to the Faeries for keeping us safe tonight. Blessed be.'"

Without speaking, each woman put their right index finger on the glass, so that they were just touching it.

"So who are we trying to contact?" Fay asked.

"Adrian."

"Lyle."

Both Maggie and Violet had spoken simultaneously. Laughing a little, Violet gestured to Maggie. "Maybe we should try Adrian first. After all, you're a strong medium, you'd be more likely to be able to reach him."

"I haven't been able to reach him up until this point, I always wondered if his spirit had already come back to Earth by the time I tried."

"Do you want to try again now?"

"Sure. Let's try to contact Adrian. Adrian Jenkins, my twin brother."

As a group they all turned to look at their fingers perched on the glass, and their breathing synchronised, becoming deeper and slower.

Several moments passed, and mentally, though Violet was trying to think of Adrian, her thoughts kept going to Lyle. She so desperately wanted to talk to him.

Suddenly she felt a tiny movement under her finger.

"I think something's happening," Keeley whispered.

Violet stared intently at the glass, determined to make sure that no one was cheating. The glass shifted slightly again.

"Someone ask a question," Leila suggested quietly.

"Are you there, Adrian?" Maggie asked.

There was a gasp as the glass suddenly shifted abruptly to the side, towards the 'Yes'.

After a moment, the glass moved back to the centre again. Violet didn't think any of the women were making it move because their faces were all as ashen as hers felt.

"Do you have a message for us?"

The glass shifted to the 'Yes' again, then quickly moved around the board, barely stopping at each letter for more than half a second at a time. Luckily Violet had thought to get a pen and notepad out, and clumsily with her left hand, she quickly wrote down the letters that were coming thick and fast.

"V-e-l-v-e-t," Maggie called out softly. The glass paused for a couple of seconds then continued. "V-i-o-l-e-t."

Violet felt her eyebrows raise as she wrote down her own name. She asked the next question.

"Do you have something to tell me?"

The glass swung to the 'Yes' then continued immediately to the letters. The urgency of the movement had them all on the edge of their seats as they struggled to keep up with the glass.

"E-a-t-a," Maggie called out, sounding slightly confused. The glass paused and they all looked at each other.

"Eata?" Beattie asked. "That's not even a word."

The glass began again.

"T-w-i-n-f-l-a-m-e-s," Maggie spelled. She split the letters up. "Twin flames?"

Violet shook her head. "I don't know. I haven't heard of that before, what is it?"

The glass started to move again, seeming almost impatient with their lack of understanding.

"L-y-l-e."

Violet wrote the letters down and felt like she was going to have a heart attack; were they really going to speak to Lyle?

"Lyle, are you there?" she asked.

The glass moved quickly to the 'Yes'.

"Are you okay?"

The glass moved slightly, still on the 'Yes'.

"Are you and Adrian together?"

Slightly confused when the glass moved to the letters instead of the 'Yes' or 'No', Violet was slow in writing the next word down.

"S-a-m-e," Beattie said softly. "Same?"

Maggie looked at Violet, her eyes wide. "Adrian, are you the same spirit who was also known as Lyle?"

The glass nearly tipped over in its hurry to move to the 'Yes'. It then moved back to the middle of the board.

Violet felt her chest constrict. Adrian and Lyle were the same person?

"Could I have saved you from dying if I had contacted you earlier?"

Fay, Leila, Beattie and Keeley all looked at Violet in surprise. Violet ignored them and stared intently at the glass, knowing that the answer was going to affect her deeply.

But the glass remained where it was.

CHAPTER FIVE

Laguz knew that all tiredness and illness in the Fifth Dimension were just inside his mind, but at that moment, he felt absolutely exhausted. He flopped back on the sand and gazed up at the wispy clouds above. He was sat on the shores of the Angelic Lake. After talking to the Rainbows, he'd gone to the Angels to seek their advice, and they informed him that Velvet was about to ask for their help to communicate with him. They'd showed him how to connect with the lake, and how to give answers through moving the glass. But they hadn't warned him how draining it would be. He felt as though he hadn't an ounce of energy left in his ethereal body.

He wished he hadn't left without answering Velvet's question, but as well as running out of steam, he just didn't know the answer. Could she have saved him? Could they have been together?

Laguz closed his eyes, and recalled his recent life on Earth. It was a sad one, that was true. He had been an alcoholic in the end, had no career or even a job, lived in a squalid rented flat, and had very little self-belief. Laguz shook his head to himself. No, even if Velvet had found him sooner, he would have been ashamed to be with her in that state; she deserved so much more than that.

Maybe Gold was right. Maybe she would have been so distracted with the task of trying to sort him out, and with being in love with him, that she would have completely forgotten her mission to Awaken.

Laguz sighed and opened his eyes again. All of the confidence boosting he'd received from the Rainbows was already dissipating. They seemed certain that he and Velvet were indeed meant to be together, but he just didn't see how that was going to be possible, or even how that would in any way help to stop the end of the world. He pushed himself up into a sitting position and looked into the lake again.

He saw Velvet in her room, staring at a computer print-out of the newspaper article of his death. Though being with him would have been a distraction, surely grieving his death was just as distracting? He watched a tear roll down her cheek and his heart ached. Surely she would be more likely to Awaken if she were happy?

His determination returning once more, Laguz hauled himself to his feet. He needed to see Gold. There must be a way for him to return to Earth. To Velvet.

* * *

Violet flipped through her notepad, reading the words the Angel Board had spelled out, for what seemed like the millionth time. She tried to read in-between the lines, but it still didn't mean much. It had been a month since they'd communicated with Lyle, and they'd tried every week since, but they'd never heard anything more. Violet couldn't sleep. Why didn't he answer her question? Was it because the answer would haunt her for the rest of her life?

She lay back on her bed and closed her eyes, but it was no use. Now, instead of the beautiful dreams of Lyle and the beach, all she saw when she closed her eyes was the photo of him in the newspaper article. She'd had nightmares where he was calling for her, begging her to come to him, but she was always too late.

She'd told Maggie about the dreams, the nightmares, and they'd talked about the possibility that Lyle had indeed been Adrian. After all, Lyle had been born just a couple of months after Adrian had died suddenly of cancer. Maggie told Violet how she'd told Adrian that if he ever met his Velvet, he was to hold onto her, and to never let her go.

They'd also both researched the Twin Flames, and 'eata'. It seemed that Twin Flames were soulmates who only came together when the world was about to end, so that they could have one final perfect reunion. A Twin Flame relationship was less about learning and more about complementing one another. It was supposedly the best relationship that was humanly possible. But no matter how much they looked, they couldn't find anything in reference to eata, as a word or as an acronym. Violet felt that if they figured that out, then they would be a little closer to understanding what it all meant.

Violet opened her eyes again and stared at the shadows on the ceiling created by her bedside lamp.

Lyle was her Twin Flame. She just knew it. The way Velvet's name had come through, and then her own, made her wonder if she was the same person that Adrian had talked about. But Adrian had died before he got to be with Velvet, and Lyle had died before he could be with her, so where did that leave her now? And why was all this happening? There must be a reason in it all somewhere. Violet just couldn't believe that any of it was merely coincidence.

Sighing, Violet sat up, glanced at her clock and groaned when she saw the time. She was going to be a complete wreck in work the next day. But it seemed pointless to try and sleep when her mind was whirling like this. She rummaged around in her bedside table, trying to find a pen so she could write in her diary, when she came across the small purple book that Amy had lent her months before. Abandoning the search for a pen, Violet settled back into her pillows and started to read about the Realms of the Earth Angels.

* * *

"Finally! Amy gave her that book ages ago. I can't believe it's taken her this long to start reading it! I'm so glad Amethyst took my advice and decided to write about Earth Angels. I reckon even I would have woken up if I'd had her books to read."

Linen smiled and offered Aria some chocolate truffles as they watched Violet through the clear lake. She took a handful and stuffed them into her mouth.

"I wonder how Laguz is getting on in his meeting with Gold."

Aria coughed, nearly choking on the truffles. She swallowed them with a gulp. "He went to see Gold?"

"Yes, it seems he's more determined than anyone gave him credit for. He really thinks there must be a way to be with Velvet."

"Is there?"

Linen was quiet for a moment. "Anything is possible, don't you think?"

Aria smiled. "I hope so."

"Is this a private viewing, or can anyone join in?"

Linen and Aria both looked up to see Laguz standing on the beach behind them. Aria patted the sand. "Feel free. Things are hopefully beginning to get interesting; Velvet's reading about Earth Angels."

Laguz sank down onto the sand next to Aria. He stared at the image of Velvet in the lake. "Is she any closer to

Awakening?"

Aria shrugged. "I think she's finally figured out that she's an Old Soul, it's definitely a good start." She turned to Laguz. "What did Gold say?"

Laguz continued to stare at the lake. "He's not making any promises, but there might be a chance that I can return to Earth."

Aria bounced up and down. "That's amazing! Why aren't you more excited?"

Laguz shook his head. "I'm just not sure I like Gold's idea much."

"How come? What do you have to do?"

"Become a walk-in."

"A what-what?"

"A walk-in. Instead of being born on Earth as a baby and growing up, I would essentially take over a body belonging to another soul. They would walk out, and I would walk in."

Aria frowned. "How does that work? I mean, how do they leave?"

"It would have to be with someone who was unconscious, and close to death. When the soul is met by Gold, he would offer them the chance to exchange with me. They'd stay here on the Other Side and I would take over their body and their life."

"But wouldn't their friends and family on Earth know the difference? I mean, you would probably have a totally different personality to them."

Laguz shrugged. "It seems to work somehow. People seem to accept that occasionally, when someone receives a knock to the head, and is unconscious for a while, their personality can change."

"Huh, I guess so. Would be a little strange though. Do you keep any of your memories, or is it still a clean slate?"

"Clean slate. Though there's a higher chance that I will

remember because I don't have to go through the growing up process. I'll be stepping into an adult body." Laguz drew swirling patterns in the sand with his fingers, still watching the lake.

"So it's just a case of waiting for the right body to become available? Surely you won't have to wait too long, humans are really accident prone, aren't they?"

Laguz chuckled. "Yeah, it's amazing they have survived this long at all."

"You know you're welcome to hang out with us until you have to go," Linen said.

"Thanks, Linen. But I think I'll spend some time in the gardens, and go visit the Rainbows again. Perhaps they'll have some ideas on how to make this work."

"Sounds like a plan," Aria said, flying to her feet. "Linen and me have some work to do, but feel free to stay and watch for a while."

Laguz shook his head. "Nah, I don't want to spend all my time spying on her. Doesn't feel right somehow."

"Fair enough." Linen flew to his feet too and took Aria's hand. "See you later, Laguz."

Laguz nodded and they disappeared with a click. He sighed and looked back at the lake. He watched Velvet for a few moments, as she went through her day, a faraway look on her face. Then he waved his hand over the surface of the water and she disappeared too. He sat and stared at the blank surface for a while before getting to his feet and heading back to the gates.

* * *

Wondering if maybe she was just imagining it, Violet looked away from where the little girl sat across from her on the bus and stared out of the window for a few minutes. She glanced back, only to find that the little girl with dark blonde ringlets was still staring at her. She smiled slightly and the little girl smiled back.

It was perhaps the tenth time that Violet had noticed children staring at her intently. No matter where she went, she seemed to feel their eyes following her. A couple of times they seemed to be reacting to her thoughts, which was crazy, but something in their eyes made Violet think that maybe it were true.

When the bus reached Violet's stop, she stood and made her way to the front. As the bus pulled away, Violet looked up and saw the little girl watch her out of the window. Above her head were the words 'please remember'.

Logically, Violet knew that the words were just part of the advert printed on the side of the bus, but it did seem like an odd coincidence. Remember what? What were all these children trying to tell her?

She pulled her phone out and called Maggie. When her friend answered, she explained the occurrences to her.

"I should think that the children probably have a message for you."

"A message? What kind of message?"

"I've been reading up on the new generations of children, it seems that they are far more enlightened than us, and that they have come here to wake us up. Perhaps they have a message of Awakening. Or perhaps you knew them in a previous life and have asked them to help you Awaken?"

Violet frowned. "As improbable as all that sounds, it does seem vaguely familiar to me."

"Well then, there's only one thing you can do."

"What's that?"

"Next time you meet one of these children, ask them."

* * *

It was just over two weeks later before the opportunity arose, and even when it did, Violet felt reluctant to take it. Violet didn't know her neighbours well, but she knew that her next door neighbour had a little girl who was about five years old. While picking up some branches from her lawn after an early morning storm one Saturday, Violet felt someone watching her, and turned to see the little girl looking at her intently through the wire fence.

Violet turned away and bit her lip. Mustering up the courage, she added another branch to the compost heap and went over to her. She smiled and crouched down so that she was the same height.

"Hey there, what's your name?"

The little girl smiled slightly, but remained silent. She nodded as if to say, "You already know."

Violet closed her eyes for a moment and suddenly saw a rose quartz crystal.

"Rose?"

The little girl grinned and nodded. Violet frowned and peered closer at her.

"We've met before, haven't we?" Violet didn't mean in this life, and Rose seemed to understand that.

"Yes, we have met." Though soft and young, Rose's voice was far wiser than her years would suggest.

"What is it you need to tell me?"

Rose smiled. She looked up at the sky then, and Violet followed her gaze to where a rainbow coloured the horizon.

"At the beginning of the rainbows, there will be gold."

Violet looked back at Rose and frowned. "Don't you mean there's gold at the end of the rainbow?"

Rose smiled and shook her head.

"Rosie! Lunch!"

Rose looked towards her house. She threw Violet a final glance. "Please remember."

* * *

"So, what do you think?"

Violet waited for Amy to digest all the information she had just given her, and to give her opinion.

"That's all she said? 'At the beginning of the rainbows, there will be gold'?"

Violet nodded. "Her mum called her in then, so I don't know if she would have said more, but somehow, I don't think she would have."

"I'm not sure if this is just a weird coincidence, or if it has anything to do with it, but I bought this for you." Amy handed Violet a small purple velvet pouch. "I saw it in the window of the crystal shop in town, and I just had to get it for you."

Violet took the pouch and emptied the contents into her hand. "Oh, Amy, it's gorgeous." She held up the clear, faceted, heart-shaped crystal.

"You're supposed to hang it in the window. It turns sunlight into rainbows."

Violet glanced up at the dark windows. "I'll hang it up tonight; maybe it will be sunny in the morning." She leaned across and hugged Amy. "Thank you."

Amy shrugged. "I hope it helps somehow."

A moment later, the doorbell rang, and Violet tucked the crystal back in the pouch and put it in her pocket. She answered the door three times until the lounge was full of chattering women.

"Right then, tonight, I'd like to talk about Earth Angels. Amy lent me this book months ago," she held up the small purple book. "And it gives detailed descriptions of the different kinds of Earth Angels, and what realms they are from. Amy has figured out that she is from the Angelic Realm, and I have figured that I am not from another realm, but that I have been a human many, many times."

Amy nodded. "I knew, as soon as I read it that you were a Wise One."

Violet blushed a little. "Personally, I prefer the term 'Old Soul'. When I think of Wise Ones I just picture old men with long white beards." Everyone giggled.

"So what am I then, Vi?" Keeley asked.

"I thought it might be better if each of you read the book to see which category you felt you fitted into, rather than me telling you which ones I think you are."

"But you have managed to fit us into the categories?" Fay asked.

Violet nodded. "I think so, yes."

"Just tell us then, I think I'd rather hear your opinion on it," Keeley said.

Violet smiled and opened the book. "Okay, well, Keeley, like Amy, you fit quite neatly into the Incarnated Angel category."

"An Angel? Seriously?" Keeley laughed.

"Absolutely. You're always there for everyone, you always listen, and you always see the best in everyone. But don't take my word for it, read this book if you want."

Keeley nodded. "Okay, I'll read it. It would be interesting to see why you think I'm an Angel."

"What about me?" Maggie asked.

Violet smiled. "You're an Old Soul too. Though I think you may have also spent some lifetimes in the Angelic Realm; you definitely have some Angelic traits as well."

Maggie smiled and nodded.

"Beattie, I think you're a Starperson. But it was a little unclear, so perhaps you've also lived in another realm at some point. And Leila, I think you are also an Old Soul, though you also have some Faerie-like traits, so perhaps you were either very good friends with the Faeries, or you have lived in the Elemental Realm at some point."

"Fay, I think you are a-"

"Faerie," Fay supplied. "I completely agree. I've been obsessed with them since I was tiny, and I also think I may even have seen some once."

Violet suddenly remembered the tiny green Faerie-like bug she'd seen outside the kitchen window, and was about to mention it when Leila spoke up.

"I've been reading about reincarnation a lot lately, and I think I'd like to try past-life regression. Does anyone have someone they can recommend?"

As the discussion turned to past lives, Violet forgot about the tiny green Faerie.

* * *

"Maybe I should visit her again," Aria mused as she licked the melted chocolate fudge ice cream from her hand. "Perhaps she just needs a bit more of a nudge in the right direction. Though the Children seem to be doing quite well."

"Yes, I'm quite impressed with Rose for getting such a clear message to her. I wonder why it is that the Children find it so much easier to remember their purpose and missions and to Awaken while on Earth."

"Maybe it's because they had such fantastic teachers in this dimension," Aria suggested as she wiped her mouth with a napkin.

Linen chuckled. "Maybe. I just wish that all the Earth Angels could remember so easily. It would make the Awakening process happen so much quicker."

"It's a shame that there are no Indigo and Crystal Children left here now. I miss having them around."

"I do too. It was like having a massive family."

Aria looked over at Linen's wistful expression. "Do you wish you'd stayed on Earth long enough to have kids?"

Linen returned her gaze. "I don't think that was ever an option for me. I think that this was always going to be my destiny."

"So if you could go back in time, you wouldn't choose to stay?"

Linen shook his head. "And miss out on being here with you right now?" He grabbed Aria's hand and squeezed it. "Not a chance."

* * *

It was a week later when the early rays of sunshine shone through the window, easing Violet out of slumber into awake. She pried her eyes open and her dream faded away when she saw the dancing rainbows on her wall and ceiling. Her breath caught in her throat as she watched them, and inexplicably, a tear rolled down her cheek. Slowly, not wanting to scare them away, Violet sat up and reached out until a rainbow of light sat on her palm. She closed her palm and her eyes, and a feeling of calm settled over her.

Flashes of what felt like memory shot through her mind. Souls of rainbow light, giving her messages. Children made of crystal. Children made of indigo blue light, living in a golden city. Golden city. Violet followed the train of thought that was slipping from her grasp. There was something about gold that she needed to remember. Something important. But it seemed to be just beyond her reach. Just before she opened her eyes though, a final image revealed itself, of an Angel in front of a globe.

Violet looked around her room, now dim as the sunlight had disappeared behind a cloud. The rainbows had gone, but aside from the feeling of loneliness, Violet felt elation. Just as the children had asked her to, she was remembering.

* * *

"Can I get you a drink?"

Violet looked up at the blue-eyed stranger next to her at the bar and shrugged. "I don't drink."

The stranger frowned. "Can I ask what you're doing stood at the bar in a pub then?" he asked teasingly.

Violet smiled and jerked her head towards the band setting up their equipment on the tiny makeshift stage. "My friend's husband is in the band. We've come to support them."

"We?"

"Yeah, my friends are over there," she pointed to the table closest to the stage, where her Sisters were sitting.

"Okay, so can I get you a lemonade, or a fruit juice?" the stranger persisted.

Violet shrugged again. "Sure, thanks. I'll have an orange juice."

The stranger beckoned to the barman and ordered her drink, then resumed his staring. Violet smiled, thanked him again, took the drink, and turned to leave.

"Wait a second," the stranger said, putting his hand on her shoulder. "In exchange for the drink, do I at least get to know your name?"

Violet hesitated for a second, but he seemed nice enough. "Violet."

The stranger smiled, and Violet noticed the dimples in his cheeks. "Nice to meet you, Violet. I'm Charlie."

"Good to meet you too, Charlie. I'd better get back to my friends." She glanced over to their table and saw that they were all watching the exchange with interest. Luckily, they were too far away to be able to hear.

Charlie nodded. "Okay, Violet, I hope to meet you again sometime."

Violet smiled but didn't respond. She had a fleeting sense of déjà vu as she walked away from him, but it was instantly forgotten when she saw the looks she was getting. She groaned internally at the grilling she was going to get from her Sisters.

"Well, well, well, has our little Sister pulled, or what?"

Violet sat down and sipped her drink, ignoring Keeley's question.

"Aww, come on, Violet, you're the only one of us allowed to pull, please let us live vicariously through you," Beattie pleaded.

Violet sighed. "There's really nothing to tell. He asked if he could buy me a drink, I said yes, he bought me an orange juice, asked why I was here, asked me for my name, then told me his name. It's Charlie."

There was a pause, and the band started playing the opening notes of their first song.

"And?" Fay prompted.

"And nothing, that was it, the entire conversation."

"So he didn't ask for your number? You're not going to meet him again?" Keeley shouted over the now thumping beat.

"No," Violet shouted back. "Look, I'm not interested, okay? It's too soon."

"Too soon after what?"

Violet rolled her eyes at Keeley. "After Lyle dying. I'm not ready to meet anyone just yet."

The women all looked at each other, unsure as how to proceed. It was Amy who spoke up.

"Vi, Lyle died months ago. And you didn't even have a relationship with him. You hadn't even talked to him for years. It's not too soon at all."

Violet sighed. "I know what you're saying is true and sensible, it's just how I feel, that's all."

There was another pause, until Keeley piped up. "Well, when you're ready to say 'fuck it' and go for it, he would make an excellent choice." She nodded to where Charlie still stood at the bar, watching Violet. "He really does have a gorgeous arse."

* * *

Laguz was sat cross-legged in room 336, his eyes closed in meditation. When his breathing was deep and even, and his mind was clear from confusion, he opened his eyes and held his hand out in front of him. Almost immediately he caught a Rainbow, and closed his hand around it.

"Greetings, Laguz. We sense you come not for answers, but for reassurance."

Laguz smiled down at his hand, he could see the rainbow-coloured light peeking out through the gaps in his fingers.

"And as always, you are right. I know now that I will be with Velvet, or at least, I will have another chance to be with Velvet, but I suppose I just need some reassurance that this is the right thing to do. That it's not somehow breaking some Universal law that says I've had my chance and I should now just leave her be."

"Do you honestly believe that?"

Laguz shrugged. "I don't know what to believe anymore."

"I know you don't really believe that. Laguz, if this course of action was in any way breaking Universal laws, do you think it would be possible?"

Laguz sighed. "I guess not. It just feels like cheating somehow, to just step into someone else's body, someone else's life, and take over."

"Fear not, Laguz, you will not be taking anything that is not offered. The soul you exchange places with will offer you their life gladly. They will never be forced to give it up against their will."

Laguz closed his eyes and rubbed them with his other hand. "I know that, and I know that this is the only way for us to try and be together. It just makes me feel a bit uncomfortable, that's all."

"We can sense the uncertainty in you, but we can assure you that you will overcome this uncertainty. The vessel you occupy in which to do so, is not important. What is important is that when you and Velvet join forces, you will Awaken the entire planet with your energy, passion and love."

Laguz smiled. "Thank you, Rainbows. I appreciate your support. I don't know how I would have coped with all of this without you."

"It is our pleasure, Laguz. We look forward to seeing you on Earth."

"Me too." Laguz opened his hand and the Rainbow Child danced away to join the others who were swirling around the room. Laguz watched them for a while, feeling better for having spoken to them. Knowing that his time on the Other Side may be short, he said goodbye to the Rainbows, then made his way through the Academy to the gardens. He passed through all the gardens with barely a glance at his surroundings, until he reached the Atlantis Garden. Before sitting down on the bench, he traced the lines of Velvet's face gently. His fingers trailed down until he reached the wooden rune pendant strung around her graceful neck with a leather cord. He wondered how his rune necklace from his life as Adrian had come to Velvet. Who had sent it? He vaguely remembered that he'd put the necklace in the carved wooden box he'd made for Magenta, then had tucked it away safely for her to find after his death, but apparently someone else had got hold of it, then somehow knew to send it to Velvet? He guessed it didn't really matter; the fact that Velvet and Magenta were friends again was more important. He knew how much Velvet valued Magenta's insights.

Feeling slightly foolish, Laguz glanced around to make sure he was indeed alone, then he leaned in and brushed Velvet's cold marble lips with his own. He hoped with all his heart that he would be able to do it for real very soon.

He pulled back and retreated to the bench. He wished Gold would hurry up and contact him. If he didn't return to Earth soon, Laguz was worried he might be too late.

CHAPTER SIX

How had she managed to get here?

Violet looked at her pale reflection in the bathroom mirror and shivered. The person staring back at her was not the person she had been just four months before. Time seemed to have a mind of its own these days, changing Violet's life at the speed of light. She felt as though she had been careening head first into complete disaster and had no way of stopping.

The door handle rattled, making her jump. It seemed she couldn't even escape to the bathroom for more than a few minutes.

"Are you nearly done in there? I've got to go!"

Violet sighed and made a face at her reflection. Slowly, she left the bathroom, ignoring the swearing as she passed Charlie in the hallway.

She returned to the bedroom and curled up on the bed, hugging her knees to her chest. She closed her eyes and tried to relax, but her body was wound too tight.

It had started off so sweetly, and had felt so right, but just a few months later, Violet was wishing that she'd heeded her original intuition.

Just a couple of days after the gig in the local pub, Violet had run into Charlie again, this time in the supermarket. In all honesty, she hadn't recognised him immediately, but he'd recognised her. Perhaps she'd been feeling a bit lonely, or perhaps she was just finally ready to move on, but for some reason, she ignored her own instinct and gave him her number. He didn't even wait until the next day to call and arrange a date.

Their first date had been really sweet. They had gone back to the pub where they'd met, had a few drinks, and then he'd walked her home, kissing her goodnight at the front door.

Their relationship had progressed far too quickly from that point onwards. It was barely a couple of weeks later when he moved into her house. At the time, it all felt right, natural, and Violet knew that no one could have stopped it from happening. But now she felt trapped. Within a month of living together, he'd lost his job and had no interest in finding another. When he bothered to get out of bed, it was either to eat, drink beer, use the bathroom, or to play his computer games. He contributed nothing to their relationship financially, and emotionally all he provided these days was abuse. Nothing she did was good enough; nothing was the way he wanted it to be.

It was ironic, Violet realised, that for so long she'd been telling Amy to get rid of Danny because of the way he treated her, and now here she was, with a guy who treated her even worse than that, and she was just putting up with it.

Why did she put up with it? Because she loved him. It was a bizarre concept, to love someone so much when they quite obviously did not have your best interests at heart. When they treated you like dirt. But Violet finally understood why Amy found it so difficult to leave Danny, why she continued to be with him, despite the affairs, the disappearances, and the way he acted like it was okay for him to do that. Though Charlie had never been physically abusive, she now understood why women stayed with men who beat them. Because the thought of not being with him was agony. Of course, being with him was just as painful at times.

Violet flinched when she heard Charlie come out of the bathroom, but he headed straight downstairs. Straight for the fridge, no doubt, for the beers that Violet had to buy him because he had no money.

She hadn't seen her Spiritual Sisters in ages either. She'd cancelled a meeting because of Charlie refusing to leave his computer game because he was at a 'really important bit', then the following week he'd insisted on an evening in together, only to fall asleep ten minutes into watching the movie she'd rented. Then the week after that she was just too exhausted to host a meeting. Charlie's lack of job meant that she'd been doing extra hours at the office - any overtime going - just to pay the rent and the bills, which were much higher since he'd moved in, thanks to his late night binge eating, alcohol consumption and continuous computer game-playing.

Violet looked at her watch. Seven-thirty on a Monday. Normally by now, her Sisters would be here, having a good gossip over a hot cup of tea, and engaging in some kind of spiritual activity or experiment. Instead, she was curled up on the bed, feeling sorry for herself. Groaning, she sat up and looked around the room, seeing clutter and debris; no trace of the calm, peaceful haven it used to be. Even her spiritual books had been boxed up and put away in the loft, because he hated that 'hocus-pocus shit'. It was easier to stop doing the things he didn't like than it was to stand up to him and do them anyway. Violet was just too exhausted to fight anymore. She knew that he was sapping all her strength, all her energy, but she didn't know how to stop it.

The phone rang and Violet jumped off the bed, but before she'd even got halfway down the stairs, she heard Charlie answer it. She stopped to listen. From the gruff tone of his voice, and the way he slammed it down, Violet guessed it had been one of her friends. But who? She took a deep breath and walked down the rest of the stairs, pausing in the doorway of the lounge.

Charlie was completely engrossed in his computer game again, a furrow of concentration on his forehead, his teeth biting his bottom lip as he killed a monster he was hunting.

Violet stared at him, wondering how she had fallen so deeply for someone who thought that violence was not only okay, but an essential part of life. Someone who loved to collect war paraphernalia and shoot at people on the TV screen. Violet herself was not a fan of violence. In her opinion, it just created more violence; it never really solved anything. Wars made no sense to her. After all, if you won, you had the blood of many men on your hands and memories that would haunt you for the rest of your life. And if you lost, you were dead. It just didn't sound like a very good idea to her.

Violet watched Charlie for a few more minutes before speaking up.

"Who was on the phone?"

There was no response as Charlie jerked his controller around, trying to scale a wall to catch another beast on the screen.

"Charlie?" Violet tried again. "Who was on the phone?"

Still no response.

Suddenly, something in Violet snapped and she strode across the room to the TV and switched it off. She wished she had a camera to capture the look on Charlie's face. But then her stomach clenched a tiny bit when his expression of shock turned into fury.

"What the fuck did you do that for?"

"I asked you a question, several times, and you didn't respond," Violet said, trying to keep her voice from quivering.

"I was just about to complete the level. I've been working on that for two damned weeks!" Charlie shouted, throwing the controller on the floor, making Violet flinch. He stepped towards her, and she shrank back, but had nowhere to go.

"Don't you dare do that again," he growled. Violet nodded mutely then stepped sideways, escaping to the kitchen. She got to the sink and leaned against the counter, her legs trembling. She heard the TV snap back on and Charlie slumping back onto the sofa. She stared out into the darkness, and vaguely recalled the night she thought she'd seen the tiny green Faerie hovering outside the window. In that moment it seemed entirely improbable.

Violet couldn't imagine that magic had ever existed in the world.

* * *

"Gold! Jeez, you scared me!"

"I'm sorry, Laguz, I didn't realise you were in your own little world," Gold said, sitting next to Laguz on the bench. "How long have you been sitting here?"

Laguz shrugged. "A while, I guess." He shifted about on the crystal encrusted bench, but knew that any feeling of discomfort from sitting still was purely in his mind.

"What can I do for you, Gold?" he asked, turning to the Elder. "Have you found a soul who will swap with me yet?"

"As a matter of fact, a soul who may be suitable has come forth, yes."

Laguz's eyes widened. He'd been joking; he hadn't dared to hope that Gold would find anyone this quickly. "Seriously?" He jumped up off the bench. "Let's do it!"

Gold smiled a little at his enthusiasm. "It's not as easy as that, Laguz, you need to talk to the soul first, make sure that it's the right decision, the right body for you. Though I do hope that it's suitable."

"You do? Why's that? I didn't think you were keen on the idea of me returning to be with Velvet."

Gold sighed. "Yes, well that was before Corduroy came along."

Laguz frowned, trying to place the name. "Who?"

"Brown Corduroy. He was the Professor of Death at the Earth Angel Training Academy."

Laguz thought back to those few days he'd spent at the Academy with Velvet and could see the face of the Professor of Death, glaring at him whenever he was in the room. He seemed like such an angry soul. "What do you mean, before he came along?"

"He has met Velvet, on Earth. They are now living together."

Laguz sat back down on the bench. "They're together? But they were so different, I mean, she wasn't even interested in him, was she?"

"They were good friends, they'd been friends through many lifetimes, but they had never been anything more."

"So why are they together now?"

"Because in all those lifetimes, Corduroy wanted to be with her desperately. He tried everything, but she was always oblivious to his advances because she didn't know how he felt. But before he left the Academy, he confessed his love for her, and she rebuffed him. But on Earth, having forgotten this, all she remembers is that he feels familiar to her, and subconsciously, she is trying to make up for all the times she has rejected him."

"So is she happy with him? Do they have a good relationship?" Laguz asked, his heart aching at the thought of Velvet being with another soul, of being too late, again.

Gold shook his head. "It was never a good union. It should never have happened. Being in a relationship based on past-life guilt is never a good thing. But because of their friendship, Velvet feels love for him, and therefore, is unable to break off the relationship, even though it is stifling her, sapping all her energy and stopping her Awakening process."

Laguz clenched his teeth together. He was beginning to get quite angry with Corduroy. How dare he mess with Velvet this way?

"Right, that does it, I don't care how unsuitable this body is, I'm taking it. I need to get back to Earth now, and get Velvet out of that relationship."

Gold raised an eyebrow. "As heroic as that sounds, and as much as I would love for you to do that, for the sake of the human race; do you honestly think that Velvet would let you? You know how independent and proud she is, if you go swooping in there, trying to save the day, do you really think that will win her over?"

Laguz's shoulders slumped. "You're right. She would just end up resenting me for it. What should I do then?"

"You should go to Earth, you should be with Velvet, but it's entirely up to her to get out of the relationship with Corduroy. She is the only one who can end it. Believe me, she will be much stronger for it."

Laguz nodded. "Okay, so no crazy heroics, got it. Can we go talk to this soul now?"

Gold scrutinised Laguz for a moment, then nodded. "Yes, let's."

Before Laguz had the chance to blink, with a click of Gold's fingers they were suddenly standing on the edge of a white mist, peering into nothingness. Laguz recognised it as the outskirts of the Angelic Realm. He knew that if he looked over his shoulder and squinted, he would just be able to make out the outline of Pearl at the gates.

"Grey, this is Laguz, the soul I mentioned to you."

Through the mist, a figure approached him, and Laguz's heart sank a little. Though good looking, the soul facing him was the complete opposite to Laguz in appearance in every way. How on Earth would Velvet recognise him if he looked like that?

Grey stepped forwards and shook Laguz's hand. "Good to meet you, Laguz. Gold tells me that you'd like to return to Earth. Can I ask why?"

Laguz smiled. "Why does a guy do anything crazy? For a woman, of course. Though she's not just any woman, she's my Twin Flame."

Grey nodded. "I understand. I wish I could have found mine. Instead I ended up marrying a girl my parents approved of." He grimaced.

"Are you still married?"

"Yes, we've been married for fifteen years now."

Laguz frowned. "Have you got children?"

"Yes, two girls, Lucy and Janie."

Laguz looked at Gold. How on Earth was he supposed to be with Velvet if he was going to enter the body of a man that already had a wife and two kids?

Laguz turned back to Grey, trying to determine what kind of man he was. "Do you love them?"

"My girls? Of course I do."

"Then why don't you want to return?"

"Because it's my time to leave. This is the time I decided on leaving Earth, and I'm ready."

"So if I don't swap with you, you'll just move onto the Angelic Realm and your body will die?"

Grey nodded. "Yes."

"What happened to you? How did you cross over?"

"I was in a car accident. Knocked unconscious by hitting my head on the steering wheel. Slipped straight into a coma."

"Will I be disabled if I take over his body?" Laguz asked Gold.

Gold shook his head. "No, the only reason he didn't wake up was because he didn't want to. There are no permanent injuries to his body, which is why the doctors are flummoxed as to why he won't come round."

Laguz was quiet for a moment as he considered all of the information. He scrutinised Grey for a while.

"Laguz? Time is running a little short, what is your decision?"

Laguz bit his lip, then nodded briefly. "I'll go."

Grey smiled. "Could you do me a favour, Laguz?"

Laguz shrugged, he figured he owed the man for letting him take over his body, his life. "Sure."

"Could you just make sure my girls are well looked after, if you decide to leave the family in search of your Flame?"

Laguz smiled. "Of course, least I can do." He held his hand out and Grey grasped it, shaking it once.

Grey turned to Gold. "Can I go on now?"

Gold nodded and stepped aside. Grey walked in-between Laguz and Gold, patting Laguz on the shoulder as he passed.

Laguz glanced over his shoulder in time to see Grey disappear into the mist. "So what happens now?"

Gold gestured in front of them, towards where Grey had appeared.

"It's time to wake up."

* * *

Violet opened her eyes. After staring into the darkness for a few seconds, she suddenly saw everything with a clarity that had eluded her for months. She expanded her awareness a fraction and listened to the heavy breathing coming from Charlie as he slept next to her, completely ignorant to her sudden Awakening.

Why had she waited so long? Unable to be near him another second, she slid slowly from under the covers, grabbed her dressing gown from the end of the bed, and snuck out of the room, taking care to miss all of the creaky floorboards. Once safely downstairs, she put the kettle on and stared out of the window. The tiniest hint of light was just appearing on the horizon.

It was as though a heavy mist had lifted from her mind. She realised just how asleep she had been from the moment that she had allowed Charlie into her life. She had felt a connection with him, and had let herself believe that this connection was worth losing herself for. But it wasn't. Their love was not the unconditional love of two souls destined to be together. Their love was much more conditional, much more changeable. How could you love someone unconditionally when really you wished they were someone else?

Violet poured the steaming water onto her herbal teabag and stirred in a spoonful of honey. She had been right when she'd told her Sisters that she wasn't ready to meet anyone else after losing Lyle. Yet again, she should have listened to her own intuition. How many more times would she ignore a strong intuition about something only to regret it later? As she sipped the sweet tea she hoped that from this point on, she would listen to herself.

A sound from behind her startled her, making her slosh some of the hot tea onto her hand.

"What the hell are you doing?"

Heart pounding in her chest, Violet set her mug down, wiped her hand on a tea towel, and with a deep, courage-building breath, turned to face Charlie.

"I want you to leave."

* * *

"Greg? Can you hear me?"

When he opened his eyes, the first thing Greg saw was dyed frizzy blonde hair. The next thing he registered was a pair of brown eyes.

"Oh, Greg, honey," the irritating high-pitched voice said. "You're awake."

Greg blinked a few times, his eyes dry. He focused on the plain face above him and frowned. "Who are you?"

The unremarkable face frowned back. "Greg? What do you mean? It's me, Carly, your wife."

Greg continued to frown, having no memory of the woman now scowling at him. Just then, a doctor entered with a smile on his face.

"Greg! Good to see that you've decided to join us, finally. My name is Dr Richards and I've been taking care of you while you've been sleeping. How are you feeling?" The doctor checked Greg's chart, and Carly jumped up to whisper in his ear.

Dr Richards smiled at Greg. "Having a little trouble remembering things, Greg? You have suffered quite a bump to the head. I should think everything will become clear in a day or two."

Greg nodded, already feeling his eyes drooping.

"I'll be right here when you wake up, sweetheart," Carly said, as the doctor left the room. Greg nodded, his heart sinking slightly at the thought. Within seconds, he was asleep.

* * *

Violet stared at her computer screen blankly, as she had

done for the past few months. Even though she was free of Charlie now, her work productivity was still practically at zero. It was a wonder that she hadn't been fired. She just didn't seem to have the energy to pick herself back up. Hours later she found herself at home again, which was now in a semi-tidy state since she'd thrown Charlie out. She had no recollection of the rest of her work day, the bus ride home or making the cup of tea that was now cold on the coffee table. She needed some help. Fast.

The knock on the door came two seconds later. Slightly unnerved by the coincidence of her mentally asking for help and someone knocking on the door, Violet didn't get up straight away. But the knocking continued, and was getting louder.

Slowly, Violet made her way to the door, worried that maybe it was Charlie, coming to beg her to take him back, as he had done the day after she'd broken up with him.

Before turning the key, Violet peeked through the peephole. It was Amy.

She opened the door to her friend, who she hadn't spoken to properly in months.

"Jeez, and I used to think I looked bad after a fight with Danny."

Violet cracked a half-smile. "Thanks a lot, friend." She waved Amy in. "Besides, we didn't have a fight, I threw him out."

Amy looked around the lounge, noting the lack of male stuff in surprise. "You mean he's gone? Seriously?"

Violet nodded.

Amy stepped forwards and engulfed her in a hug. "Thank the Goddess for that. I thought I was going to lose you, you know."

"I'm sorry I haven't been in touch, it's just, well, Charlie didn't like all the spiritual stuff and I just-"

"Uh uh, no excuses. I should have been round here

more, not been so wrapped up in all my own drama. But what's done is done. Now we need to sort you out." She pulled her mobile out of her handbag and pressed a few buttons. "Time for an emergency Spiritual Sisters meeting, I think."

Shaking her head, but smiling all the same, Violet headed to the kitchen to make some fresh cups of tea.

"Thank you, Angels," she whispered.

* * *

"Huh, well I'm not an Angel, I'm a Faerie."

"I think you'd make an excellent Angel," Linen commented, eating the cherry off the top of his cupcake.

"I don't think so," Aria retorted. "They're way too... angelic."

Linen chuckled. "That is the general idea you know. What I meant was, you've done some very good deeds, I'm sure the Angels are proud of you."

"I wonder if Amethyst would be proud of me," Aria mused, grabbing another cupcake from the plate.

"I'm positive that she would be. Have you visited her lately?"

"Nah, she's finished with the Faerie books, she's moved on to writing about Saints now, I think. And I am definitely *not* one of those."

Linen chuckled again. "Maybe one day you will be."

"Hah, I don't think so! Don't you have to suffer a lot and die in loads of pain?"

Linen shook his head. "Not necessarily, no. But I can understand why you'd be put off."

"Hmm, I'm quite happy here to be honest. Though I was wondering something."

"What's that?"

"When the Rainbows finally leave for Earth, what do

we do then? I mean, we're staying here because of them, but they don't really need us. When they're gone we really will have no excuse to stay here."

Linen shrugged. "I don't know. What do you want to do?"

"You mean we can choose?"

"Aria, you know that we have free will, just as the humans do."

"I guess so. I'm just not sure what would be a good idea. I mean, I don't want to become a human. I don't think going back to the Elemental Realm would be a good idea either, because it's still on Earth, and the humans are wrecking it. And I don't really want to hang out in the Angelic Realm forever." She looked around her quickly to make sure no one was listening. "I mean, don't get me wrong, it's great here, I love it, I really do, but it's a bit boring."

"So you've ruled out most options. What about going to another planet?"

Aria made a face. "Huh, I hadn't thought of that. I'm not sure, most of the aliens I met were a bit odd, and they were really funny shapes, too."

Linen smiled. "So where else is left in the Universe?"

"I'd rather be at the School than anywhere else, I think. As long as you're there though," Aria added.

"But we won't have any students left soon, like you said."

"How about we change it into something else again? It went from being the Earth Angel Training Academy to being the School for the Children of the Golden Age; we could change its purpose again."

"To what? A Leprechaun School?"

Aria shook her head, laughing. "No, silly, I was thinking more along the lines of something that might help with the Awakening."

Linen was puzzled. "It sounds like you've been giving

this some thought. What did you want to change it to?"

"Okay, don't laugh, but how about changing it into a retreat for humans? I mean, I know they go to the Angelic Realm to progress and all, but what if we offered them an alternative? Try to Awaken them here, then offer them a chance to return to Earth, only this time maybe they'll have more chance of Awakening? I mean, it might help out the Earth Angels a little if we're sending educated humans back to Earth."

Linen was silent as he thought about Aria's idea. A slow smile crept onto his face. "Do you know what, Aria? I think you may be onto a winning idea there. Fancy pitching it to Gold?"

Aria grinned. "You really think it's a good idea?"

"No, Aria, I think it's a brilliant idea."

* * *

Greg couldn't stop himself from rolling his eyes for the hundredth time as Carly fussed over him again; this time it was about the arrangement of the cushions he was sitting on.

"Seriously, Carly, I'm fine. You can go shopping now, I'll call you on your mobile if I need anything, I promise."

Carly sighed. "But I don't want to leave you when you've only been out of hospital for a day, what if you have a dizzy spell or something? I don't want to come home and find you collapsed on the floor, I just don't know what I would do!"

Oh my good God, was the woman annoying! How on Earth had he ended up marrying such a drama queen? Greg was very happy that his memory still hadn't returned - it wouldn't surprise him if he'd blocked out the previous fifteen years for the sake of his own sanity.

"Honestly, darling," Greg said, wincing inwardly at

using the endearment; it sounded false even to him. "I'll be fine, I promise."

It was a strange feeling, having to learn about his own life. He'd looked at photos of himself with his family over the years, with his two girls, but he felt no recollection, no sentimentality, no connection whatsoever. He didn't even really recognise his own face. When he went past the hallway mirror earlier that day he'd jumped, thinking there was a stranger in the house. The doctors seemed surprised by his amnesia - it seemed quite severe considering that the blow to his head hadn't left any other lasting damage.

Carly finally gave up fussing and left the house, after making sure he had a drink, food, the cordless phone, all the phone numbers he could possibly need and even all the remote controls lined up next to him. Though it should have been nice, having someone look after him, he just felt stifled. Hospital was preferable to this, at least the nurses left him alone most of the time. He felt a bit nervous about the coming afternoon when he was going to meet his daughters for what felt like the first time, but other than that, he just felt a bit bored.

It wasn't as though Greg had no memories at all, but the only face in his mind was the one he had yet to see. She haunted his dreams every night, and every time he saw anything purple she surfaced in his mind again. He hoped that at some point he might meet her, it seemed important somehow.

Greg sighed; he was even bored with his own company. He picked up the TV remote. Might as well see what daytime TV had to offer. He picked up a packet of crisps and flicked through the channels, finally deciding on a particularly crazy episode of the Jeremy Kyle show. When he saw the topic he laughed, nearly choking on a crisp.

"Maybe it's a sign," he muttered to himself.

CHAPTER SEVEN

"Things have been pretty crappy for both of us recently, and though we're making great progress, I think we both need a bit of a boost, so I've booked us on a retreat."

Violet's eyebrows shot up. "What? Seriously? But you don't have that kind of money, Ames, I couldn't possibly-"

"Nope, sorry, I'm not listening to any excuses. You're coming with me whether you want to or not. Besides, my Nan gave me some money to cheer myself up after breaking up with Danny, so it's her treat, not mine." Amy smiled, but Violet could still see the slight strain beneath the surface. Though he'd been a prize-winning asshole, Amy had really loved him. Violet's heart ached. She knew how Amy felt; despite everything, she'd really loved Charlie.

"Maybe you're right. I know I could do with getting away. So where are we going?"

"It's a small place in the middle of Wales, they have little camping pods where you sleep, and they run courses on various spiritual things, but their main focus is on relationships."

Violet grimaced. "I think I've had enough of men to last me a lifetime."

"Hey, you can't give up, what if your soulmate is out

there, waiting for you, and you've stopped looking?"

"Then he'll just have to come and find me, won't he?"

Amy shook her head, smiling. "Anyway, we're going on Friday, first thing in the morning, and we won't be back 'til the following Friday."

"A whole week? It's a bit short notice getting the time off work."

"Like I said, no excuses. We are going. I don't care if you have to fake a broken leg to get the time off, I am putting you in my car and driving you to the retreat on Friday morning."

Violet smiled. "What did I do to deserve a friend like you, Amy?"

"Don't know, but it must have been something quite spectacular!" Amy glanced at the clock. "The others should be here in a moment; we'll have to tell them there won't be a meeting next week."

"Shall I tell them you're whisking me away for a romantic break?" Violet asked, wiggling her eyebrow suggestively.

"Oh, darling, if I ever decide to be a lesbian, you'll be the first person I'll call, but I'm afraid I like my men too much."

Violet laughed. "I wish I could say the same, but right now I think I would be better off becoming a nun."

Amy looked at Violet and tilted her head to the right. "Hmm, yeah, I can just see you in a habit. Black and white would really suit you."

Violet swatted Amy on the shoulder then went to answer the door.

"Hey, Fay, Beattie, how're things?" she greeted her Sisters then went to the kitchen to boil the kettle while they settled into their usual chairs. While Violet was in the kitchen, the doorbell rang again, signalling the arrival of Maggie, Leila and Keeley.

Once settled in the lounge, Violet made the weekly

announcements, including the cancellation of the following week's meeting, and then they started on their new topic. Despite not having a meeting for several months while she was with Charlie, they had fallen back into their Monday night routine as though nothing had happened.

"So, who's brought something with them that can be used as a pendulum?"

Everyone except Fay held up their objects. "Sorry, Violet, I totally spaced out on bringing something."

"That's okay, you can use one of my pendulums," Violet said, handing Fay a crystal pendulum made from rainbow fluorite. "Now then, hold the chain or string with your thumb and forefinger, and let the pendulum dangle down. I find it easier to start with it swinging in a neutral position, just back and forth." Violet got her pendulum swinging, then looked around to see if everyone else was doing the same. "Then ask aloud, or in your head, for the pendulum to show you what a 'yes' answer looks like. Note any changes in direction, and keep your hand as still as possible."

Violet's pendulum swung immediately to the right, in a clockwise circle. Though she'd been using a pendulum for a while, it still delighted her when it moved by itself. She saw the same amazement and joy on the faces of her Sisters as their pendulums also began to move in response to their thoughts.

"Okay, now swing it back into neutral, and ask it what a 'no' answer looks like. The first time I asked for a 'no' it was quite weak, but it will get stronger with a little practice." Her own pendulum swung to the left, swinging in anti-clockwise circles when she asked it for a 'no'. She loved dowsing. Though her answers were never a hundred percent accurate, they were right more often than they were wrong, and when she found herself stressing out over something, it usually reassured her that everything in fact was going to turn out okay.

"Once you know what your 'yes' and 'no' look like, you can start asking it questions. You can ask questions you know the answers to at first, to test your accuracy, but then you can ask it virtually anything you like."

"Anything?" Fay asked, not moving her eyes from her crystal pendulum.

"Yep, anything. What will happen in your future, what's happening in the present, what course of action would be best to take; anything that's on your mind."

Without another word, the Sisters all put their pendulums into neutral and began asking questions, their lips moving silently as they stared at their swinging object.

Violet bit her lip. There was a question she'd wanted to ask, but hadn't had the courage to. Was breaking up with Charlie a mistake? Should she have tried harder to make it work? She did still love him, still missed having him around, despite everything. Taking a deep breath, Violet silently asked the pendulum then closed her eyes, afraid of the answer. A few seconds later, she opened her eyes and sighed in relief. According to her pendulum, it was the right thing to do. She asked her next question: was she ever going to meet a soulmate who loved and respected her, and who treated her well? Again she closed her eyes, afraid that it would tell her no, and that she would end up an old spinster with too many cats.

Her second sigh of relief caught Amy's attention, and her friend looked up from her own swinging pendulum. She shook her head slightly in response. She would tell Amy later, though she was sure from the look of relief on Amy's face that she was probably asking similar questions.

After a busy evening of dowsing, Violet was just putting the mugs and plates in the sink when Maggie came into the kitchen.

"Hey, Violet. I hope you don't mind, but I've got a message for you."

Violet set the china down and turned to her friend, refusing to get her hopes up too high. "From Lyle?"

Maggie shook her head. "No, sorry, I don't know who it was from, but I got an image of a flower, which is called Lunaria," she smiled sheepishly. "I had to Google it to identify it. And the message was 'Believe in what you see, feel and dream, not in what you think you know'." Maggie shrugged. "Seemed a little random to me, I wondered if you would know what it meant."

Violet shook her head slowly. "Not really, was there anything else?"

"Actually yes, the last thing that came through was the image of a tiny green Faerie."

"A green Faerie," Violet echoed, her gaze wandering over to the kitchen window where she thought she'd seen a Faerie. "Believe in what you see," she whispered. Could she? Could she honestly believe that Faeries really existed?

* * *

"Woo! Go, Magenta! I'm so glad that she got my message. Just in time for the retreat as well. Must congratulate the Angels on orchestrating that one. I'm looking forward to trying to talk to Velvet in her meditations. Let's just hope she listens to herself this time."

"Yes, it does all seem to be coming together now, doesn't it?" Linen commented, taking a handful of peanuts.

"Yep, it does. How is Laguz doing? Have you checked on him recently?"

Linen shook his head. "No, the last I saw of him, he'd come out of hospital and was being driven crazy by his newly acquired wife."

Aria's eyes were wide. "How weird would it be to go to Earth to a ready-made family and not know them? I wonder how long it will take for him to break away from her. I mean, Velvet's got rid of Corduroy, so Laguz and Velvet can be together now."

"I'm not so sure she's ready just yet, to be honest. I think she needs a bit of time to herself, to open up again, reconnect to the Universal energy. After all, we weren't able to connect with her through her dreams the whole time she was with Corduroy; so she'll need a chance to shake off all the negativity and regain some of her old sense of self."

"Hmm, I guess," Aria said, munching on a chocolate covered marshmallow. "It just seems so silly, all this waiting around, all these rules that humans follow."

"That's because you're not a human."

"Yeah, yeah, and I never will be, if I have anything to do with it. Though I am looking forward to being able to do more to help them, if I can. When are we meeting Gold?"

"He said he'd call when he had a spare moment. I figured we could just stay here until then. After all, like you said, there's not much work to be done right now."

"Shall we check on Laguz?"

"Why not." Linen waved his hand over the lake and the image changed.

"It's still weird to see Laguz like that. I mean, he's blond and green eyed here. Do you think Velvet will recognise him?"

"I hope so. The world is depending on it."

* * *

"What are you looking at?"

Greg quickly closed down the internet browser and looked over his shoulder at Carly, who was stood a foot behind him, her hands on her hips.

"Nothing," he said.

"Nothing? That didn't look like nothing to me. That looked like a camper van."

"I was just browsing on eBay, and saw an advert for camper vans. I've always wanted one."

Carly frowned. "You have? I never knew that."

"Guess I never mentioned it."

"And what exactly would you do with a camper van? Those things are tiny, you'd never fit me, you and the girls in it to go on holidays, so it would be a bit pointless, wouldn't it?"

Greg gritted his teeth, unsure as to how much longer he could endure her whining, grating voice.

"You're right, dear, I was just looking out of interest. It would be completely impractical to buy it for the family."

Carly nodded her head curtly, obviously used to winning the arguments, and stalked off towards the kitchen.

Greg turned back to the computer and went back on eBay. Of course it would be an impractical buy for the family, but if he were on his own, then it would be perfectly practical…

"Four thousand, three hundred and fifty," he muttered to himself. That was definitely doable. He had about twenty thousand in his own savings account. He could easily buy the camper and still have enough to live on for several months. If he was careful and picked up odd jobs, maybe even a year or more. After all, it wasn't like he could go back to his old job as an engineer - his amnesia meant that he had absolutely no idea how to do the job he'd apparently done for the last ten years. Decision made, Greg put a bid on the slate blue camper van, then logged out, carefully wiping the history on the internet browser, so that Carly wouldn't be able to see what he'd done. It irked him that he didn't have his own private computer. He had a work laptop, but it was password protected, and of course, he couldn't remember any passwords either.

Greg headed straight upstairs, to the master bedroom; avoiding the kitchen where Carly was slamming pots and pans around in a dramatic effort to make the dinner, and the lounge where his two girls, who really were two strangers, sat watching TV and pretending to do their homework. Once the door was closed behind him, he had a quick look through the wardrobe, but decided he'd only take essential clothing. After all, he felt no attachment to any of it. He'd just pick up what he needed as he went along. In terms of possessions, the only things he intended to take were the necessities - a toothbrush, his notebook and his deodorant.

He sat on the bed and mentally planned his escape. He wanted to just go, disappear one night with no note, no explanation or forwarding address, but that idea made him feel too guilty. As much as he felt nothing for Carly, he did feel responsible for the girls. But then the house had very little mortgage, Carly had a full time job, and a joint account with more than enough to keep them comfortable.

The only problem with disappearing without a trace would be that Carly would call the police and begin a massive search, assuming that he'd got lost or something because of his amnesia. No, he needed to leave a note. That way, she wouldn't come looking for him. The last thing he wanted was to end up as a picture on a milk bottle.

The auction for the van ended at midnight; he'd keep an eye on it, to make sure he won. Then he would see how quickly he could pick it up. Hopefully he'd be gone by the end of the week. Four more days, surely he could last that long?

* * *

"I really don't know how to thank you for this, Amy, you really are an amazing friend." Violet settled back into the car seat and buckled herself in.

Amy started up the engine and smiled at her. "You can

send my nan a thank you note if you want. Now then," she reached over and put a CD in. "I vote that we do nothing but relax and think happy thoughts from now until we get back next Friday. Agreed?" The music began; a classical song by Bach.

"Agreed."

"Excellent. Now then, next stop, Middle of Nowhere, Wales."

Violet giggled. "You do know where you're going, right?"

"Nope, no idea, but Susie here knows exactly where we're going," she said, gesturing to her Sat Nav. "So fear not, I will get you there in one piece."

"I trust you."

"Good! Should think so too."

Feeling the stress in her shoulders begin to melt away, Violet closed her eyes and listened to the soothing melodies coming from the speakers. She'd never really been a massive fan of classical music, but it certainly was calming. As she hovered on the edge of falling asleep, a new song started, and instantly she was swept into a dream.

She looked around her and smiled at the familiar surroundings. The waves lapped onto the golden sand, nearly touching her bare toes. She breathed in the salty air and looked out towards the sea. For some reason, she expected to see someone there. The music rose and fell around her, the sun warmed her shoulders, and the waves continued lapping, but no one came.

"Vi? Are you okay?"

Violet jolted awake and looked at her friend. "What?"

Amy frowned. "I was asking you if you were okay, you're crying."

Violet raised her hand to her cheek and wiped away the tears. She shook her head. "I fell asleep. I was dreaming, I guess."

"About what?"

Violet closed her eyes and the dream came back to her. "It was the same beach from the dreams I used to have of Lyle. But though I expected him to turn up, I was all alone."

Amy frowned. "I didn't realise you were still dreaming about him."

"I'm not. That's the first dream I've had of that beach since the day he died. It must have been the song."

"The song?"

"The one that was playing just now, when I fell asleep. I'm sure it was the same song that they played at Lyle's funeral."

"It must have just reminded you of him then."

"I guess it must have."

A silence settled between them then, and neither of them spoke until they hit the border of Wales.

"Croeso i Gymru," Amy read. "Feels like we're entering another world."

"The Welsh do sometimes seem like they're from another planet," Violet remarked, thinking of some of her more unusual Welsh friends.

Amy giggled. "I wouldn't say that too loud, we've only just got here, I wouldn't want to offend anyone."

"How long have we got to go anyway?" Violet asked, shifting in her seat, trying to get the feeling back in her stiff legs.

Amy peered at the Sat Nav. "Susie reckons about twenty minutes. Can you last that long?"

Violet nodded, looking out of the window at the passing scenery. It did seem a little otherworldly. The mountains in the distance reminded her of the *Lord of the Rings* movies. She loved that trilogy. She'd wanted to move out to New Zealand for months after seeing it.

After what seemed like a very long twenty minutes,

Susie told them to turn into a very narrow, bumpy driveway that seemed to take them deep into the woods. Turning on her lights in the gloom, Amy concentrated on missing the biggest of the potholes.

After a few minutes, they drove into a small clearing. Amy parked the car and turned off the engine. When they stepped out of the car, the silence was deafening.

"Wow," Violet whispered. "I'd forgotten what silence was like."

"It is a retreat. Wouldn't be much good if it was too noisy, would it?"

The two women got their bags from the boot of the car then followed the carved wooden signs to the main house; a surprisingly modern structure that looked like it had been dropped there from the future.

"Not quite the old-style Welsh cottage I was expecting," Violet said.

"Looks just like the pictures on the internet."

"I didn't know there were pictures."

"That's because I wanted every bit of it to be a surprise," Amy replied, hoisting her bag a little higher on her shoulder. She always packed far too much.

When they reached the front door, before Violet could ring the bell, she noticed the sign above it.

"The Twin Flame Retreat," Violet read. Twin Flames… that was what had come up on the Angel Board, from Lyle, surely that couldn't be a coincidence too. She turned to Amy. "Did you choose this place because of the name? Because of what came up on the Angel Board?"

"Actually no, that was just a happy coincidence. This retreat just happened to be the cheapest and seemed to be offering the kind of courses that both of us need right now."

Violet looked back at the sign, noting the symbol of two figures with flames for wings carved into the wood.

She'd noticed the symbol on the signs from the car park and had wondered what they meant. Reaching for the bell, she'd only rung it once when the door swung open and they were greeted by a lady with curly blonde hair and a huge smile.

"Welcome! I hope you didn't have any trouble finding us, we're a little bit out of the way here."

Amy and Violet stepped into the house. "We had no trouble, Susie got us here just fine."

The lady frowned. "Susie? Aren't you Violet and Amy?"

Violet smiled and set her bag on the floor. "Yes, I'm Violet, this is Amy. Susie is the Sat Nav."

"Oh! I see. I'm afraid I'm a little technologically challenged myself, I prefer a good old fashioned map."

"Me too," Violet agreed. "I prefer to see the whole route rather than just be fed little bits of it a time."

"Ah ha, I see we will have to do some meditations on seeing the bigger picture, I think you will enjoy them. Now then, if I could just get you to sign in the guest book - you can leave comments at the end of the week if you wish. Then I will show you to your sleeping pod and you can get settled in. Afterwards we'll have some tea and cakes and chat about what you wish to do during your stay."

"Sounds great," Amy replied, signing her name and Violet's in the guest book. Violet picked up her bag and they followed the lady outside. They followed a wood-chip path through the trees until they came to a structure that reminded Violet a little of a hobbit house, only it was made entirely of wood and had a normal, though small, door on the front. They stepped inside and were a little amazed at how big it was inside compared to the way it looked outside.

"Right, I'll be in the house when you're ready, don't worry about ringing the bell, just come on in. Oh, and I forgot to introduce myself! I'm Esmeralda and my husband, Mike is around somewhere. You'll meet him later, at dinner." With a little wave, she left, closing the tiny door behind her.

"Which bed do you want?" Violet asked, gesturing to the two single beds made up beautifully with embroidered cotton linen.

"The green one."

Violet took the other one, which had lilac coloured sheets embroidered with lavender flowers. When she got closer, she thought she could even smell some lavender. She flopped onto the bed, then looked around the pod.

"Hey, where do we go to the toilet?"

Amy laughed, and pointed to the door. "Welcome to the great outdoors!"

* * *

Greg stood outside the house he had tried to think of as home, shivering slightly in the cold night air. He felt nothing for the building in front of him, which was good, because he'd just slipped out, leaving a note in the kitchen, and was about to get a taxi to a hotel before going to collect the camper van in the morning. He had no clear idea of where he was going to go, but he felt a strong need to get out of the country, at least for a little while. He didn't trust Carly not to call the police, despite him leaving a note explaining everything.

Finally, the taxi arrived, and Greg threw his rucksack onto the back seat before climbing in. Without another glance back at the dark house, Greg gave the taxi driver the hotel address and they sped away into the darkness.

The driver wasn't chatty, so the forty minute journey passed silently, as Greg mentally tried to make some kind of plan. He reckoned that going to France would be the best first step. He'd just drive to Dover and get on the next ferry.

Then, well, he wasn't sure what then. Drive in a southerly direction and see what happened.

In the hotel, he felt too keyed up to sleep straight away. He felt a sense of anticipation and excitement, though he didn't know why. He flicked through the channels on the TV twice, but didn't find anything particularly interesting. He switched the TV off and sat on the bed, staring at the blank screen for a while. It felt a little like he'd been sent from another planet. With no memory of his life before the accident, it felt as though he didn't know anyone. Except for his dreams. The dark-haired woman haunted him still, and he knew he wouldn't feel right until he saw her face for real. If she even existed, that was. Finally feeling a little bit sleepy, Greg flicked the lamp off and got underneath the covers. He closed his eyes and hoped for another visit.

* * *

"So, Gold, what do you think?"

Gold nodded slowly. "I think it's a very interesting idea, though how effective it will be, I cannot be sure."

"But it's worth a try, right?" Aria pressed. "I mean, the Earth Angels need all the help they can get, it would make things so much easier if what they were saying triggered some kind of memory within the humans."

Gold smiled at the small green Faerie. "I admire your spirit, little one; therefore I say you should give it a try. Turn the School for the Children of the Golden Age into the Academy of Awakened Humans."

Aria smiled. "I like the sound of that. What do you think, Linen?"

Linen smiled back. "I think it sounds great. And I think Gold would agree with me when I say that I think you should be the Head of the Academy."

Aria's eyes widened and her mouth dropped open.

"What? I couldn't possibly be the Head of the Academy."

"Why not?" Gold asked. "It was your idea after all."

"Do you really think I could do it?" Aria asked.

"Without a shadow of a doubt," Linen replied. "You've been amazing as my assistant."

Aria looked from Linen to Gold then back again. Though she had her doubts, she finally nodded. "Okay, I'll do it. Hey, does this mean I get a bigger desk?"

Linen laughed. "If you want one, sure. Though I don't think it would be any tidier if it were bigger."

"My desk isn't messy," Aria protested. "It's organised chaos, just the way I like it."

"Right, well, shall we leave Gold to it? I'm sure he has plenty of things to be doing."

"Thank you, Linen. I'm glad you asked to see me, I wish you the very best with this idea. Oh, and I wouldn't wait until the Rainbows have left, they won't mind if you begin straight away. From now on, I will offer the humans crossing over a place at the Academy. It will be interesting to see what the response is." Before Linen or Aria could respond, with a click, Gold was gone.

"I guess we'd better get a move on then," Aria said, holding her hand out to Linen.

"Lead the way, Headmistress."

With a giggle, Aria clicked her fingers and they vanished.

CHAPTER EIGHT

"Good morning!" Esmeralda called out to Violet and Amy as they entered the dining room the next day.

"I hope you both slept well?"

"Yes we did, thanks," Amy replied, sitting down at a table for two. "I'm sorry we didn't join you last night for a chat, I think we were both more tired than we realised."

Esmeralda waved her hand dismissively and placed a menu in front of them both. "Don't you worry about it, that's what this retreat is all about - relaxation. I'm just glad that you both got plenty of rest."

Violet smiled. "Yes, though I must admit I felt much better when I found the bathroom."

"Oh dear, I forgot to point that out yesterday, didn't I? I do apologise. We are in the country here, but we do still have a few luxuries."

Violet studied the menu briefly, her stomach was grumbling. "Could I have the herbal tea and the pancakes with strawberries?"

Esmeralda nodded. "And for you, Amy?"

"I'll have a coffee and some toast with raspberry jam, please."

"No problems, I'll be right out."

"Are we the only guests at the moment?" Amy asked, gesturing around the empty dining room.

"Yes, you are indeed, though we're expecting a couple more guests to arrive tomorrow."

Esmeralda went out to the kitchen to get their breakfast and Violet and Amy settled back into their seats.

"It's so quiet here," Amy whispered. "It's like we're meditating even when we're not."

"I know what you mean. I can never quiet my mind enough to meditate properly at home. But here, I can actually imagine doing it."

After a leisurely breakfast, Violet and Amy met Esmeralda outside in the meditation tent. It looked like a miniature circus marquee. Once inside, it was like stepping into a giant marshmallow. There were white scatter cushions covering the floor, and billows of white fabric draping down from the centre of the ceiling to the edges. Violet silently wondered how they kept it so immaculately clean. They removed their shoes, and stepped inside, sitting on cushions opposite each other, with Esmeralda on one side.

"My husband, Mike, will be along to join us in a moment, to make up the circle. But before he does, I would like you both to just think about what it is that may need healing within you. Or even what question you would like answered. It seems that there are many mysteries in life, and though it appears that the answers are not available to you, in truth, every answer you could ever possibly need is within you. All you have to do is to listen. Also, asking the right question is where most people become unstuck. Ask the right question, and the answer will come."

Violet and Amy both nodded then closed their eyes.

What needed healing? Violet wondered. Part of her said 'Everything'. It seemed like the last few months had been the most tumultuous, testing times of her whole life. She wanted to heal the pain she felt for not finding

Lyle in time. She wanted to heal the pain caused by her relationship with Charlie. Bizarrely, she even needed to heal the pain of losing Charlie. She had really loved him, though she wasn't sure why. She'd felt like she'd known him her whole life, which was why it had hurt to make him leave. As for questions she needed answering, of the hundreds that swirled around her head, there was only one thing she felt she really needed to know - what should she do now? She felt lost. She had no idea what her next move should be. There were so many things she wanted to do with her life, but she just didn't know how to make them happen. So that would be her question. She opened her eyes and looked at Amy, who seemed to be going through a similar internal dialogue. Esmeralda was simply sat cross-legged, hands resting lightly on her knees, a look of deep peaceful serenity on her face.

A few minutes later, Esmeralda's husband, Mike, joined them. For some reason, he looked nothing like Violet imagined he would, yet he looked quite familiar. She wondered if she had met him before.

Once introductions were made, Mike settled down and Violet watched him quickly sink into a meditative state. She breathed deeply and closed her eyes. Once their deep breathing was in unison, Esmeralda began to speak.

"Now, we're going to go on a journey together, but before we go, I want you to have a clear question in your mind. By the end of our journey, you will have the answer that you seek. You start off on a small bumpy path, which you walk down steadily, noticing the beautiful scenery that surrounds you."

Violet was quickly drawn into the vision, noticing fields of sunflowers either side of her as she walked down a narrow country lane.

"At the end of this path, you reach a gate. You open the gate and step through, closing it behind you. When you look up, there is a building in front of you. This is your house."

Violet closed the gate and looked up to see a beautiful white cottage, with roses growing up the front of it. She noticed she was no longer surrounded by sunflowers, but instead had the sea behind her; the waves gently lapping against the rocks.

"I want you to walk to the front door, enter your house and then walk into the front room. I want you to notice the décor, the furniture, if it's neat and tidy or a mess, anything that you can see."

Violet stepped through the white wooden door and into the front room. There were faded floral sofas, stone flooring, French-style white painted chairs, a dining table, and a bookcase filled with books.

"Now walk through that room into the kitchen, notice again anything you see or even smell."

Violet walked into the kitchen and was overwhelmed by the smell of drying herbs. Bunches of herbs were hung over the Aga, and though the kitchen was old, everything was scrubbed and clean.

"Now for the next few minutes, I want you to explore the rest of the house, taking note of any details." Esmeralda was silent as Violet left the kitchen and went through the front room to the stairs. She climbed the wooden spiral staircase, and from the landing upstairs, went into the door on her right. It was a spacious bedroom, very simply decorated with a double bed, two bedside tables, and a beautiful blue rug covering part of the whitewashed wooden floor. There was a large window looking out to the sea, and Violet crossed the room to stare out at the view for a few moments. Then she left the bedroom and entered the other room, which was a large bathroom with an old-fashioned bathtub and sink. The décor was again very clean, bright and neutral. The third door on the landing led to what looked like a guest room, with clean, mismatched towels set out neatly on the end of the bed. Violet soaked in as much detail as possible, then headed back down the stairs. She was about to open another door when Esmeralda spoke again.

"Now wherever you are in the house, please go back to the kitchen and then exit the house out the back door."

Violet followed her instructions, leaving the final room unexplored. She left the house and found herself in a beautiful garden, filled with fruit trees, a large veggie plot and statues of Unicorns, Faeries and other mystical creatures.

"In the garden, there's a spade next to some earth that has been dug up recently. I want you to go over to it and dig a small hole."

Violet saw the spade and the earth in the centre of the veggie plot. She went over to it and started digging. After a few seconds, she hit something.

"You should find, not too deep down, a small box."

Violet dropped the spade and knelt down next to the hole. She reached in and uncovered the box with her hands. She pulled it out and set it on the ground. Despite looking old and battered, the metal box was surprisingly light.

"Now I want you to open the box. Your answer is inside."

Slightly hesitant, not knowing what might be revealed, Violet flicked the clasp on the box and lifted the lid. Inside was a single sheet of paper, folded in half. She pulled it out and unfolded it to read the two words written on it. *La Rochelle.*

"Now, once you have found your answer, I want you to leave it in the box, replace the box in the hole in the ground and cover it over with earth. Then walk around the house, leave through the front gate, and make your way back up the path."

Violet followed the instructions, feeling a little puzzled

as to what her answer meant. She left the garden and watched the sea for a moment, inhaling the fresh salty air, which reminded her of her dream of the beach. Then she set off up the path, glancing back at the house a couple of times, trying to memorise every last detail that she could. She saw the sunflowers again, their brown faces basking in the afternoon sunlight, which felt warm on her skin.

"We are now back where we began our journey. In a few moments, I will count backwards from five, and when I reach one, you will open your eyes. Five…four…three…two…one. Now, when you're ready, open your eyes."

Just as Violet was about to open her eyes, she saw a figure among the sunflowers, waving to her. But before she could see who it was, Amy's voice broke her concentration and she opened her eyes.

"That was amazing, I could see so much detail! I've never been that good at guided meditations before, that was so cool."

Esmeralda smiled at Amy. "Would you like to share your experience? Did you get the answer you were looking for?"

Amy frowned. "I think so, I mean, yes I did, but I suppose a small part of me was just hoping for a different answer." She looked up to see everyone looking a bit confused and laughed. "I asked for the name of the man I'm supposed to be with. And the answer was Nick." She looked around the circle. "Anyone know any Nicks who are single by any chance?"

Violet laughed. "Sorry, no, but I'll keep an eye out for you. Were you hoping it would say Danny?"

Amy nodded slightly. "Yeah, which is crazy, because Danny and I really were completely wrong for each other. Maybe this Nick guy will be a better match."

"I have no doubt that he will be," Esmeralda said, patting Amy's hand. "It was an excellent question to ask, seeing as we are at the Twin Flame Retreat. Who knows, perhaps this Nick is your very own Twin Flame. What about you, Violet? Did you receive an answer to your question?"

"I'm not sure. Does anyone know what 'La Rochelle' is?"

"It's a place in France, I think, on the coast," Mike said. "Was that your answer?"

Violet nodded. "Yes it was. Just those two words: La Rochelle."

"What was your question? Amy asked.

"It was a bit of a broad question, I just asked what was next for me."

"Planning on going travelling anytime soon?"

"Well, I have always wanted to travel around Europe. So yeah, I guess so. Maybe I need to visit La Rochelle?"

"Was there anything else you saw that could help?" Esmeralda asked.

"There were fields of sunflowers, and the house was a white cottage right on the coast, I could see and smell the sea."

"Perhaps there is such a place in La Rochelle. You'll have to go there and find out - then let us know how it goes."

"Maybe I will."

"Right then, who's ready for a bite to eat? Meditation always makes me a little hungry."

Violet and Amy nodded.

"I'll see you in a bit, I have some things to finish off in my shed," Mike said, leaving the marquee.

"What answer do you think he got?" Amy asked.

"He gets the same one every time. No matter what question he asks, the answer is always the same."

"What is his answer?" Violet asked, feeling a bit nosey.

Esmeralda smiled. "I don't know, he won't tell me. Anyway, let's go back to the house and get some food going, shall we?"

* * *

Greg inhaled the salty air and smiled. He'd be at Calais in less than two hours, and he had no idea what to do when he got there. He had no destination in mind, but he preferred the coast to inland; for some reason he felt it was important to be near a large body of water. He felt much more at home on the ferry surrounded by water than he had in his own house with Carly. So it made sense to stick to the coastline, maybe head west, then skirt around the edges of France. He was hoping to meet some like-minded travellers along the way, to make the journey a little less lonely.

He briefly wondered what had happened when Carly had found him gone, leaving nothing but a note. Then he decided that it didn't matter, as that ship had most definitely sailed. He wasn't the same person who'd married her, who'd had children with her. He felt absolutely nothing when he looked at her. But he had made sure they were provided for, so he couldn't feel too guilty for his abrupt disappearance. He breathed in another deep, salty breath then exhaled slowly. From now on, he would only look forwards. What was in his past was gone. All that lay ahead of him was a new life, a new shore. A fresh beginning.

"Excuse me? Do you have the time?"

The woman's voice jolted him out of his reverie and Greg glanced at his watch before looking up into a pair of light grey eyes.

"It's just after six."

The woman smiled, her eyes twinkling. "Going on holiday?" she asked.

"Uh, no, well, sort of. A long holiday, I think," Greg replied.

"Okay," the woman said, laughing. "Sounds interesting.

I'm Leona, by the way," she said, holding out her delicate hand.

Greg shook it gently. "Greg. Nice to meet you, Leona. Are you going on holiday?"

Leona gestured to her rucksack. "Not exactly. Going on an adventure. I've packed what I need to survive, I've got a destination in mind for my first few nights and after that, who knows?"

"You're more organised than me, that's for sure. I've not brought much at all and have no destination in mind whatsoever."

Leona smiled. "It is rather organised for me actually, I usually do what you're doing, just go with the flow, drift along the breeze and see where it takes me." She looked around. "Though I don't think I'd go with no luggage at all."

Greg smiled. "I do have a few things, they're in my camper van, parked downstairs."

"See? You are organised. You have transport figured out, and a place to sleep."

"I guess so. I suppose I'm just not used to going with the flow and having no clear plan. Or at least, I don't feel like that's what I'm used to."

Leona frowned. "I'm not sure I understand."

"I wouldn't expect you to. About two months ago I was in a car accident, got knocked unconscious and was in a coma for a while. When I woke up, I had no memory of my life whatsoever."

"None at all?"

"Nope, nothing. I have a wife, two kids, a house, a job, even a cat. But I remember none of it. I looked at pictures, spoke to friends; none of it triggered any memories."

"Wow, that's crazy. I mean, you see that happening in the movies, but I don't think I've ever known anyone in real life who it's happened to."

"Now you do," Greg said, smiling.

"So what happened then? I mean, how come you're here now?"

Greg looked away. "I'm not very proud of the next part, to be honest."

"You didn't kill them, did you? And now you're on the run from the police?" Leona asked, her eyes wide.

Greg laughed loudly, causing a few people to turn and stare. "No, no, don't worry, it's nothing like that. I just couldn't handle it anymore, being with a woman I felt nothing for, stifled by her fussing. So I bought a camper van on eBay, left a note and snuck out at night."

"A note? Couldn't you at least have told her face to face? She was your wife, even if you couldn't remember her. You must have loved her once."

"You know, I already feel terrible, there's no need to make it worse. But no, I couldn't have said goodbye to her in person because she would never have allowed it. In fact, I was a little surprised I wasn't stopped earlier by the police. I half expected her to send out search parties."

Leona frowned. "She must love you a lot then, to not want to let you go?"

Greg shook his head. "No, she didn't love me. She loved the man I was before the car accident, before the coma. I'm not that man anymore."

Leona was quiet for a while. Greg enjoyed the silence, broken only by the ferry engines, the lapping of the waves against the sides and the chatter of the people around them.

A chilly wind started up and Leona rubbed her arms. "I think that's enough sea air for me for now. I hope you have a good holiday, Greg," she said, holding out her hand again. "I'm sure your destination will become clear in time."

Greg shook her hand again, feeling a little like he'd known her for much longer than a few minutes. "Thank you, Leona. I hope you have a great adventure. Maybe our paths will cross again."

"You never know. It's a pretty small world." Leona hefted her rucksack onto her shoulder and went inside, waving over her shoulder as she went.

Greg stayed by the railing, the wind whipping around him. The sunlight was beginning to fade by the time he could see land in the distance. He went inside to warm up.

An hour later, Greg was on the road heading west, trying to get used to driving on the right, instead of the left. He saw a café on the roadside and his stomach noisily reminded him that he'd only had breakfast that morning, and nothing since. He indicated and pulled into the car park, taking up two spaces with his van.

He locked his door then went to the café entrance. Once inside, he paused for a moment before heading to an empty table. He picked up a menu and was pleased to see some things he recognised. He was going to have to brush up on his French pretty quickly though, otherwise all he was ever going to eat was chips and sweet pastries.

He ordered a hot chocolate, a cheeseburger and some fries, which arrived pretty quickly. He dug in, and was halfway through when a voice made him jump.

"We really must stop meeting like this."

He looked up to see Leona, her rucksack on her shoulder, smiling at him.

"Wow, it really is a small world. Please, join me," Greg said, gesturing to the seat opposite him.

"Or this just happens to be the closest café to the ferry port in Calais, and naturally we were both hungry after the journey," Leona said, sliding into the chair, setting her rucksack on the floor with a thud.

"What have you got in there? Bricks?"

Leona laughed. "It feels like it, but no. Just all the essentials. You know, clothes, books, chocolate, et cetera."

"I don't envy you having to carry that around France."

"I'll be pretty fit by the end though, don't you think?"

Greg laughed. "I guess that's one way of looking at it. So, have you eaten already?"

"No, I haven't."

Greg waved at the waitress, and she came over. Leona ordered in broken French, and Greg smiled to himself. He wasn't the only one who needed to learn the language fast.

An hour later, having finished their food and deciding it was getting late, Leona and Greg paid the bill then stepped out of the warm café into the cool night air. Greg had been toying with the idea of offering Leona a lift to wherever she was headed, but didn't know how to.

"It was good to see you again, Greg," Leona said holding her hand out again. "I hope our paths cross once again sometime."

Greg shook her hand, trying to think of a way to approach the idea without seeming too lecherous. "Where are you headed now?"

"I'm going to stay with a family in Vimoutiers. They're HelpX hosts. They house and feed me in return for me doing a few hours' work for them each day. They have a vegetarian hotel and restaurant."

"That sounds really good, do you know how you're getting there?"

"They said they'd pick me up from their nearest train station, but I was trying to save money by not using public transport too much, so I was going to walk and hitch."

"Hitch-hiking? By yourself? Don't you think that's a bit dangerous?"

Leona smiled. "In the UK? Yes, definitely. In France it's not so bad. Don't worry, I'm an excellent judge of character. I can spot a person with bad intentions a mile off."

"That's decided then."

"What is?"

"I'm giving you a lift." Greg gestured to his blue camper van. "Your chariot awaits, fair maiden."

Leona smiled. "Are you sure?"

"Absolutely. I would be honoured to be your first hitch."

"In that case, I couldn't possibly refuse. Let's go!"

* * *

Aria couldn't help but beam when she saw the new sign that Linen had created in the foyer of the Academy.

"The Academy of Awakened Humans," she murmured to herself. "Headmistress - Aria."

"Do you approve?"

"It's brilliant!" Aria squeaked, flying around Linen in a mad circle before grabbing him for a hug. "I can't believe I'm going to run the Academy! When I first got here I never dreamt this could possibly happen."

"'There are more things in Heaven and Earth, Aria, than are dreamt of in your philosophy'."

Aria frowned. "That sounded unlike you, Linen, did someone famous say that?"

Linen smiled. "Am I not intelligent enough to speak like that?"

"I didn't say you weren't intelligent, just that it didn't sound like you."

"Well, you were right; it's a line from a Shakespeare play."

"A what play?"

Linen shook his head. "A writer on Earth. Never mind. What I was trying to say is that so much more is possible than we could ever imagine. Even our dreams and imaginations aren't as grand as they could be. We can think bigger and crazier and still never reach the limits of the Universe."

Aria smiled and looked back at the new sign. "Does that mean you think that this idea will work? Awakening humans before sending them back to Earth?"

"I think it's entirely possible that it will help, yes. I also think we could do with thinking a little bigger, too."

Aria raised an eyebrow. "Oh yeah? How?"

"Laguz going back as a walk-in had me thinking. Why don't we ask Gold if that can be done more often? So when people are in comas, or on the edge of our world and theirs, they can swap with another soul, though not just any soul - an Awakened human. Or even an Earth Angel."

Aria thought for a minute. "Do you think it would be a good idea to have so many people in the world with no memory of their lives previous to whatever nearly kills them?"

"That's a point that will need to be addressed, but surely, if the souls who are leaving are ready to leave their lives, then that life has run its course anyway. What this will allow us to do, is to send souls into adult bodies so they can Awaken quicker. Yes, sending Awakened humans back to be born again and grow up is a good thing, but there's quite a long wait for them to mature and remember. Whereas if they're already older, then hopefully the Awakening and Remembering will be a speedier process."

Aria bit her lip. "I can see what you mean. After all, if the humans don't Awaken soon, there's not much longer left, is there?"

Linen shook his head. "No, the Indigos and Crystals were optimistic, and I can see many changes have occurred on Earth, but not big enough changes for them to experience the Golden Age, I fear."

"I wonder what the Golden Age is like," Aria mused. "If no one has ever experienced it, then how will they know when it's the Golden Age? I mean, if it's brand new in the entire lifetime of the Universe, how will we know it when it arrives?"

"That's what I love about you, Aria, you surprise me so often with such deep questions, and yet they simply come from your innocent need to know more."

Aria blushed. "Are you saying that you don't think I'm intelligent?"

"Of course not. To be honest, I would be surprised even if Velvet had come out with such an intelligent question."

Aria pushed Linen playfully. "No, you wouldn't. Velvet was such an Old Soul, she had oodles of intelligence. Anyway, back to my question. How will they know it's the Golden Age? I mean, couldn't the Earth be experiencing the Golden Age right now without us realising it?"

"I very much doubt that, there's too much violence, chaos and disaster in the world right now."

"So the Golden Age is the absence of anything negative? But how can positive exist without the negative?"

Linen smiled. "There you go again. You're right of course. Velvet said much the same thing to me. There cannot be good without bad, light without dark. Of course, right and wrong and good and bad don't really exist, it is merely our own experience and opinion that makes them one or the other. What is good luck on one side of the world is bad luck on the other."

Aria was quiet for a moment. "So perhaps the Golden Age is not a world where negativity doesn't exist, but instead is a world where everyone's perceptions of things are different. So instead of seeing the bad in someone dying, they see the release, the good, and celebrate the life that the person had," Aria's eyes lit up as she delved into her own theory. "And instead of seeing disease or pain or anger or disaster as bad, they see the bigger picture, they see the pattern, the reason, the truth behind it, and accept it as a part of life. Maybe that's the Golden Age."

"You are amazing, Aria. You will make such a good

Head of the Academy. Because I believe you could well be onto something. Maybe that could be the focus of the Academy of Awakened Humans, to inspire them to see things from a new perspective. To help them to see events in a different light."

Aria beamed in pleasure. "I think you could be right about the walk-in thing though, you should ask Gold."

"I will. In fact, I may go now, before the first lot of humans arrive. You probably need a bit of time to plan your first lesson and your welcome speech?"

Aria's eyes widened. "This is so scary! I guess I should go and practice a bit. I'll be in the office."

Linen patted her on the arm, then leaned in for a quick kiss. "You'll be absolutely fine. I'll meet you back at the office." A click later, Linen disappeared, leaving Aria staring up at her name in green glitter on the wall. She remembered her first day at the Academy when Velvet had made their room numbers appear on their hands in purple glitter. She smiled and wondered if she could do the same. Like Linen, she'd learnt a bit of the Old Soul magick. She decided to go back to the office and give it a try. It would make for an impressive start to her welcome session. With a click of her own tiny fingers, Aria vanished.

CHAPTER NINE

"I love it here, Amy. Do you think we could just live here, in this pod, forever?" Violet asked as she stretched out on her lilac bed on the third night.

"It is amazing here, isn't it? I don't think I've ever felt this relaxed in all my life. Especially seeing as the food is all home-made and we don't have to do any chores or anything. And the meditations have been really cool. Are you really going to go to La Rochelle?"

Violet smiled. "I've been thinking that going travelling would be a good idea. I have some money saved up due to the fact that I've had no life for the past few months. Charlie did his best to try and run me dry, but I kept putting a little aside, just in case."

"That was a good idea. I wish I'd done the same," Amy grimaced.

"Why don't we go together? I could get an old car, we could share the driving. I'm sure we could camp or find cheap accommodation. And I'm sure we could do some odd jobs while we travel to make a little money to keep us going."

Amy was quiet for a bit. "When are you planning on going?"

"Not immediately. My rental lease on the house doesn't run out until February. I was thinking of going then."

"Eight months," Amy mused. "I'm sure I could get some money together by then. I mean, I'm not spending much living at my parents house." She smiled. "It sounds like an incredible idea, though I'm not too keen on the idea of camping in February."

Violet laughed. "Me either. Eight months should give us enough time to research some alternative accommodation, though."

Amy bounced up and down on her bed. "This is so exciting! What kind of car should we get?"

Violet laughed again. "Why don't we leave it up to the Universe to decide?" She glanced at her watch then sat up. "Hey, didn't Esmeralda say she would be showing that spiritual movie in the lounge at eight?"

Amy nodded. "Yep, she was going to show us *The Secret.*"

"It's five to eight now, we'd better get shifting."

"Okay, let me just stick some shoes on. Hey, maybe she'll have more of those amazing courgette and lemon cakes."

Violet shivered. "As tasty as they are, it still seems wrong to put such a hideous vegetable in a cake."

"Oh hush, if it tastes good, who cares what's in it?"

"True. You ready yet?" Violet stood impatiently by the door. "I don't want to miss any of it."

"Okay, okay, I'm coming. You're not going to be all bossy like this when we're travelling, are you?"

Violet and Amy bickered light-heartedly all the way to the house and let themselves in. It already felt a little like home to Violet. She would love to live in such a beautiful place, though she still preferred a slightly more traditional look.

The lights hadn't been dimmed yet when they arrived in

the lounge. They were greeted by Esmeralda and the other people who had come for the retreat. They took a plate and some more unusual cakes, then settled in from of the large TV screen.

A while later, the DVD finished and Violet looked down at her plate and realised she'd been so absorbed in the movie that she'd forgotten to eat her chocolate and beetroot cake. She started to nibble on it as Esmeralda switched the TV off and put a lamp on.

"So what did everyone think?" she asked.

"It was interesting," one of the other retreat residents, Tony, said. "I mean, I've heard of the Law of Attraction before, but the idea that we should be grateful for having what we want before we have it is a new concept to me."

"It's not easy though is it? To believe that you have something even when you don't. It's like lying to yourself, isn't it?" Amy asked.

"No, because if you truly believe it's possible to have the thing you want, then it shouldn't be difficult to imagine already having it, and thanking the Universe for that," Rebecca, Tony's partner, said.

"It's just reprogramming yourself, really," Violet said, in-between mouthfuls of cake. "It's changing the way you see things, the way you perceive things. As a rule, I know I personally focus on the lack of something, rather than the abundance of it. If I could get myself to focus on having plenty as opposed to thinking of all the things I wish I had, but don't, then I'm sure my life would change for the better."

"I think that one of the main problems is not that we don't have what we want, but that we don't know what we want. And if we don't know, then how is the Universe supposed to know?" Tony asked.

"Tomorrow, there's an exercise we can do to help you identify the things you want in your life," Esmeralda said as she refilled everyone's mugs. "By narrowing down what you wish to see in your life, you are able to focus on these things as if they are already in your life, and your narrow focus is likely to manifest them quite quickly."

"I thought that being spiritual was about being open? About having a broad range of interests and knowledge?" Amy asked.

"Certainly, that is an aspect of spirituality, but it is more difficult and lengthy to attain something if your mind and heart are in twenty million places at once. Also, the broader your interests, the more likely you are to have a lot of clutter, and clutter is definitely not conducive to the manifestation process."

"I think that's why I'm looking forward to travelling," Violet said. "You have to be so much more selective with your possessions. At the moment, I'm renting a two bedroom house and it's just crammed full of junk. It's no wonder that all I'm attracting in my life right now is more junk."

"Don't wait until you go travelling to get rid of things, do it now, then your travelling plans will go more smoothly," Tony said. "What will you do with anything you want to keep but don't want to take travelling?"

Violet shook her head. "I'm not keeping anything. It's all going. A clean slate. There are no memories that I wish to keep from my past that I have physical objects for. My parents have all the old photos; there isn't really anything else that needs to be collecting dust in their attic."

Rebecca raised her eyebrows. "I wish I were that brave. I don't know how I could get rid of all my stuff. Even though I know that most of it I will never use again, or even look at ever again, it feels like it's a part of me, part of what made me who I am."

Violet shrugged. "It's all energy, so yes, those objects could well hold your energy within them, but I think that if they are never used, or disturbed, then it's just stagnant energy. And surely, it will attract more stagnant energy, which is not really what you want in your life, is it?"

"You're absolutely right, maybe I do need to get rid of some of that stagnant energy," Rebecca agreed.

"I'll help, sweetheart," Tony said, squeezing Rebecca's hand.

"Yeah, yeah, I know you, you'll just hire a skip and launch it all in without a second thought. You have no sentimentality whatsoever."

"Hey, that's not fair. I just prefer to keep my memories in my head rather than in a box."

"But you know how awful my memory is. I couldn't keep all my memories in my head."

"You could always write them down, or photograph them. I know whenever I've had to throw away a broken object that I loved, I've taken a photo of it. A notebook or some digital photos won't take up nearly as much space as the actual objects, and who knows, perhaps they'll bring as much joy to someone else as they did once to you."

"I think that's one of the best ideas I've heard in a long time, Violet," Esmeralda said. "It is such a great way to de-clutter, yet still preserve the memory."

"Better yet," Violet added. "You could photograph the item, scrapbook it, and add some journalling to the page which explains what the item meant to you. If you can't be bothered scrapbook a photo of the item, then you know you can happily get rid of it without worrying about losing the memory of it."

"That would make a great workshop, Violet. Would you be at all interested in running a workshop here with us?"

Violet's eyes widened. "Really?"

"Absolutely. We're always looking for original ideas for retreats and workshops. I think that your idea would make an excellent weekend workshop. People could bring five items they want to get rid of but are keeping for sentimental reasons, photograph the items, scrapbook them and write about them, then ceremonially either give the item away or burn it."

"I would love to do that, Esmeralda. Who knows, it might even inspire me to get rid of some of my clutter, too. After all, I'd have to do some example scrapbooks. I've got lots of materials I could bring for people to use. We could even do the photographing and printing as part of the workshop, and they could go home with a lighter load and a beautiful scrapbook of memories."

"Excellent, I will do the write-up on our website as soon as possible. We'll work out the cost of the workshop while you're here this week. What dates would you be available?"

"On the weekends? Any would be fine, I don't really do much on the weekends."

"Okay, I'll put a few dates up and see what response we get. I can think of quite a few regulars we have who would be interested. I'll also send out an e-mail to everyone on our mailing list."

"I think we're going to turn in," Tony interrupted, pulling a sleepy Rebecca to her feet. "Thank you for a great evening. I think I may have to book Rebecca on that workshop, might get a bit more space in the house then." He smiled and nodded to them, then gently guided Rebecca out the door.

"I'm afraid I'm quite tired too," Amy said, yawning. "Would you mind if I turned in?"

Esmeralda shook her head. "No, of course not, you two should go and get plenty of rest. Tomorrow we'll do the exercise I mentioned, along with some visualisation exercises and also a creative one."

"Sounds good." Violet stood and stretched. She put her empty plate and mug on the table. "See you at breakfast."

Amy and Violet left the house and made their way up

the dimly lit path to their pod.

"I think that the workshop idea is brilliant, Vi. Though I hope it's not going to stop you from going travelling, I'm really getting into the idea."

"Don't worry, Amy, the travelling is still most definitely happening, but with the extra money from the workshops, we might be able to afford a camper van!"

* * *

Greg wiped his forehead with the heel of his hand and rubbed it on his jeans. It was only noon and he was already breaking into a sweat. He'd decided to see if he could be of any help at the place he was taking Leona to. Turned out the hosts were happy to have extra hands, especially as they didn't need to provide an extra bed. In return for a few hours of work a day, they were feeding him and providing hot showers and internet access if he needed it. He felt it would be a good idea to register on the HelpX website himself. He couldn't just keep following Leona and hoping they had room for one more. He hoped he would be able to travel with Leona a while longer though. He wasn't attracted to her in the sense that he would want an intimate relationship with her; it was more that she felt like his sister. There was a definite bond between them, and as Greg hadn't felt any connection to his actual family, it was nice to have the feeling of kinship with someone.

"How's it going?"

Greg looked up and saw Leona holding a glass of lemonade and a large cheese salad baguette. He took the lemonade gratefully and downed it in nearly one gulp. "Thanks, I needed that," he said, handing back the empty glass. He took the baguette and bit into it.

Leona smiled. "Obviously you're not used to hard work."

Greg swallowed his mouthful and frowned, he wiped more sweat from his forehead. "It's strange, I feel like I should be able to do this with no problems, but my body doesn't feel the same way."

"I've been thinking a bit about what you said about having no memory of your life, your kids or your wife. Have you thought that maybe it's because you're actually a different soul to the one who previously inhabited your body?"

Greg's frown deepened as he considered Leona's words. "What you've just said sounds utterly improbable and bizarre, yet at the same time it makes a lot of sense. But is that even possible?"

"For souls to swap places? Why not?"

"How do you know about all this stuff?"

"I've read a lot and attended many workshops. There are a lot of theories out there, and one of them is that many of the people on Earth at this moment are originally from other realms, other planets, other dimensions. But they've come here to be humans, to bring about an Awakening. Then there are walk-ins, where a soul has had enough of their life here, but instead of allowing the body to die when the soul leaves, it is simply taken over by another soul. That's when you get people waking up from comas with no recollection of their lives previous to their near-death experience."

"Wow, you really do know a lot about this. So you think that I could be a walk-in? What are you then?"

Leona smiled. "You mean you haven't figured it out yet? Give it a guess."

"Give me some options to choose from at least, I'm new to all of this."

"Okay, there are Incarnated Angels, Faeries, Mermaids and Leprechauns. Then there are Starpeople, who are aliens from other planets, and Old Souls, who are humans who have had thousands of lives spanning the ages, and usually at some point they would have had lives as magickal beings - witches, sorcerers, et cetera."

Greg's eyebrows raised as he tried to take in all the information and figure out what Leona might be. "Taking into consideration your spontaneous nature, your love of adventure and your appearance, I'm going to hazard a guess and say Incarnated Faerie?"

Leona grinned. "You got it in one! Pretty impressive considering you haven't read the characteristics of each realm. If you had, it would have been even more glaringly obvious. Mind you, by Faerie standards, I'm quite quiet really."

Greg smiled. "So you're a Faerie, or you were one in a past life. That's really cool."

Leona laughed. "It's a good feeling, knowing why I act, think and feel the way I do. I always felt a bit odd when I was younger, like I didn't really fit in anywhere. Once I realised why, I relaxed a bit, enjoyed life a lot more." She tilted her head and studied Greg for a moment. "I can't quite decide about you. Especially as being a walk-in, you probably don't look like your soul should."

"It's weird you should say that. Since I woke up, whenever I see my reflection I'm always surprised."

"What do you expect to see when you look in the mirror?"

"This is going to sound strange, but I always expect to see green eyes and long blond hair." Greg ran his hand through his thick black hair. "It's not like I ever could have had blond hair in this life."

"No, but it makes sense though, from what I've sensed about you."

Greg sat on the low stone wall surrounding the vegetable garden where he'd been weeding and motioned for Leona to do the same. "What have you sensed?" He continued to eat his forgotten baguette.

"A mixture, actually. I don't think that you belong to just one category. I'm getting a strong sense of knighthood. You like to rescue people. That, I've seen first-hand. You have a gentle nature though, so I don't think you were a warrior Knight, more of a kind, genteel Knight, who upheld the law and tried to make things fair for all. So you are an Old Soul, who was a Knight, maybe more than once. But I also sense another life that you've had, which would have incorporated the qualities of the Knight, but in a different way."

"In what way?"

"It's the long blond hair and green eyes thing that clinched it really, but I suspect that you had a past life as a Merman."

Greg laughed. "You think I had a fishy tail and lived underwater?"

Leona nodded. "Yep, I'm pretty certain of it, in fact. I can lend you some books to read, so you can see for yourself."

"I'd like that, this is all very intriguing. It's not every day you find out you're a Knight and your only friend in the world is a Faerie." He expected Leona to laugh with him, but instead she was studying him closely again."

"I'm not the only friend you have in the world. There's someone else, a woman, with long dark hair and brown eyes."

The image of the woman who haunted him every night in his dreams flashed through Greg's mind. He nearly dropped his last bit of bread. "How did you know that?"

Leona smiled. "I just got a glimpse of her. But I suspect that she is part of your future, as well as your very distant past. You haven't met her yet, have you?"

Greg shook his head.

"Don't worry, you will. She's out there. And if it's meant

to be this time, then your paths will cross."

"But when?"

Leona grinned. "At the right time and not a minute sooner." She stood up. "Now, I'm going to get on with peeling the potatoes. You'd better carry on digging, otherwise we won't get fed tonight."

Greg laughed and picked up his trowel. "We should talk about this some more later."

"Sure, I'll find those books for you. See you later." With a wave over her shoulder, Leona went back to the old farmhouse.

Greg chewed the last of the baguette and looked out at the view across the French hillside. He looked at the work yet to be done and sighed. He wished his body was more up to the task. At least some good would come of the working holiday though. He may actually be a bit fitter by the end. He wondered about everything Leona had just said. It seemed so fantastical. Could he possibly have been a Knight in a past life? Or even a Merman? He wasn't even sure if he believed that such things as Faeries and Merpeople existed. But disbelief aside, something felt right about all the things Leona had just told him. And she even seemed quite Faerie-like; her movements were fluid and graceful, she was so light on her feet and quite small in stature and build. Greg hoped that she may have more to tell him. Especially about this mysterious dark-haired woman that he'd dreamt of since he woke up. At least now he knew that she did in fact exist. He hoped that it wouldn't be long before their paths crossed. He had a feeling that everything would change when they finally met.

Greg threw all of his energy into digging out the weeds in-between the vegetable plants and lost himself in the concentration of his task. The afternoon slipped by and before long, Greg looked up to see the cloudy sky darkening as the evening approached. He got up and stretched, then put the tools away in the shed before joining Leona in the kitchen. They were the only volunteers at the hotel at the moment, so they were eating with the family who owned it.

The evening meal was a noisy affair, but the home-made food certainly made up for it. Later, Greg and Leona went back to his camper van and he made them both a hot chocolate on his tiny gas stove.

"So how do you know that I'm going to meet this dark-haired woman? And how do you know it's in the future? Surely you couldn't have read that in your books too?"

Leona shook her head. "No, I just get images sometimes, of people or events or just symbols, and they usually relate to something that is about to happen in the future."

"So you're a psychic?"

Leona shrugged. "I don't know, I've never used the ability to tell people their futures or make any money from it. Mostly it just comes in handy to know whether I need an umbrella or not."

"You can predict the weather? My God, you should have become a meteorologist; the weather people in the UK are useless."

Leona laughed. "Yeah that's true, I don't think I've ever had to rely on their predictions though, so I'm lucky."

"I'll have to ring you for the weather report in the future then," Greg said, smiling.

"You know, the woman I glimpsed in your future, she seems very familiar to me. I have the feeling I may have dreamt of her myself. Or perhaps met her in a past life."

"Really? That would be a very strange coincidence, wouldn't it?"

"There are no such things as coincidences. Anything that seems like one has happened deliberately."

"You believe in fate? What about free will?"

Leona shrugged. "There are several different possible

futures, and we choose the one we wish to experience, but each future is still set out before us."

"Which one should we choose? How do we choose it?"

"There is no 'should', there is no right or wrong either. We choose our futures with every word spoken, action taken or thought in our minds. It's not always a conscious choice. In fact, most of us would appear to have chosen the exact future that we did not want to experience, but because our thoughts have been so heavily focused on that which we do not want, that is the future we experience. It's the Law of Attraction."

"The Law of Attraction? You mean like attracts like?"

"Yes, like energy attracts like energy. For example, when you're having a bad day, your energy is at a lower vibration and therefore you will attract other people or events that are at that lower vibration. Whereas when you're having a good day, your energy is at a higher vibration, and you will attract people and events that are at the same level of vibration."

"So if your day starts badly, you may as well just get back into bed and stay there?"

Leona laughed. "That would seem like the best thing to do sometimes, but no, not necessarily. Just because your day begins badly, doesn't mean it has to stay at the same level all day. You can consciously change your energy vibration."

"By thinking happy thoughts?"

She laughed again. "Yes, in a way, but it's not enough to merely think happy thoughts, you have to feel them. In every cell of your being, you have to let the negativity wash away and consciously imagine everything going your way, going well. It's not the easiest thing in the world, but it's certainly possible."

Greg shook his head. "This is all amazing to me. I mean, you seem to know so much about all of it."

Leona shrugged. "I was shown much of it. Growing up, I would get images in my mind and then would see them come true. I used to talk to the Faeries whenever I was outside. They showed me a lot. I also had a very understanding mum who encouraged me to experiment, to listen, to remain open to nature."

"Wow, I can't believe you could actually talk to Faeries. Could you really see them?"

Leona smiled. "So it's easy to believe I was a Faerie in a past life, but not that I could see them and speak to them as a child? You're funny."

Greg smiled back. "Yeah, I suppose that is a bit weird. Weirder still is the fact that all of what you're saying makes perfect sense to me. I mean, I've never read anything about this, or even spoken to anyone else about it, but, well, I don't know, somehow…"

"It triggers a memory in you? Brings things back that you have long forgotten?" Leona guessed.

Greg met her eye. "Yes, that's it exactly." Despite the fact that he wasn't attracted to her in that way, and the fact that part of him knew it would be wrong, in that moment, Greg found himself leaning towards Leona.

Before their lips could make contact, Leona leaned back and put her finger to his lips.

"This won't make any sense just yet, but I promise you that it would be a mistake. I know that you feel a connection to me, but it's purely because we are linked by the woman you have been dreaming about. We're not meant to be together, we're not even soulmates."

Greg sighed and leaned back. "I'm sorry, I don't know why I did that."

"I do. You were lonely, you felt a connection to me. It's perfectly natural." Leona leaned forwards and wrapped her arms around Greg, pulling him tightly to her. He relaxed into her embrace and sighed again.

"Thank you, Leona."
"You're welcome, Greg. That's what friends are for."

CHAPTER TEN

If Aria had been a human on Earth at this moment, she would have been sweating profusely as she nervously surveyed the large human audience listening to Linen, who was doing a general introduction to the Academy.

"Now, I would like to introduce the Head of the Academy, Aria. Aria was a student of the original Earth Angel Training Academy, and the Assistant Head of the School for the Children of the Golden Age. She has a wealth of experience to share with you, and I am happy now to leave you in her very capable hands."

After that very impressive-sounding introduction, Aria struggled to make her legs work and carry her to the front of the stage. For the first class, Linen had decided that they should assume more human, Old Soul-like appearances, so that the human souls would focus on their words, rather than their Faerie appearances. Later on in the course, they would reveal their true selves to reinforce the fact that the other realms really existed. They had found a guest teacher, Bk, who had stayed at the academy since the Earth Angel Training days. He had agreed to speak to the humans about Starpeople. They'd also found an Angel called Jasper who'd agreed to speak to the humans about the Angelic Realm, and a Mermaid called Feefee who would talk to them about the Merpeople. Each would explain the plight of their realms, and help the humans to identify Earth Angels when on Earth. They would also reveal their true selves in the hope that the shock factor would securely fasten the memories of the Academy in the humans' souls, which might give them a better chance of Awakening when they either were born again as a human, or became a walk-in.

Since Linen had asked Gold about increasing the number of walk-ins, and he had agreed, word had spread throughout the dimension, and they had scores of former Earth Angels coming to them asking to re-join Earth as a walk-in. While they waited for suitable bodies to become available, Linen was running through some Awakening ideas and techniques with them, which is where he disappeared to, leaving Aria to face the human souls by herself.

"The world will be going through some dramatic changes in the next few short years. Soon, an Awakening will come about, whereby all who dwell on Earth will become consciously aware of the energy that surrounds them; of their ability to create the world they live in and of the fact that unless they respect the Earth and her nature, then they will not live to see the many possible years to come." Aria had been rehearsing her words and at first she felt they were too stiff and formal, but standing tall on the stage, in flowing glittery green robes, she felt more authoritative than she had ever felt in her entire existence.

"The purpose of this Academy is to help you, when you return to Earth, either as a baby or as a walk-in, to Awaken, to recognise Earth Angels, and to aid them in the process of Awakening the whole world. I know it may seem like a daunting prospect; just Awakening yourself can be a lifetime's work and a huge challenge. But if just even a few of you who attend this Academy manage to do so, then the Awakening process will accelerate beyond what any of us can imagine right now, and the world will experience the Golden Age for the first time in the entire existence of the Universe. Never in billions or trillions of years has any civilisation ever experienced it."

A tentative hand went up in the air as Aria paused, mentally trying to remember the next part of her speech.

"Yes?" she asked, gesturing to the soul.

"If no civilisation has ever experienced it, how will we know when we are experiencing it? I mean, we won't have anything to compare it to."

Aria smiled. "It's interesting you should ask that, I asked the exact same thing. And the explanation given to me, by Linen, was that when the Golden Age comes about, it won't be a world with no negativity or bad things, but a world where everyone sees the value of those things, indeed, the value of all things, and lives in harmony with all that happens. Therefore, the changes the Golden Age will bring won't necessarily be physical ones, but mental ones. Everyone's perceptions of events will shift. They will realise that everything is energy and as such, they can have anything they wish to. But also, that they don't actually need that much to not only survive, but to live a full and happy life. Happiness doesn't come from owning or attaining things or people, it comes from the place deep inside where you are secure in the knowledge that everything is exactly as it should be. Everything happens for a reason, and instead of labelling it good or bad, we should appreciate it for how it changes our lives. We should appreciate the value it has." Aria found herself pacing back and forth a few steps at the front of the stage, as she gathered steam. None of this had been what she had rehearsed, but it flowed from her now, and she figured it must be making some sense, because she could see everyone listening hard, but not looking confused.

"My own story is a great example. I am originally from

the Elemental Realm; this is a realm that we will talk about in more detail in a moment. I was a Faerie. My job was to help the grass to grow. Sounds like a simple job, a simple life. And it was, until the humans decided to remove the grass and build things there instead. I moved around several times until it got to the point where there were more grass-growing Faeries than there was grass. I was jobless and homeless, feeling quite sorry for myself, when I met the recruiting souls from the Earth Angel Training Academy. They convinced me to join the Academy, and return to Earth as a human, to try and change the way the humans were treating the Earth. Now, I must admit, though I was looking forward to the prospect, the more I learnt, the more I realised that I couldn't give up my wings. In fact," Aria smiled in anticipation of their reaction.

"I miss them now, so," she clicked her fingers and her robes vanished, her legs, arms and body shrunk, and her glittering green dragonfly wings reappeared behind her, supporting her as she hovered above the stage. There was a huge gasp from her audience, and some even began to clap. Aria was sure that it would be a memory they wouldn't forget in a hurry.

"This is my natural appearance. So, as I was saying, I wished to remain here, as a Faerie, and help with the School for the Children of the Golden Age, which is what I did. All of my fellow classmates from the Academy graduated and heard the call to Earth, and then it was just me and Linen and the Children. Now that all of the Children except for the Rainbows are on Earth, I decided it was time that we did more. Which is why you are all sat here now. So everything I perceived to be bad, worked out just fine, and all that was good, well, was probably even better than I realised. Now, before we move on, are there any questions?"

A hundred hands shot up in the air, and Aria smiled.

* * *

Violet took one last look around the pod and sighed. It was the last day of their retreat and they were packing up before the final meditation. She hefted her bag onto her shoulder and left the pod, following Amy down the woodland path. She wished with all her heart that she could stay. She was looking forward to coming back to do the workshops, which she and Esmeralda had set dates for, but she wished she didn't have to leave now. The thought of returning to her old job, of being stuck in front of the computer screen, typing up letters, inputting seemingly meaningless data; it just all seemed so pointless. With a sigh, she put her bag in the boot of Amy's mum's car, and Amy slammed it shut.

"I wish we could stay," Amy said, mirroring Violet's thoughts.

Violet nodded. "I'm struggling with the idea of returning to my old life, I have to admit. It feels like everything has shifted somehow."

Amy nodded. "I know what you mean. It feels like this is what we are meant to do. Like we are meant to help people Awaken in the way that Esmeralda and Mike are."

Violet tilted her head. "There's something very familiar about that idea." Then she shook her head. "Anyway, let's go get some breakfast. I'm looking forward to this final meditation. Esmeralda said it would have something to do with our past lives."

"Yeah, it would be funny if we all knew each other back then, wouldn't it?"

"No, it would be right." Violet linked arms with Amy and they walked back through the trees to the house.

Esmeralda was there to greet them "I wondered where you two had got to. You're normally the first to breakfast."

Amy laughed. "We were just loading up the car."

Esmeralda frowned and ushered them into the dining

room. "I'm going to miss you two. I think this has been my favourite retreat so far."

"It has been an amazing week, we were both just saying that we didn't really want to leave," Violet said, sitting down at their usual table.

"I'm not one to wish time away, as I believe that every moment is precious, but I hope that the dates of your workshops come quickly, I look forward to working with you, Violet. And Amy, please feel free to come with Violet as a guest."

Amy grinned. "I'd like that. I'm sure I can be helpful somehow."

Esmeralda waved her hand. "I would just be happy to have your company."

"Thank you, Esmeralda."

"Now then, the usual for you two?"

Amy and Violet both nodded, not even bothering with the menus in the centre of the table. Esmeralda went to the kitchen to prepare their breakfast. Tony leant over from his and Rebecca's table.

"We look forward to seeing you then too, we've both booked places on the workshop you're doing, Violet."

Violet was surprised. "What, even though you know it was borne simply of a random conversation in the lounge?"

Tony laughed. "I think you know much more than you give yourself credit for. I'm looking forward to your insights, and of course," he nodded at Rebecca. "I'm looking forward to de-cluttering the house a little too."

"Hey," Rebecca protested. "You have to bring things of yours to get rid of too, you know. We're not just bringing all of my stuff."

Violet laughed. "I look forward to seeing you both again. It's been fun this week."

Tony nodded. "Yes, I hope we can keep in touch. I

would love to know if you ever make it to La Rochelle."

Violet frowned. "How did you know about that?"

"Amy was telling us about the meditation you did, where you dug up the box. It sounded great. Oh, and don't worry, Amy, I'll let you know if I meet any good-looking men called Nick."

Amy blushed. "Thanks, Tony. We'll have to exchange numbers or e-mails before we leave today."

"Definitely." Tony saw Esmeralda enter the room with the breakfast tray. "I'll leave you two to enjoy your food." He turned back to Rebecca and continued poking fun at her for being so messy.

"Here we go. Herbal tea and banana pancakes with cream and strawberries, Violet, and a strong coffee and toast with raspberry jam for you, Amy. Enjoy, I'll meet you at the meditation tent later."

"Hey, Esmeralda," Amy called after her. "What exactly is the final meditation we're doing?"

Esmeralda smiled. "It's our favourite, one of the first that we developed ourselves. You'll see. I think you'll really enjoy this one, Amy."

Amy turned to Violet. "Sounds interesting." She bit into her toast. "I want to take a few pictures before we leave, so I can put them up on my desk, and remember the relaxation techniques we've learnt when things get stressful at work."

"That's a good idea, I might do the same. Though I might just end up daydreaming about what it would be like to live here."

"Oh, I'll probably do that too. Though I must admit, I can't see you living somewhere as far inland as this."

Violet frowned. "No?"

"No, I think the place you described to me from your meditation is more like you. Who knows, maybe that place really exists in La Rochelle. Maybe that's where your Twin

Flame is."

Violet laughed. "Anything is possible."

A while later, full and rehydrated, Violet and Amy made their way to the meditation tent, and went inside. It was lovely and warm as usual, and Tony and Rebecca were already there, getting themselves centred and calm, their breathing in sync with one another.

Violet and Amy joined them, leaving enough space for Esmeralda and Mike to make the circle complete.

Violet very quickly slipped into a calm state of mind, her breathing slowing and becoming deeper. She heard Esmeralda and Mike enter the tent and take their places. After a few moments, it was Mike who spoke.

"When Esmeralda and I first met, we knew instantly that we had a deep connection to one another. We were lucky, we were both in places in our lives where we had figured ourselves out, we were comfortable in our own skins, and most importantly, we were both available."

Violet opened her eyes and saw them smile at each other, the devotion and adoration plainly clear.

"But it wasn't until we had been together a while that we realised just how deep this connection was. Just how far back our histories together spanned. We realised that if we meditated together, we could actually access these ancient memories, and see the path our lives had taken until now. We developed our own meditation that inspired the Twin Flame Retreat. This is the meditation we are going to do now. It's the only one that I lead, mainly because Esmeralda gets so deeply entwined in the past memories that she forgets the words."

Esmeralda punched Mike lightly in the arm. "Don't listen to him. He just likes this one because it reminds him just how lucky he is to have me."

Mike grinned. "Oh yeah, that's why. Right then, let's all get our breathing calm and relaxed. This meditation is slightly different; once I have led you to the door, when you open it, you are on your own. I will give you ample time to spend with your ancient memories, in which you may learn more about yourself, and of course, more about your Twin Flame. I will then bring you back slowly to that door, and back to full consciousness. But during that time through the door, I won't speak, because I wouldn't want to disturb you. Although, if you find yourself unable to access your memories, or you've finished and there's still silence, if you concentrate hard enough, you should be able to see the memories of the others here today. That is of course, if they let you see them. Though I can't imagine that any of us would want to hide who we were from anyone present. Right, enough explaining, let's begin."

Violet closed her eyes and concentrated on her breathing. Mike began to speak in a lower tone than his normal speaking voice, and he led them through a maze of sorts, with many twists and turns, until Violet found herself in a room with a row of different coloured and shaped doors. Each one bore a name. She looked around and saw her fellow group members stood by her side, all looking at the doors. She decided to do things a little differently. Instead of going straight through the door with her own name on it, she followed Mike through his door, making sure she left it slightly ajar so she could get back out easily. Once through, she looked around her in wonder. She was in the most incredible garden, with a large waterfall that made rainbows appear on every surface. Even the ground seemed to shimmer under the bright, sunny sky. She looked ahead and saw Mike sitting on an elegant golden bench in front of the waterfall. But he wasn't alone, Esmeralda was with him. Violet moved closer so she could hear their words.

"Tomorrow's first class should be interesting, shouldn't it?"

"Well, considering Velvet doesn't seem to have any idea

what we've all come here for, it should be very interesting." They watched the waterfall in silence for a while, enjoying the quiet. Violet was shocked and surprised to hear the name Velvet mentioned. The same name mentioned with her own on the Angel Board in a message from Lyle.

"It's not our place to say anything," Esmeralda said abruptly. "I already said more than enough this morning, but she was not open to the information. I think we should hold back from giving anything more away. Everything must unfold at its own pace."

Mike nodded. "You're right, as usual. I just hate to see people struggle unnecessarily."

Esmeralda leaned onto his arm. "I know you do," she said softly. "But it is quite necessary."

"I guess we will see."

"Yes, we will."

They were silent then, just watching the glittering waterfall. Sensing she had witnessed the memory in its entirety, Violet backed up, and felt behind her for the door. She slipped through it, unnoticed by the two on the bench. Back in the room of doors, Violet wondered whose memory she should look at now. She decided to peek in on Esmeralda's, just in case she could glean any more information about the woman named Velvet.

She reached for the ornate door handle and gently pulled the circular door open. She stepped inside and found herself in another garden, only this one was filled with golden statues and crystal encrusted benches. She saw Esmeralda and Mike sat on the bench in front of a statue of a Merman with green emeralds as eyes. She found herself drawn to the statue, and had to force herself to concentrate on listening to the conversation, which was the reason why she was there.

"I was very impressed with Velvet this morning, I think that she may be finally seeing the big picture," Esmeralda said.

Violet became aware of another presence, and saw a beautiful Angel in lilac, with feathered wings, standing beside her behind the bushes. Her eyes widened and she nearly gasped. Though she believed in Angels, to actually see one like this was incredible. The Angel seemed completely unaware of her, so she turned away and forced herself to concentrate on listening to the conversation.

"Well, Emerald, I do truly hope so. Without her presence on Earth, I think our mission to reunite the Flames may well be impossible." Mike smiled at Esmeralda. "Though I know we would still do our very best."

Violet's eyes widened at Esmeralda's name. It made sense; she wore a lot of emerald green clothing.

Esmeralda smiled back at Mike then looked up at the statue of the Merman, diverting Violet's attention to the statue once again. Who was he? He seemed so familiar.

"I think once she realises that she will have the chance of another life with her Flame, there will be no problems in convincing her she must return."

Violet realised that Esmeralda's pointed look at the statue was actually meaningful. Velvet's Twin Flame must have been the person who had inspired the statue. If he seemed familiar to Violet, did that mean that she was in fact Velvet?

"Yes. I remember watching them in Atlantis. I don't think I'd ever seen two souls so intertwined with one another, so in sync. It was as if they were one."

"I remember, too. I remember hoping that I would one day experience what they did while in human form."

"We will, I promise you from the very depths of my soul that when we reach Earth I will find you. I won't rest until we are together again."

Esmeralda smiled and leaned her head on his shoulder. "Oh, Mica. If you retain even an ounce of your romantic nature when you reach Earth, I have no doubt that we will indeed be together again."

"Hey, Am, what are you doing? I've been looking for you everywhere!"

The Angel next to Violet jumped out of her skin, and so did Violet. The tiny high pitched voice seemed so loud in the quiet space. Her eyes widened when she saw the green Faerie, it looked so much like the one she'd seen outside her kitchen window just months before.

"Shhh!" the Angel hissed. She looked back over her shoulder at Esmeralda and Mike on the bench, but they seemed oblivious to what was happening right behind them. Violet decided to leave as the Angel and Faerie began to have a heated discussion. For some reason she didn't want Esmeralda and Mike to catch her spying on their memory, and her mind was whirling with all the new things she'd heard. She could be Velvet. Her Twin Flame was a Merman, they'd been together in Atlantis, and somehow, the green Faerie had appeared outside her kitchen window one night. It was all too much to take in.

Violet found herself back in front of the line of doors again, and worried that she might not have much time left to explore, she ignored the rest of the doors and reached for the handle of her own, which was a beautiful shade of purple. She took a deep breath and tried to clear her mind of the whirling confusion, and of any expectations she had of what her past might contain.

This time, Violet wasn't confronted with a single memory, but with several simultaneously. She saw herself in flowing purple robes stood on a stage talking to hundreds of Angels, Faeries, Mermaids and others; she saw herself sat behind a huge desk, talking to a man in yellow robes. She gasped when she saw herself talking to her friend and colleague, an Angel with sparkling golden wings who looked exactly like Amy. She saw the small green Faerie again, as well as Esmeralda and Mike, who seemed so attached to one another. She saw herself visiting someone called Magenta, and gasped when she realised it was Maggie. She saw the man in yellow playing the piano, surprised that it was the same piece of music that had played at Lyle's funeral. She was even more surprised to see her visions, the same dreams that she'd had of Lyle just a few months before he died. The memories came thick and fast, streaming through her consciousness until suddenly it all became still, and she found herself sat on the same bench Esmeralda and Mike had been sat on, in front of the gold Merman statue.

"I wish you were here already, Laguz," she found herself saying, knowing that she had said the same words in her past life. "I wish you would help me through all this craziness," Violet paused. "I wish I could know with absolute certainty that we will be together on Earth. How will I find you? I have seen so many people on Earth miss meeting their soulmate by mere minutes or inches - how do I know that it won't be the same for us?" She sighed. "With all the uncertainty of the future of the human race, I wish I could be certain about being with you."

Violet was quiet for a moment, then she smiled and began to hum the song that seemed to be the theme tune for both her and Lyle, and for Velvet and Laguz. Violet hummed louder, feeling a tear fall from her now closed eyes. Her humming slowed and became quieter and she bowed her head, sad that it seemed she was always missing her chance to be with her Twin Flame.

"Velvet, my love."

Violet stopped humming and slowly opened her eyes. She looked up and blinked once, then three more times in quick succession.

"Laguz?" she whispered.

His heart-stopping smile made her catch her breath. She wrenched her eyes from his to look at where his statue stood, but it was gone. She looked back at him, her eyes wide.

"This isn't a dream?" Violet reached out to touch his face gently, completely lost in her memory now, forgetting everything that had just happened. When her fingertips met his cheek, it was like she'd been given an electric shock.

"You're real," she breathed. "How is this possible?"

"You wanted me to be here. You wanted certainty. So here I am."

"It's that simple? All I had to do was say that I wanted you here, and you would come?"

"Yes."

Violet leaned forwards and her lips met his. It felt so natural to be with him like this. She had forgotten what it felt like to be held so lovingly. She closed her eyes and ran her hand through his long hair. He responded passionately, drawing her closer to him.

After a few minutes, she pulled back, slightly breathless. "Can you stay?"

"There's nowhere else I would rather be."

Violet smiled and grabbed his hand. "There is somewhere else I would rather be," she said, her eyes sparkling. She raised her other hand, clicked her fingers, and the memory disappeared. Violet felt bereft at the sudden loss of his warm hand, then suddenly more memories came rushing through: Laguz leaving, herself lost in grief, bringing the lightning upon herself, then going to the Angelic Realm. She saw Magenta and Laguz become twins and realised finally the full connection that they had struggled to work out months before. She saw herself remembering that she could play the piano, and that it was she who had composed the piece of music, for Laguz, in their life in Atlantis. She saw the Academy change into the School, and all the Children of the Golden Age: the Indigos, the Crystals and the Rainbows. Then, finally, she saw herself leave the

Academy, thinking that she and Laguz would never meet. But then she saw something, something that she was sure wasn't her own memory, but that had been put there for her to see when she was open enough to receive it. She saw Laguz return to the Academy and find that she had already left, and then him following her to Earth. She saw him reborn as Lyle. Then she saw how his life had ended and her heart felt as though it were torn in two. All those dreams! Why had she ignored them for so long?

"Now then, I want you to conclude the current memory, and find your way back to the door. Make sure to close it behind you, and we will journey back through the maze to the present moment." Mike's voice, though quiet and gentle, jolted through Violet like an unpleasant shock. She wasn't ready to leave yet! She was beginning to understand so much; surely she could have a little more time? But she couldn't resist the instructions Mike was giving her. Entirely against her will, she left the stream of memories, and found herself standing back in front of the door bearing her name. She ran her hand over the engraved nameplate, and it shimmered, changing to Velvet, then back to Violet again. It seemed that it would be up to her now to find out the rest.

She went back through the maze and at Mike's instruction, slowly began to feel her body again, sat on the cushion in the meditation tent. When she finally slowly opened her eyes and looked around, she saw Amy, Esmeralda and Mike, and promptly fainted.

CHAPTER ELEVEN

Despite only meaning to stay at the vegetarian hotel for a few days, nearly three weeks later, Greg and Leona were only just packing up to leave. They'd met several more helpers and other travellers, who had recommended other hosts. They had decided to stick to Greg's plan to stay as close to the sea as possible and skirt around the coast of France. They had also decided to travel together, having enjoyed each other's company. Greg also loved Leona's uncanny ability to See the future. The weather reports were particularly handy.

After a lengthy goodbye, complete with double kisses and lots of hugs, Leona and Greg were finally on the road. Leona as the navigator and feeder, Greg as the driver. They kept up a steady stream of conversation for the first three hours, then were lulled into silence by the seemingly never-ending fields that rushed by.

Greg saw a sign indicating a café was coming up in a couple of miles and decided a pit-stop was needed. Leona had fallen asleep a few miles back and the map had slipped off her lap onto the floor.

Greg pulled into the small, rustic roadside café and parked. Leona didn't stir. He switched off the engine and at that moment, Leona woke up.

"What happened? Where are we?" She sat upright and looked around. "What did I miss?"

Greg laughed. "Nothing much, I thought it was time for a sugar break, I'm beginning to get a bit sleepy."

"Oh sorry, Greg, when did I fall asleep?" Leona asked, stretching.

"Not too long ago. Come on, I'll treat you to something chocolatey and hot."

Leona smiled. "Sounds good to me, lead the way."

They jumped out of the camper and Greg locked it, even though theirs was the only vehicle in the car park. The sun was nearing the horizon, and the light was already fading as they walked to the tiny café.

"Un chocolat chaud et un pain au chocolat, s'il vous plait," Greg said to the tired-looking waitress when she came to their table. He motioned to Leona to make her order.

"Same please," Leona said, closing her menu.

The waitress nodded disinterestedly and took the menus with her.

"You should be practising your French," Greg teased. "What will you do if we split away from one another? You'll starve."

"Just because you were the star pupil at the hotel! How come you picked it up so quickly anyway?"

Greg shrugged. "Don't know, guess I must have been French in a past life."

"Typical, you Old Souls really do know it all, don't you?"

Greg laughed. "I honestly don't know, I'm just learning about myself right now, just as you are getting to know me. In fact, it feels like you know me better than I know myself."

"But you felt like you fit the description in the book I

lent you?"

"I think so, I mean in general, but I don't know if some of the things fit. I mean, I've never seen the *Lord of the Rings* or *Harry Potter*, so I don't know if I would like them. But the description of the Merpeople also felt like a good fit. So I think you were right before, I am both."

"An Old Soul Merman." Leona tilted her head to look at Greg. "I think that's exactly right."

"I definitely think it could be right about the clothing thing, too." He tugged at the collar of his shirt. "Modern clothing doesn't feel particularly comfortable to me."

Leona's eyes lit up. "In that case, we are going to have to find a Renaissance Fayre along the way. You would absolutely love it."

"The book mentioned those Fayres; it did sound like a good idea."

"So are you going to grow your hair out and wear it in a ponytail?" Leona teased.

Greg laughed. "If gets to be any longer than a quarter of an inch it's just tight curls." He ran his hand over his shaven head. "I don't think long hair is ever going to be on the cards."

"You could grow it long then dreadlock it."

"And have to live with an afro in the meantime? I think I'll pass, thanks." Greg sipped the hot chocolate that was placed in front of him. The rich, thick, molten chocolate revived him a little, giving him the sugar hit he needed.

"I swear the French just melt bars of chocolate into mugs for their hot chocolate. There can't be any milk or hot water in this at all," Leona said appreciatively, taking several savouring sips, then taking a giant bite of her chocolate pastry.

"This definitely is my favourite drink now. Any other hot chocolate is just going to pale in comparison."

"Absolutely. So, at the next place, we'll have to see if

anyone has the *Lord of the Rings* or *Harry Potter* on DVD. I really do think you'd like them."

Greg raised an eyebrow. "My French may be good, but it's not good enough to watch whole movies."

Leona laughed. "I mean the English version, dummy. There's no way I'd sit through a dubbed movie with all the wrong voices that are out of sync, anyway."

Greg laughed with her. "Okay, we'll see if anyone has an English version. I'm intrigued to see if I do enjoy them, and therefore fit into the category even more."

"I can't imagine having to learn who I am all over again. It must be quite freeing in some ways, getting to choose anew what you like and don't like, without any real influence from your upbringing. Well, from this life anyway. As you found out, if there's anything that you don't like, you can just get rid of it."

Greg winced at the reference to his wife and kids, whom he hadn't thought about in the last three weeks. "You know I feel awful about what I did. I just couldn't bear to be with someone I didn't love or even like. It felt wrong. It felt like I was deceiving her, and myself. And who wants to live like that?"

"You'd be surprised. There are thousands, probably millions of people in the world who live just like that. In loveless relationships borne out of need, or worse, out of being forced to by family or religion."

Greg shuddered. "I got off lightly, I guess. At least I could leave."

"Do you think she's tried looking for you?"

Greg shrugged. "I don't know how she would begin. I didn't take a mobile phone, left no forwarding address, wiped all my e-mails and records of buying the camper, and she knows that I wouldn't go to anyone I apparently knew before the accident, because I have no memory of them now. So where would she look?"

Leona was thoughtful for a moment. "Maybe you should ring her, at least let her know that you're okay, and make sure she's okay?"

Greg looked a little embarrassed. "That would be a little difficult."

"Why's that?"

"I have no idea what the number is. I never memorised it because I never really left the house."

"We could always look online, I'm sure we could find her number listed. We have your last name, maybe your address is on your driving licence?"

Greg frowned and drank the last of his hot chocolate. "Leona, I know you mean well, and I do appreciate it. But do you think we could just drop this now? It's better this way. If I contact her now, I'd just be giving her the false hope that I might be coming back. I told you before, I'm not the man she loves. That guy just doesn't exist anymore. She's much better off without me, and so are the girls."

Leona sat back and held her hands up in surrender. "Fine, I won't mention it again, I promise."

"You're not bringing this up because you've Seen something, are you?"

Leona shook her head. "No, I haven't Seen any contact between you and your family in the future."

Greg nodded. "Okay. Seen anything else recently?"

"Yep, if we don't get back on the road soon, we're going to be driving all through the night to get to our next stop."

Greg laughed and finished the last tiny bite of his pastry. He wiped his mouth with a paper napkin then stood up and took his wallet out. He left the money for the bill and a tip for the dour waitress.

"Come on then, navigator. Try not to fall asleep on me this time."

* * *

"Hey, stranger!" Aria called out as she flew along the lake in the Angelic Realm. Linen looked up from the glassy surface to greet her.

"Hey, yourself. Taking a breather? How did the welcome session go?"

Aria hovered next to Linen for a moment before landing in the sand and grabbing a handful of nachos.

"It was amazing! I don't know where all the words came from, but it really sounded like I knew what I was talking about! I couldn't wait until later, so I changed back into a Faerie a bit early. I really missed my wings. You're still looking the same?"

Linen looked down at his Old Soul appearance. "Yeah, I don't mind being like this. It makes you move a little slower, but it helps to think more like an Old Soul, somehow."

"That's exactly how I felt! It was like I was channelling Velvet's spirit or something. I even used some long words too! I only left when Bk arrived. I figure I've got at least half an hour while he tells them all about aliens." Aria munched on some nachos then turned her attention to the surface of the lake. "What are we watching?

"I just thought I'd quickly check in on Velvet and Laguz's progress towards one another. Velvet's has been amazing. She did a meditation with Emerald and Mica - do you remember them? They were second years. Anyway, it was a meditation to unearth memories of their Twin Flame, and Velvet realised who she really was, who Laguz was, and even saw much of what happened at the Academy."

"Wow," Aria breathed. "That's so amazing! She can't fail to Awaken now!"

"She realised that the Faerie she saw outside the kitchen window was you."

Aria squealed. "That's amazing! Wow! I can't believe it, she must have really believed what she saw. Woo!" Aria flew upwards and went round in a few celebratory circles.

"Laguz is currently travelling across France. He's left his wife and kids, and has met a Faerie, who is an Awakened Earth Angel, and who I have to admit, is doing a pretty damn fine job of Awakening Laguz right now."

Aria stopped circling momentarily. "Who's the Faerie? Do I know them?"

"Do you remember when Velvet was trying to induce visions? There was a Faerie trying to help her?"

"Leon? Oh cool, how is he?"

"She. It seems Leon decided to live as a female human this time."

Aria shrugged. "Good for him! I mean, her. Oh, you know what I mean. It's good that Laguz has met her though, now he can't fail to properly Awaken either. Honestly, things couldn't have worked out better if they tried!"

"Yes, and that's what worries me slightly."

Aria frowned. "I'm afraid I don't understand."

"Don't you get the feeling that it's all a bit too good to be true? That surely there must be some cataclysmic event looming on the horizon?"

"Right, that's it, you need to change right now; you're becoming far too boring and serious. You need your wings back, immediately."

Linen laughed. "Maybe you're right." He clicked his fingers and his body shrank and his wings returned. He flew up to meet Aria. "Wanna race?"

"You're on! Ready... Go!"

* * *

Three months had passed since the retreat and Violet was slowly getting used to being in her boring job, and doing her normal, boring routine again. But there was a difference. She was now reading all the material she could get her hands on concerning Earth Angels, Atlantis, Wicca

- anything that might give her some useful information on what exactly she was supposed to do.

When she had come round from her fainting spell, she'd asked immediately for a pen and paper to write down all the information she had gathered during the meditation. She didn't admit to Esmeralda or Mike that she'd spied on their memories, but from the looks they gave her, she reckoned they knew. They seemed happy about it though, which made sense, considering their conversation in the garden. It seemed that they thought she was an important part of the world Awakening that was supposedly about to happen. Since the meditation, Violet had dreamt very vivid dreams, which she wrote down when she woke up. Pieced together, they seemed to be more memories of her past life on the Other Side as the Head of the Earth Angel Training Academy.

It was a slightly intimidating prospect, supposedly being a key part of a global shift that was to change the fate of the entire planet. It seemed more like something out of a superhero comic or movie. Violet didn't feel like she possessed any such super powers. Until the past year, she had been a very normal, exceptionally unexceptional human being. But her foray into her past life had definitely cleared up a few things she'd been wondering about recently. The situation with Lyle and Maggie and Adrian now made sense. They felt a connection because they had been so close in their past lives. And Amy! Her friend and fellow professor and so much more, it was no wonder they had hit it off immediately and had remained close friends.

The other thing it had explained was the strange way that children always looked at her whenever she was out anywhere. Some would even turn around in their pushchairs to look back at her. Violet had been wondering what the significance was. Could it be that they were the Indigo Children or the Crystal Children, trying to wake up her up? She had dreamt of a conversation she'd had with an Indigo Child, where she'd told him to remind her, in any way possible, of why she was on Earth.

Violet took a sip of her herbal tea and sighed. The problem was, despite all of her reading and remembering much of her past life, she still didn't know what to do. Lyle was still dead, and she was still just an ordinary person with a boring job. How was she supposed to change the world?

She fingered the wooden pendant that she wore around her neck every day. Another thing that had become clear through seeing her memories was the significance of the rune pendant. Her Twin Flame's name was Laguz, and in her memories of him on the Other Side he wore a similar pendant around his neck. She recalled the memory where he'd come back to the Academy to find her gone. She saw him put the rune necklace around the neck of the statue he'd created of her. Somehow, that act on the Other Side had brought the pendant to her now, she was sure of it.

It was the day before her workshop at the Twin Flame Retreat. She was looking forward to seeing Esmeralda and Mike again, and spending the weekend with Amy. She wondered if she should talk to Esmeralda about everything she'd remembered, and see if she could help her in any way. It made sense to. She'd wanted to help her when she was Velvet, why wouldn't she jump at the chance to now?

Violet glanced at the clock. It was past eleven at night and she hadn't packed yet. She sighed and hauled herself to her feet, and after putting the dirty mug in the already full sink in the kitchen, she went upstairs to bed. Though her mind seemed full of confusing thoughts, when her head hit the pillow, her mind went blank and she was asleep in seconds.

"Velvet? Can you hear me?"

Violet blinked and turned around to face the small green Faerie.

"Aria! You scared me."

The little green Faerie flew closer. "You remembered my name! That's amazing! Now then, I know you sometimes struggle to remember your dreams, so I'll be brief and to the point. You and Laguz will be together again." She held up a tiny hand as Violet began to cut in. "Shush, just listen to me. I know that Lyle is dead, but Laguz is here on Earth, now, and you two will meet, and you will be together. But you have to be open to it! If you close off to the possibility you'll miss him again, like you missed Lyle. Although with all those dreams you got, I don't know how you managed that one." Aria shook her head. "Anyway, I promised to be brief, sorry. Okay, this is the message you must remember - you will be together! Okay? You will." Aria flew to Violet and touched the rune pendant around her neck. "We're doing everything possible to make it happen, but it'll only happen if you let it, okay?"

Violet nodded.

"Oh, and say hi to Leon for me, okay?"

Violet blinked. "Who?"

She looked around her, but she was alone. "Aria? Where are you? Who's Leon? Aria!"

Violet sat up in bed suddenly, and looked around her. She was vaguely aware that she'd called out. While sleep still clung to her she fumbled in the darkness to turn her bedside lamp on and grab a pen and her dream diary. By the time she got the pen to work, the only word she could remember to write down was 'Leon'.

Frustrated that she couldn't remember any more, Violet threw the pen and notebook down and clicked the lamp off. She tried to re-enter the dream, but the rest of the night was a dreamless one.

Feeling restless and agitated the next morning, Violet got up a whole hour earlier than she needed to and had a long shower. Something was hanging on the edges of her consciousness, bothering her, but she didn't know what it was.

Amy arrived to pick her up at ten o'clock, by which time Violet still had wet hair, but had managed to throw some clothing and essentials into her bag. She was just putting the bag in the boot of Amy's car, when she remembered her dream diary.

"Hang on a minute, Amy, I've forgotten something," she said, dashing back to the house. She unlocked the door and took the stairs two at a time. She ran into her bedroom which was so messy from the morning's packing that you couldn't see the floor, and grabbed her dream diary from her bedside. She glanced around, trying to see if there was anything else she'd forgotten, then ran back downstairs and out the door, locking it behind her. By the time she got in the passenger seat beside Amy, she was shattered.

"Are we ready now?" Amy asked with a smile, fully used to her friend's complete disorganisation.

Violet nodded. "Yep, let's go."

Amy started the engine and they set off, both lost in their own thoughts for a while.

"So have you figured out some kind of structure for the course?"

"Yes, it took me a while, but I've got it all broken down into time slots, and I've got all the materials, don't worry."

Amy frowned and slowed the car. "Materials? Where? You didn't put anything in the car besides your suitcase."

Violet's hand flew to her mouth. "Oh, shit! I left them in the lounge. I had them in a box ready."

Amy was already indicating to pull into a side road and turn around. "Dear me, Violet, I think I should be the organiser and navigator when we go travelling, otherwise we may well find ourselves in deep trouble.

"I can't believe I did that," Violet said as they headed back to her house.

"What did you go back to get then?"

Violet held up her notebook. "My dream diary. Thought I might need it."

Amy shook her head and pulled back into Violet's street, bringing the car to a stop. Violet unbuckled her seatbelt and jumped out of the car. Cursing at her forgetfulness the whole way, Violet unlocked the door again and dashed into the lounge where her box of materials for the workshop sat on the coffee table. She grabbed it and dashed back out the door again. She put it in the boot with their bags then got back in the car to find Amy flicking through her dream diary.

"Who's Leon then?" Amy asked, handing the book back to her and pulling away again.

Violet frowned. "Leon? I don't know, why?"

"Because that's what you've written in your book in big letters. I figured the name must mean something."

Violet flipped to the current page in her dream diary and saw the name in her own messy handwriting. "Huh, I guess it must have been something I dreamt. I don't remember writing it down, to be honest."

Amy shrugged. "Oh well, I'm sure it'll come back to you if it's important."

Violet snapped the book shut and put it in her handbag. "Yeah, I'm sure you're right."

She leaned over and switched the CD player on. It was the same classical CD they'd listened to on their trip months before.

"Sorry, I would have put some other CDs in, but I find classical stops me from getting tensed up when I'm driving."

Violet shrugged. "It's cool, I found it quite relaxing on our last trip." She leant back in the seat, and let the music lull her into sleep.

"Who are you?"

Violet peered into the darkness. She knew someone was there, but she couldn't make out their features.

"It's me, Velvet. It's Laguz. I'm here."

Violet tried to walk towards the voice, but instead found herself walking into deep water. Before she could utter his name, the water suddenly rose up over her head, and she drowned.

"Violet! Wake up!"

Violet came round, gagging and coughing. She opened her eyes and looked around wildly. They were parked in the woods by the Twin Flame Retreat.

"What happened? How are we here already?"

Amy laughed. "You slept the whole way. You were completely out of it. I only woke you up because we were here. I could have left you in the car but you'd have got cold. Why were you gagging?"

"I was drowning. I couldn't move; the water came up over my head."

Amy frowned. "That's a horrible dream, I'm glad I woke you up now."

Violet took in a deep shuddering breath. "Yeah, it was horrible. Not a nice way to die at all."

"You died?" Amy shuddered. "Maybe you shouldn't live by the sea after all."

Violet shook off the feeling of dread that lingered and forced out a laugh. "Anyway, let's get in there, they're going to be wondering where we've got to. What time is it?"

"It's just after two. Hopefully there might be some lunch, I'm starving."

Violet laughed. "You're always hungry. Come on." She got out of the car and retrieved her bag and the box of materials from the boot. Amy grabbed her bag and slammed the boot shut.

"Can you manage all that by yourself?"

Violet nodded. "Yep, I've got it."

They made their way down the woodland path. The autumn leaves made a thick, colourful and noisy carpet underneath their feet. Before they reached the house, the door swung open and Esmeralda came out, in her apron and slippers.

"You're here!" she called out, coming down the path to help Violet with the box. "It's been far too long! How are you both?"

"Good, you?" Violet responded, gladly letting Esmeralda relieve her of the box.

"Good! Things have been quite busy. We usually find that it's busier here in the Autumn."

Amy frowned. "How come? I would have thought less people would come here in the Autumn, with the days becoming colder and the darker."

Esmeralda smiled. "It's the cold and the dark that makes them come here. If they're on their own, or are in a relationship that needs help, or are just feeling a bit down, then Autumn and Winter seem to make them feel worse. Which is when they come to us."

They reached the front door and went inside. Violet and Amy soaked in the warmth for a moment before taking their shoes off.

They left their bags by the door and headed straight to the dining room to have some food. The three of them talked non-stop throughout lunch, catching up on the events of the past few months, but Violet didn't mention what she really needed advice on. After the retreat, she'd told Amy vaguely what she'd seen, but hadn't gone into great detail. For some reason, she was holding back from telling her best friend everything, mainly for the fear of seeming big headed. Amy had seen her Twin Flame in the meditation; a dark-haired Angel called Nicholas. She'd remembered a time they had spent together in the Angelic Realm. As far as Violet had seen, they hadn't been reunited at the Academy, so Amy hadn't remembered any of that particular life.

Once the food had gone, Amy and Violet made their way to the same pod they'd stayed in before and settled in. The workshop participants would be arriving at six o'clock so they had plenty of time to relax. Violet's stomach churned slightly at the thought of running the workshop, but then apparently in her past life she'd spoken to hundreds of people with ease. She wondered how it was possible to be so different from one life to the next.

She glanced over at Amy, who was lying on her bed, and realised she was asleep. Hoping that she might catch Esmeralda with a few moments to spare, Violet quietly left the pod, smiling as she heard Amy begin to snore.

She made her way to the house and let herself in, then followed her nose to the kitchen where Esmeralda was baking a chocolate cake and singing along to a song on the radio.

"Mind if I join you?" Violet asked.

Esmeralda jumped and turned around. "Oh, it's you, Violet! You made me jump! I wasn't expecting anyone to come in, please excuse my out of tune warbling."

Violet smiled. "Sorry, didn't mean to scare you. I think your singing sounded good though, you have a nice voice."

Esmeralda laughed. "No need to be polite, we are friends after all." She turned the volume on the radio down then carried on mixing the melted chocolate into the mixture. "Everything okay?"

Violet was quiet for a moment, trying to figure out how to start. "I don't know. At the retreat, when we did that meditation, well, it was amazing. The amount of information that came flooding through was just incredible. But even now I have all that information, I still feel completely in the dark. Rather than give me answers, it just seems to have raised more questions. And I'm just not sure what I should do."

Esmeralda smiled. "You listened to mine and Mike's conversation, didn't you? Or conversations, I should say."

Violet raised an eyebrow. "You knew I was there?"

Esmeralda nodded. "Yes, and I was hoping you would. So you've remembered your life as Velvet and you've remembered the Academy?"

Violet nodded. "Yes, but I don't really understand. I mean, if I was that influential there, how could I be so ordinary and boring now? How am I supposed to make any difference to anything?"

Esmeralda set her spoon down, went over to Violet and put her hands on Violet's shoulders.

"My dear, how could you possibly think that you are ordinary and boring? Have you no idea the impact you have had on the lives of the people in your life? Even the ones who you have known for seconds will have been affected. Never, ever underestimate yourself. Yes, you are capable of being so much more than you are now, but you are already brilliant, you have already made a difference. And don't ever forget that."

By now, Violet was a deep shade of red. "Umm, thank you."

Esmeralda shook her head. "Have some confidence, woman! Repeat after me. I am brilliant."

Violet turned a deeper shade of red. "I am brilliant," she repeated quietly.

Esmeralda shook her head again. "Right, that's it. What time is it?" She swung around to look at the clock on the wall. "Perfect. Let me get this cake in the oven, then we're going for a little walk." She bustled around the kitchen, finishing the cake in record speed and putting the timer in her pocket. She pulled off her apron and grabbed Violet, marching her to the front door. Violet put her boots and coat back on, and Esmeralda did the same.

They set off around the back of the house, following a tiny path through the woods. Esmeralda didn't say anything, but set a steady pace that Violet struggled to keep up with. By the time Esmeralda came to a stop, Violet was breathing heavily and the light was beginning to fade.

Esmeralda turned to Violet and pulled her along, into a clearing. It was then that Violet realised that they were in fact standing on the edge of an old quarry. There was a rickety old fence to supposedly keep people out, but there was nothing substantial to stop them from falling into the disused pit.

"Now then, I want you to repeat after me, but this time, I want you to shout it like your life depended on it."

Violet glanced nervously at the drop below her, taking a small step back from the edge. She didn't honestly think Esmeralda would endanger her life, but she didn't want to take any chances. She nodded.

"Okay. I am brilliant."

"I am brilliant!" Violet shouted as loud as she could. She actually surprised herself. She didn't think she'd ever shouted so loudly. The echo of her voice ricocheted around the empty quarry and seemed to travel for miles.

Esmeralda smiled. "Now that's more like it. I am beautiful."

Violet glanced at Esmeralda who nodded encouragingly.

"I am beautiful!" Her echoing voice agreed, going round in circles again before fading away. Though her throat felt a little scratchy, Violet was beginning to feel better already.

"I am powerful."

"I am powerful!"

"I am healthy."

"I am healthy!"

"I am love."

"I am love!"

"I deserve the best."

"I deserve the best!"

"I am open to the good of the Universe."

"I am open to the good of the Universe!"

When the last echo died, Violet looked at Esmeralda, who was now grinning.

"How do you feel now?"

"Amazing."

"Do you believe that? That you deserve the best? That you are powerful?"

Violet had to stop herself from shrugging and shying away from the question. She stood straight and looked Esmeralda in the eye.

"Yes, I do believe that."

Esmeralda's grin got wider. "In that case, my work here is done." She reached into her pocket and looked at the timer. "Excellent timing. By the time we get back, the cake should be about ready."

"Perfect." Violet hooked her arm through Esmeralda's. "Lead the way!"

* * *

"How come out of that whole dream, all she remembered was 'Leon'?" Aria moaned as she nibbled on a piece of caramel fudge.

Linen shrugged. "I did tell you to keep it brief. Velvet only seems to remember the odd detail of her dreams."

"It was brief! Well, sort of. Can I try again?"

"If you think it will help. Personally, I think Velvet has to Awaken by herself."

Aria sighed and finished off the fudge. She licked her fingers and dried them on her dress. "Do you think she ever will? Properly Awaken, I mean."

"I think she's more than capable of it, and she couldn't possibly have more people in her life to help her than she already has-"

"But?" Aria cut in.

Linen sighed, and manifested more fudge for himself. "But I get the feeling that perhaps it won't be as simple as it could be."

"Since when has being human been simple?"

Linen laughed. "That's true."

"Are you still getting feelings of cataclysmic events?"

Linen laughed again at the tone of Aria's voice. "I do feel like something big is going to happen."

"Something big *is* going to happen! Velvet and Laguz will get together, they'll have lots of Rainbow babies, wake up the whole world and the Golden Age will happen for the first time!"

Linen shook his head at the over-excited Faerie. "Where do you get your incredible faith and enthusiasm from?"

"I don't know. I guess I never thought of myself as being the faith-type, but I just know that everything will work out just fine. It has to."

Linen nodded. "Let's hope you are right. Do you fancy going to the Leprechaun Garden for a bit? Feels like we haven't been there in ages."

Aria smiled. "I do have some time before my next session with the humans." She flew up and held her hand out to Linen. "Let's go!"

CHAPTER TWELVE

"Joyeux Noël!" Greg said, raising his glass to clink Leona's.

"Right back atcha," Leona replied, taking a sip of the mulled wine. "Mmm, this is my second favourite drink of all time, after French hot chocolate."

Greg nodded in agreement as he took a sip. "Most definitely." He looked around the interior of the camper; they had fairy lights strung up in an attempt to be festive.

"Though I'm sure you've had better Christmases where you actually had heating and a family around you, I'm really glad that you're here this Christmas." He shrugged. "I can't quite explain it, but I feel like you've woken me up. Like you've come into my life to open my eyes to everything." He laughed. "I'm sorry, you're probably thinking I'm crazy."

Leona smiled and shook her head. "I know what you're trying to say. And I feel like that too. Like I was meant to meet you so that you would finally get a clue."

Greg nearly choked on his wine as he laughed.

"I'm having a good time here with you, Greg, you feel like family to me. Like a big brother. All my siblings are a lot younger. So it's nice, having an older one."

Greg got his coughing under control and frowned.

"Hey, not that much older. How old do you think I am anyway?"

"Oh, I don't know, maybe a few thousand years old?" Leona asked innocently.

Greg rolled his eyes. "I didn't mean in total, I meant in this lifetime."

"Yeah, so did I," Leona replied, still acting innocent.

"If you didn't have a glass of wine in your hand I would sock you one. I'm not that old at all, I'm only…" Greg stopped mid-sentence and frowned again. He got up then, setting his wine down on the counter and found his passport tucked in his folder in the cupboard. He flicked to the back page and quickly did the maths.

"Thirty-five!" he exclaimed. "I can't be that old surely?" He put the passport away and dug around in his coat pocket for his wallet. He found it and took out his driving license. He looked at it and shook his head. "Jeez, I'll be thirty-six on the fourth of February. I do *not* feel that old."

Leona patted the couch. "Hey, come here. It's not that old, really."

Greg slumped back down on the couch and drank some more wine. "I just didn't realise. How crazy is that? I didn't even know how old I was. I'm really not Greg, am I?"

Leona shook her head. "Nope, most definitely a walk-in."

"Do you think I'll ever remember who I was before? Before I walked-in to this body, I mean."

Leona shrugged. "It's possible. I think that when you meet the woman in your dreams, it will become clear."

"Velvet."

"Sorry?"

"The woman you saw, the one I keep dreaming of. Her name is Velvet."

"How do you know that?"

"Because she told me, in my dream." Greg set down his

empty glass and leaned back. "Do you think I will actually meet her?"

"I'm certain of it. And you know how accurate I am." Leona smiled.

"It's true, you've not steered me wrong yet." He took a deep breath. "Right, I promise to cheer up now." He leant over and reached underneath the couch cushion. "It's only a small thing, but I got you a little something, seeing as it's Christmas." He handed her a badly wrapped package, just as she reached into her pocket and pulled out a beautifully wrapped package about the same size.

"Oh, Leona, you didn't have to get me anything."

"And neither did you, but we both did, so let's both enjoy them." They swapped gifts and Greg waited until Leona opened hers first. Inside the crude brown paper wrapping was some tissue paper. She pulled it open carefully and found a silver Faerie pendant on a delicate silver chain. Greg shrugged, feeling embarrassed.

"I hope you like it, I saw it in the gift shop in that tiny village we visited a couple weeks ago and it reminded me of you, so I thought maybe you'd like it."

Leona smiled at him and held it out for him to fasten around her neck. As she leaned forward she gave him a kiss on the cheek.

"I love it. It's really beautiful, thank you, Greg. Now," she said, gesturing to his present. "Open yours."

Greg carefully unwrapped the package, which was a box wrapped in shiny blue paper. He pulled the box open and pulled out a wooden pendant on a leather cord. He smoothed his thumb over the engraving.

"What is it?" he asked, feeling slightly foolish for not knowing.

"It's a rune, called Logr. I was in that tiny crystal shop we stopped by two days ago, and it caught my eye. I just felt compelled to get it for you, I don't really know why though."

"What does it mean?" Greg asked, reaching up to tie it around his neck.

Leona shook her head. "I don't know. I've never really studied runes. I only know that it's called Logr because the shop owner told me."

Greg fingered the pendant that was now securely around his neck. "It's really cool, thank you."

Leona smiled. "You're welcome. I guess we must have been in tune with one another, both buying necklaces. Perhaps it means we've been spending too much time together."

Greg laughed. "Yeah, although it doesn't really feel like it. I mean, I've enjoyed every minute."

Leona nodded. "Me too. So," she said reaching for the deck of cards. "Ready for me to thrash you again?"

Greg groaned. "It's a good thing we never play for money, you'd have cleaned me out by now."

"That's not a bad idea, how about a gambling game, just for Christmas?"

Greg shook his head. "Hell, no, I'm not stupid. I think I'll keep my wallet in my pocket, thanks."

Leona laughed. "Suit yourself. You never know though, this could be your lucky night."

"And my name could really be Santa," Greg said dryly. "Just deal the cards; you're not getting any cash out of me."

"We'll see."

* * *

"Merry Christmas, Amy! So glad you made it here, the weather is crazy, isn't it?"

Violet stepped aside to let her friend in. Amy stamped her feet on the mat, trying to get most of the snow off.

"My God, the ice is so bad at the end of your road! Don't you get gritters down here?"

"Guess they must have forgotten us. Get your shoes off and get in here, I've got the mulled wine on the stove already."

Amy followed Violet into the kitchen, through the lounge which looked like Santa's grotto. Violet loved Christmas. She always went all out when it came to the decorations, even if it was only her who would really see them.

Mulled wine in hand, they sat in the lounge. Amy was quiet for a while, mesmerised by the twinkling Christmas tree lights. After a while, she turned to Violet.

"I know we weren't doing presents this year because we're both saving up for the trip, but I made you a little something." She dug into her handbag and took out a small parcel.

"Aww, Amy, thank you. I actually made you something, too." Violet got up and picked out a parcel from underneath the tree.

Amy took the parcel and handed Violet hers. They opened them together, and then both laughed when they saw the contents. Amy had made Violet a brightly covered notebook with ribbons tied around the metal binding, and Violet had made Amy a white leather notebook with the wings of an Angel in gold on the front.

"I guess we both had the same idea!" Violet said, flicking through the pages.

"I saw the state of your dream diary and thought you might like something nicer to record them in."

Violet smiled. "Thanks, Ames, that notebook is pretty tatty." She tapped the cover of the new notebook. "I love it."

Amy turned the leather notebook over and looked at the binding. "This is really great too. You could sell these, you know."

Violet shrugged. "I just had some leather left over from another project and thought I'd give bookmaking a go. I made a few others as presents this year, seeing as I'm trying to save up for our trip."

"About our trip," Amy said, suddenly excited. "I have some great news!" She reached back into her bag and pulled out her purse. She handed Violet a cheque. "My nan has decided to give me my inheritance now, rather than when she dies. So we don't have to worry now, we can definitely get the camper van!"

Violet looked at the figure on the cheque and her eyes widened. "Wow, Amy, that's amazing. But surely you'll want to put this away, and save it?"

Amy frowned. "What for? A rainy day? Come on, Violet, this travelling trip is the only thing keeping me going through my crappy job and living with my parents! It's my money and I want to use it for our adventure."

Violet smiled. "This time I think I definitely need to send your nan a thank you card. This trip is going to be amazing."

Amy bounced up and down on the settee. "I can't wait! Can we go a bit earlier? Now we don't have to save up as much?"

Violet laughed. "We'll see."

* * *

Aria smiled. The Academy of Awakened Humans was a success. Some of the humans had already been called back to Earth. Aria hoped that their session here would help them Awaken. It seemed like Velvet was taking forever to Awaken properly; when would she start listening to her intuition? To her inner voice? At least the Angels seemed to be getting through. Aria was glad that Athena, Emerald and Mica had found their way into her life. And Magenta.

It was amazing really, considering the size of the world, that they had all found each other.

Although, it had probably been engineered that way; Gold was pretty influential when it came to these matters. She wouldn't be surprised if he'd been pulling the strings.

"I hope you're not thinking too hard there, it might hurt."

Aria looked up and stuck her tongue out at Linen, who had just entered the office. "Very funny. I was just thinking about how successful my Academy is. So there."

Linen grinned. "It is very successful, you should be extremely proud of yourself. The walk-in programme with the Earth Angels is also going very well; we've already had three transitions so far."

"God, are we good or what?"

Linen settled behind his desk and flicked through his notebook. "We're good. Hey, you available later? I wanted to check on Velvet again."

Aria nodded. "I have another break in a bit." She looked at the clock. "Oh no! I'm going to be late for the session!" She flew up and zoomed to the door, which barely had time to vanish before she went through it.

"See you later, then," Linen called after her, chuckling to himself.

* * *

Greg breathed in deeply and smiled. Though the winter had been quite a harsh one, it was just beginning to warm up a little, and the sea breeze was pleasantly cool instead of bitterly cold. Greg took in the scene around him, and hugged his knees a little closer to his chest. The waves were rolling gently onto the sand below, and the seagulls were calling out to one another. Greg closed his eyes and inhaled the cold salty air. He loved being near the sea. Though he felt a twinge of sadness whenever he was at the beach, he also felt a deep sense of belonging. And considering his feelings of detachment and of being a bit lost, it was really important to him.

"Thought I might find you out here."

Greg turned and smiled at Leona. "I think it must be the Merman in me. I just feel drawn to the sea."

Leona settled herself on the grass and leaned slightly into him. He automatically put his arm around her and pulled her closer. She shivered a little.

"Thanks. It's still a little cold to be sitting outside. Though I daresay it's warmer here in February than it is in England."

"I would agree with you, but I was only in England during the summer. That I remember, I mean." He shrugged. "It doesn't seem too cold right now. I was thinking of going for a swim, actually."

"Are you completely mad? It'll be freezing in there. You'd get cramp in about five seconds, and you're kidding yourself if you think I'd come and save you."

Greg laughed. "Okay, okay. I'll wait another week or two, it'll be warmer then."

Leona shook her head. "You're on your own on that one. I find it hard enough to keep warm as it is." She shivered again, as if to prove her point.

Greg pulled her closer still. "Shall we head back to the house for a hot chocolate?"

Before Greg had even finished his sentence, Leona was on her feet. Laughing, Greg got up with her and they made their way up the grassy path through the dunes. When they reached the rocks, Greg helped Leona up, then they held hands until they reached the door of the cottage. Their hosts had gone away for the weekend, leaving the house and pets in their care.

Inside, Leona headed straight for the kitchen and

started making the hot chocolate. Greg fed the hamster, the goldfish and the two cats, then joined Leona at the kitchen table next to the window overlooking the sea.

"I would love to live somewhere like this someday. Right on the beach."

Leona smiled. "I can see that, I can see you living here."

"Is Velvet with me?" Greg asked, his tone teasing but his eyes serious.

"It wasn't a vision. I can just imagine you living here, by the sea. I haven't had any visions of Velvet for a while, actually."

Greg frowned. "Why do you think that is?"

Leona shrugged. "I don't know, it probably doesn't mean anything. Or it could mean that I'm no longer having visions of her because your meeting with her is imminent."

Greg stared out of the window at the water. "I wish there was some way of knowing what's going to happen."

"Life would be boring though, if you knew what was going to happen. Where would the mystery and challenge be?"

Greg smiled. "I'm sure I've been told that before. Besides, you get to see bits of the future, so where's your mystery?"

"That's it though, I only See bits. I don't See the whole picture. And usually only for other people. It's rare for me to See something of my own future."

Greg was silent for a while.

"Drink your hot chocolate. It'll go cold."

Greg picked up the mug, still staring at the sea, and took a sip. "It's good, thanks."

"I wish I could tell you that it'll all work out, Greg, but I can't. It doesn't work like that. Predicting a person's life path isn't like predicting the weather. Just one tiny decision, a change of mind, a change of timing even, can change the entire course of someone's life. I could predict now that you will meet Velvet at a certain time and date, then she or you could make a choice that changes it. It's just too difficult to tell. All I can say is this, you need to keep positive that you will meet, and you need to remain open to the opportunities that come your way. If you get a gut feeling to do something, then do it. If your inner voice is urging you to go a certain way, even if it's not the normal way, then go."

Greg looked at Leona. "Thank you. I'm not being off with you for not giving me assurances. It's not your job to reassure me, or to make me feel better. But somehow you manage to anyway." He reached across and put his hand on hers. "Thank you. Really, I don't know what I'd have done without you."

"You'd have survived, I'm sure."

"But not thrived. Right, let's lighten the mood now, how about a drive into town for a drink?"

Leona smiled. "It's okay, I know you're not much of a drinker, we can stay in tonight. I want to beat you at cards again, anyway."

Greg groaned. "I'm not sure my poor ego can take any more."

Leona laughed and reached for the battered deck of cards. "Aww, come on, please?"

"Fine, but I'm not going to pretend to enjoy it."

"Excellent, I'll deal."

* * *

"I can't believe this is it! We're finally on our way!" Amy squealed as they pulled away from her parents' house in their second-hand purple camper van. Violet carefully pulled out of the street and smiled at Amy.

"I know, I thought your parents were going to keep us

there forever with all those goodbyes."

Amy laughed. "Yeah, you'd think that they'd stop treating me like a child by now."

Violet shrugged. "They just care about you. It's sweet really; my mum just drives me mad."

Amy laughed. "I like your mum, she's cool. Anyway," she switched on the Sat Nav and programmed in their destination. "Only a few hours to go until we hit the coast, get on the train and get to France! I think I'm more excited about going to La Rochelle than you are," she said accusingly.

"I just don't know what will happen there, and part of me is kind of dreading it."

Amy frowned and dug in the food bag for a chocolate bar. She unwrapped it and bit a piece off. "I wonder why that is," she said through her mouthful.

Violet shook her head. "I honestly don't know, it's just this odd feeling I have. I asked Maggie what she thought, but all she got was a vision of a beach. She couldn't See anything else."

"I guess we'll find out soon."

"So you still think we should head straight there? There's so much we could see on the way, it seems a shame to just make a beeline there."

"You really are resisting it, aren't you? My feeling is, it's not anything terrible you're sensing, it's the fact that you might meet your Twin Flame, and you're not sure you're ready."

Violet smiled ruefully, indicating to turn onto the motorway. "You could always read me like a book. You're right, in a way. I mean, I have been thinking about it all, and if Laguz found a way to come back last time as Lyle, then it's not so far removed to think that he may have found another way to come back now. But what I don't understand is, if he was reborn again after dying as Lyle, wouldn't that make him only a few months old? I mean, it would be a little strange if I was destined to be with my Twin Flame who is actually 25 years younger than me."

Amy laughed. "It's not impossible, stranger things have happened."

"Hmm, it's just a weird concept, that's all. I guess that's why I'm dreading it."

"I'm sure it'll all work out fine, you'll see."

The hours seemed to fly by, and soon they were at the Channel Tunnel, waiting their turn to board. Once in France, after a little confusion in the beginning, they managed to get the Sat Nav to work out the most direct route to La Rochelle.

"Seven hours? Oh, that's not bad at all. We should be there by the early hours."

Violet raised an eyebrow. "That's a lot of driving. To be honest, I'm kind of tired already." She yawned, but Amy was having none of it.

"Then we'll share the driving. Shall I drive now? Or do you want me to swap with you in a few hours?"

Violet sighed. "I'm okay for a bit. Let's just get going. We *are* stopping for food though. I'm not going the whole day on crisps and chocolate bars."

"That's fine. We can just park somewhere and sleep in the back whatever time we get there anyway."

"Okay. Don't expect me to be very cheerful tomorrow though."

"Don't worry, Violet, I never expect you to be cheerful in the morning."

* * *

Greg woke up at six-thirty in the morning and couldn't get back to sleep. He got out of bed and looked out of the tiny cottage window at the waves crashing on the beach below.

There was a sense of anticipation within him that he didn't understand. Something was about to happen, and he felt simultaneously excited and terrified, and somehow he knew that it would change everything.

Feeling wide awake and slightly irritated with himself, Greg pulled a jumper on over his t-shirt and joggers and went downstairs to get the log fire burning. While their hosts were away, they were staying in the house rather than in the camper, which you would have thought would be a bit warmer, but first thing in the morning it was just as cold inside as it was outside. Within minutes, Greg got a roaring fire going and poured himself a cup of tea.

He sat at the dining table and warmed his hands on his mug, while staring out at the water. The sky was getting lighter by the second, and soon the sun would be peeping over the horizon. A movement to the left made Greg look, and he squinted into the hazy dawn light. A figure was walking along the sand towards the rocks. He watched as the figure climbed the rocks down near the water, seemingly looking for a particular spot. Without realising it, he found himself walking to the back door and out of the cottage; something was screaming a warning inside him. He watched the figure perch on a rock quite high up from the sea. He was at the gate when the figure stood, and he held his breath. It came out in a gush when he saw the tiny camera in the person's hand. They weren't going to jump, they were just trying to take a photograph. He was about to turn back to the cottage when the figure jerked suddenly, losing their footing. The mug was smashed on the path and he was running before the person had even hit the waves churning below.

* * *

Despite all the driving and the late night, Violet found

herself unable to sleep once they'd found a suitable place to park. They'd finally reached La Rochelle at three in the morning. Amy had fallen asleep immediately, and began snoring indelicately straight after. After lying in bed for a few hours, Violet put a few layers of clothing on and decided to go for a walk along the beach. She grabbed her camera and put it in her pocket. She figured she may as well make use of her early morning. She opened the door quietly and left the camper. She locked it even though there was no one else in sight. It seemed that not many people enjoyed camping in February.

Once on the sand, Violet stopped and inhaled deeply. She loved the sea. Living inland in England had felt quite stifling at times. There was nowhere to escape to where you could just go for a walk and let all your worries blow away in the breeze. She shivered and decided to keep walking to keep warm. The sun wasn't far from rising and the stars were just fading away in the coming dawn.

She decided to climb up on the rocks to get a photo of the sunrise. It would look amazing from up there. The climb left her feeling slightly breathless, but she knew it was worth it when she brought her camera up to frame the shot. She turned to find somewhere to sit and watch it rise, but as she turned, she lost her footing and before she even had time to scream, she was plunging into the rocky water below.

CHAPTER THIRTEEN

"Welcome home, Velvet. Though I daresay I'm not terribly pleased to see you."

"Gold! Oh, it's so good to see you!" Velvet ran forwards and threw her arms around the Elder. "It's been so long, how are you?"

Gold extricated himself from her embrace and stepped back. "I'm perfectly fine. You, however, aren't so good."

Velvet frowned, then it suddenly all came back to her. "Oh, Goddess. I'm dead, aren't I?"

Gold nodded slowly. "I'm afraid so, yes."

"But I can't be! I went to Earth to help with the Awakening, I can't die yet, it hasn't happened, I haven't helped enough, I haven't done enough." She buried her head in her hands. "Oh, Gold, I've really, truly messed up, haven't I?"

"It would appear so, Velvet. Just when I thought you were beginning to listen to your Angels, you go and do something stupid like that."

"Listen to my Angels?"

"Amy said to you last night not to go swimming in the sea, remember?"

"But she was joking! And besides, it's not like I intended

to go swimming, I slipped! Oh, Gold, this cannot be the end, I haven't done anything I set out to do."

"I'm sorry, Velvet, truly I am."

Velvet was quiet for a while, thinking. "Was Laguz really Adrian and Lyle?"

Gold nodded. "Yes, he missed you twice, and now you've missed him."

"What do you mean? Is he back on Earth? How?"

"He went back as a walk-in. He took over the body and life of a soul who wished to leave Earth. He went back for you, Velvet."

Velvet's face crumpled. "How is it possible that we've missed each other again, Gold? Are we really just not meant to be together?"

"That's not for me to decide," Gold said, but Velvet noticed his right eye had begun to twitch.

"Gold, what aren't you telling me? Please, is there some way to fix this?"

"We don't have much time. I just need to know one thing."

"What?"

"Do you believe you can do it? Do you believe you can change the world? Bring about the Global Awakening? Take the planet into the Golden Age?"

Velvet swallowed hard. Then she remembered standing on the edge of the quarry with Esmeralda, shouting affirmations. She straightened her shoulders.

"I can do it. I just need one more chance."

Gold nodded. "I was hoping you would say that. You'd better go. You've been unconscious for a good few minutes now."

"Am I badly injured?"

"Would that change your decision to return?"

"No."

"Then it doesn't matter. Go now. And good luck."

Velvet smiled at Gold and squeezed his shoulder before turning and walking into the thick mist.

"You're going to need it."

* * *

"Velvet? Come on, Velvet, please wake up."

As Violet became aware of the voice calling her, she also became suddenly aware of the crushing pain in her left leg, and that she was soaked to the skin. She moaned.

"Velvet? Can you hear me? I need to call an ambulance, but I don't want to move you. Can you wake up?"

Violet opened her eyes and found herself staring at a deep brown pair of eyes and a very good looking, yet very concerned face.

"My leg hurts," she whimpered.

"I know, I need to get you medical attention, but I haven't got a phone with me. Would it be okay if I carried you? Do you hurt anywhere else?"

Violet flexed the rest of her body and aside from a few aches, couldn't find any other serious pains. "I think I'm okay otherwise." She shivered. "Just cold. Please, I just need something for my leg."

"Okay, I'm going to lift you now, really slowly, okay? Just to the house up this way. Tell me if anything hurts."

Violet nodded and gritted her teeth. The pain as her leg left the sand was excruciating. She didn't dare look at it in case the sight of it made her feel sick. She wondered what kind of damage she had done to cause so much pain.

She closed her eyes and felt her rescuer carry her carefully but quickly up the dunes. "What's your name?" she asked.

"Greg. We're nearly there now, just stay awake, okay?"

Violet nodded, but didn't open her eyes. She heard a door open.

"Leona!" Greg shouted. Violet heard a scuffle then footsteps coming down the stairs.

"What is it? Oh my God, is that... What happened?"

"I need you to call an ambulance. She fell off the rocks into the sea. She's hurt her leg quite badly and stopped breathing for a couple of minutes. She was unconscious for at least ten minutes after she started breathing again."

Violet heard movement and the sound of someone dialling the emergency number.

"Velvet? Can you still hear me? I'm going to lay you down on the settee okay? I need you to stay awake while we wait for the ambulance."

Violet nodded again, feeling herself drifting slightly. The pain was receding and she felt like she was floating.

"Velvet? Can you hear me?" A hand shook her gently. "Please, Velvet, you need to stay awake. Leona, are they coming? She keeps fading out on me. I'm worried about the blood loss."

Violet heard the word blood and her stomach turned. She felt someone touch her leg and she jerked in pain.

"Velvet, I'm sorry, I just needed to stem the bleeding a little until the ambulance arrives. You need to try and stay awake okay?"

Violet nodded through the red haze that clouded her vision. Salty bile rose up in her throat and she gagged. Greg helped her to sit up while she coughed.

"You're going to be okay, Velvet, they'll be here really soon."

Violet finally opened her eyes again, and looked into the deep brown ones. But then she made the mistake of looking down at her leg. Her trouser leg had been torn off at the knee and she could see bone protruding from her shin.

For the second time that morning, Violet slipped into oblivion.

* * *

"Violet? Can you hear me?" Greg bit his lip as he held Violet's hand. The ambulance was hurtling along and the paramedic was trying to tend to her broken leg. He spoke no English, and Greg's French, though not terrible, wasn't good enough for anything medical, so Greg just left him to do his job and tried his best to get Violet to wake up.

He'd met Amy briefly. She'd heard the sirens and had come out to find her friend being put in the back of the ambulance. He'd convinced Leona to bring Amy in the camper to the hospital. He couldn't leave Violet now. Of course, he'd felt a bit stupid for thinking that her name was Velvet. She did look a lot like the woman he was dreaming about, though. Maybe she was the same person.

He stroked the side of her face lightly. "Violet," he murmured. "Please wake up."

At the hospital, he finally had to separate from her while they rushed her into the back. She was still unconscious, and Greg was worried that she may have hit her head when she fell. Maybe he'd been wrong to move her. Maybe he'd made her injuries worse. He was pacing up and down the waiting room when Amy and Leona arrived.

"How is she?"

"I don't know, she was unconscious until we got here, then they took her away."

"How did Violet end up in the sea?" Amy asked.

"She fell off the rocks. I think she was trying to take a photograph."

Leona's eyes were wide. "How did you manage to get her out? How did you even see her?"

Greg tiredly recounted the morning, which seemed to be stretching out forever. It was only now that the adrenaline was wearing off that he realised he was still dressed in waterlogged clothing. He shivered.

"I'll go get a blanket, you must be freezing," Leona said, heading for the reception desk. She returned with a blanket. "The lady on reception said that maybe you should get looked at too. You could be suffering from shock." She wrapped the blanket around him.

Greg shook his head. "I'm not in shock. I'm just a bit cold."

"Well, I'm in shock; I did not See this one coming. You'd think that with all my visions of Velvet, I could have warned you how dramatic your meeting would be."

Amy frowned at Leona. "Velvet? Why does everyone keep saying that? Her name's Violet."

"It's a long story," Greg cut in.

"Okay." The three of them lapsed into silence. Greg couldn't keep still; his foot tapped impatiently against the lino floor.

After what seemed like hours, a doctor finally approached them.

"Are you Violet's family?"

"No, I'm her best friend, we were travelling together. This is Greg, the man who saved her, and Leona, his girlfriend." The doctor was continuing before Greg had a chance to correct Amy.

"Violet is stable now, she lost some blood through her leg wound and she had a bump on the head as well as other bumps and abrasions. She's been sedated so that we could set her leg and cast it, but she should be coming round very soon, if you would like to go and sit with her."

"Thank you," Amy said. "I'd like to go see her."

"Me too," Greg added quickly.

"Follow me, I'll take you to her."

The three of them followed the doctor down a maze of white corridors, until they reached Violet's room. The doctor left them at the threshold.

Amy went in first and gasped when she saw her friend

hooked up to an IV, her leg covered in plaster and various gauzes covering parts of her body.

"Violet?" She sat on the chair beside her and carefully touched her friend's hand, but there was no response.

Greg went to the other side of the bed and leant over to stroke the side of Violet's face. She blinked, then groaned.

"Violet?" Amy said again, but Violet was staring at Greg. Or, rather, she was staring at Greg's neck. She reached up with her free hand and touched the wooden pendant.

"Laguz," she whispered.

Greg frowned. "Laguz?" Violet's eyelids flickered and her hand slumped back to the bed. Within seconds she was asleep again.

Greg turned to Amy and Leona. "Any ideas?"

"Laguz is the name of the rune on your pendant. Violet has one that's almost identical to it," Amy said. She went through the bedside cabinet until she found Violet's belongings that had been removed when she came into hospital. She found the wooden pendant and handed it to Greg.

"I still don't really understand any of this."

Amy shrugged. "Neither do I, Violet hasn't told me everything that's happened recently. We went on a retreat a while back, and we did a meditation, and I know that lots of things came up in it, but she didn't tell me what. You'll have to wait until she's awake for all the answers."

"Leona?"

Leona shrugged too. "I haven't Seen anything that might help, Greg. I wish I had. All I know is that Violet is almost identical to the woman in my visions, the woman you called Velvet."

"The name Velvet came up when we used an Angel Board and spoke to the spirit of a friend of Violet's. It seemed to imply that Violet had been called Velvet in a past life."

Greg shook his head and looked back at Violet's peaceful face. "All of this is just so crazy. But I swear, though I only met her this morning, I feel like I've known Violet forever."

Leona smiled. "I know I have met her before."

"When we first met, we both felt the same way. Now, we couldn't imagine not being friends," Amy added.

"I guess we'll just have to be patient and wait for her to wake up and explain everything to us."

"Let's hope she can."

* * *

"Unbelievable," Aria breathed. "Velvet is so lucky that Laguz was there to save her!" She nibbled on her banana cake, still riveted to the scene playing out in the lake.

"Lucky? Don't you know by now that there's no such thing? That everything that happens in the Universe happens by design and not by chance?"

Aria tore herself from Velvet's life for a moment to look at Linen. "You know, sometimes I forget that you're actually a Faerie when you say things like that."

Linen shrugged. "I suppose I just find it all fascinating. That the humans are creating their lives with every thought, and yet they don't even realise. That people and circumstances are put into place by the Angels, and they have no idea of the significance. Don't you find that interesting?"

"Do I find it interesting that humans are a bit stupid and completely oblivious?"

Linen laughed.

"No, I don't find it interesting, I find it incredibly annoying! I mean here we are, cheering them on, hoping they will remember, and yet they blunder about with no idea about anything. Which is why I'm finding this," she gestured to the lake, where Velvet was recovering from her incident in hospital, "so amazing. The fact that Velvet has remembered some of her past life as Velvet, and that she is telling others about it. I find that interesting." She turned her attention back to the lake, watching attentively as Velvet and Laguz's relationship seemed to be growing.

"I love you, Aria."

Aria turned back to look at Linen, a puzzled little smile on her face. "I love you too, Linen. Now can we watch some of this quietly now?"

Linen chuckled. "Of course. I'm sorry for being so noisy."

"You're forgiven."

* * *

"So because of the rune pendant, you think I'm Laguz?"

Violet reached out to touch the pendant around Greg's neck and smiled. "It just seems like too strange a coincidence otherwise. I mean, you said yourself that you have no memory of your life before you had the car accident, that you have no connection to your family at all, that you didn't even recognise yourself. And the date you woke up was just a few months after Lyle died."

"Leona said I could be a walk-in. That I've stepped into the body of a soul who wanted to leave."

Violet nodded. "It would certainly make sense." She looked into Greg's dark brown eyes, searching for the familiar sparkle she had known throughout their lifetimes together. "I think you came back for me."

Greg looked away towards the waves that were rolling in. "I have to be honest, none of this makes a lot of sense to me. I'm not as well read in this world of walk-ins and soulmates and past lives. Well, at least if I am, I don't remember much of it."

"But how do you feel about it all? Your soul remembers, even if you don't, and your soul lets you know these things through your feelings."

Greg looked back at Violet and shook his head. "There you go again. The things you say, they just don't sound right coming from a girl in her twenties."

Violet laughed. "I know, I know, I sound like an old lady. Always have, I'm afraid."

"No, not old, just wise. Wise far beyond the number of years you have been on Earth."

"By that reasoning, past lives must exist then," Violet teased. She shifted her leg, wincing at the aching pain.

Greg caught her expression. "Are you okay? We can go back up to the house for a bit if you're uncomfortable."

Violet shook her head. "No, no, I'm fine. It's just so good to be outside after being cooped up in hospital. Besides, I love being by the sea."

Greg raised an eyebrow. "Really?"

Violet laughed. "Yeah, despite the slight drowning incident, I do still love the sea. Somehow, I feel at home here. Like I belong."

"Now that does feel right to me. I feel the same way. Are you sure you weren't a Mermaid in a past life?"

"Now you've got to be kidding, I don't think it's possible for Mermaids to drown."

Greg chuckled. "True. I don't think you have the swimming abilities of a Mermaid. So what are you then?"

"I'm an Old Soul. Like you." Violet squeezed Greg's knee. "Although you were a Merman for a few lifetimes too, which is why your swimming is far better than mine."

"It's so strange that I had to read a book to figure that out, yet you know it already."

Violet smiled. "That's because I know you."

"So we've been together before?"

Violet smiled. "Yes, we have. A few times. Though the

most recent time was on the Other Side, at the Earth Angel Training Academy."

"We were students there?"

Violet shook her head. "No, I was the Head of the Academy. You, well, you were just visiting."

Greg was quiet for a while. "I'm sorry, it's just that none of this is ringing any bells. It feels like you're describing someone else's life to me. All I remember is waking up in hospital. There's not much else." He paused again as a memory surfaced. "Although, I did dream about you."

"Really? What happened in your dream?"

"I don't remember now, I just remember your face, and that your name was Velvet. Leona said that she had Seen your face before, too, and that I would meet you at some point soon."

"I guess she was right." Violet looked up at Greg to find him staring at her intently. She smiled. "What is it?"

"There's something I've been wanting to do since you opened your eyes after I pulled you out of the sea."

"There is?" Violet whispered.

Greg leaned closer to Violet until his lips brushed against hers. Violet closed her eyes and lost herself in his kiss.

* * *

"Go, Laguz!" Aria shouted, spilling chocolate covered raisins all over the sand.

"Aria! I was enjoying those." Linen tried to retrieve them, but it was impossible to brush the sand off.

"Manifest some more then," Aria sang as she flew around in a happy dance. "Don't you realise what this means? Laguz and Velvet are back together again! This calls for a celebration!" She came to a sudden halt. "Do you know what else this means?"

"What?" Linen asked, digging into the new bag of raisins.

"You were wrong! No cataclysmic events of doom!"

Linen coughed as he nearly choked on a raisin. "Um, aren't you forgetting the incident where Velvet died? Wouldn't you call that a cataclysmic event?"

Aria shrugged. "But she's okay now. Besides, if that hadn't happened, Laguz wouldn't have saved her and they wouldn't be together right now. It's all worked out just fine."

Linen shook his head and grabbed another handful of raisins. "It still could have been a disaster; Velvet could have chosen to stay here."

"She wouldn't do that, the Awakening is too important to her, it's her entire life mission and purpose."

Linen chewed thoughtfully. "I don't know, I think a large part of her mission is to be with Laguz, too. I think she'd find it difficult to Awaken the world without him by her side."

Aria frowned. "That's okay then," she gestured towards the lake. "As far as I can see, they're doing just fine. So the world is in safe hands."

"I hope that's true. Humans are funny creatures. It's always when you think that everything is going right that it then all goes wrong."

"Jeez, even with your wings in place you're a worrier. Lighten up, Linen." Aria poked him in the side. "It'll all work out, you'll see."

* * *

A few weeks later, Violet, Amy, Greg and Leona were back on the road. They had camped in their vans in La Rochelle until they managed to arrange a stay with another HelpX host a little further down the coast. They weren't travelling too far so that Violet could go back to the hospital to have the cast removed in two weeks' time.

Greg and Violet had become even closer, so Violet now travelled with Greg in his camper while Leona had joined Amy in hers.

"Shall we stop for some food?" Greg asked. Violet snapped out of her thoughts and smiled at him.

"Sure, Amy and Leona are still behind us, aren't they? They'll see us pull in."

"Yep, they are." Greg indicated at the turning and glanced in his rear-view mirror to check that Amy was following - she was.

He parked in two spaces in the car park, and switched off the engine. He jumped out of the camper and walked around to the passenger door. Violet opened the door and was carefully trying to step down when Greg grabbed her around the waist and swung her down, making her shriek. He set her feet carefully on the ground then pulled her in for a kiss.

Though things had been going slowly, their relationship was deepening daily. Violet had explained a little more about their lives as Velvet and Laguz and about the Academy, but she had been a little vague with some of the details of Adrian and Lyle. She'd barely mentioned Charlie; his name had only come up briefly, and it was when recounting a bad experience. She found it difficult to think of any good times she'd had with him.

She mentally shook herself and lost herself in Greg's kiss, her arms wrapped around his waist, her eyes closed.

"Jeez, you two, get a room why don't you?"

Greg and Violet pulled apart slowly and Violet laughed. "That's a good idea actually," she nodded her head towards the back of the van. "Shall we?"

Greg laughed and took her hand. "Let's get some food first, then later we'll find somewhere a little more secluded."

Violet grinned. "Sounds like a plan." She gripped Greg's hand tightly as they slowly made their way into the café. Her leg was mending slowly, but it still ached if she stood on it for too long or walked any kind of distance. At least she no longer needed her crutches.

The rest of the day passed quickly in a blur of driving. They were headed to a farm on the west coast, a little further south of La Rochelle. The hosts there needed people to help them renovate their barn. When they reached the farm, they parked the campers, were introduced to the entire family, grandparents and all, then had a meal.

"Shall we go check out the beach? The stars are amazing tonight," Violet asked, staring up at the sky as they walked to the camper.

"It's a bit cold out tonight."

"Then we'll take some blankets with us." Violet squeezed his hand. "Please?"

"Okay, but I'm driving us there, I don't want you walking on that leg for too long."

Violet gave him a mock salute. "Yes, sir."

It took a few minutes to find the right turning, but eventually they found the sandy trail that led right down to the beach. It was completely deserted.

Torches and blankets in hand, Violet and Greg made their way carefully to the shoreline, where they could hear, but not see, the waves.

"This will do." Violet shook the blanket out and laid it on the sand, before carefully sitting on it. Greg joined her and pulled the other blanket over their legs. He lay down and pulled Violet down with him. She nestled into his side.

"I don't think I've ever seen the stars so clear before. It's like you could reach out and touch them."

"They are beautiful," Greg agreed. "But so is the woman in my arms right now."

Violet looked up at Greg and smiled. She kissed him on the neck and he sighed.

"I still can't believe all of this. I mean, the way we met, all that happened in the past, it just all seems so unreal."

Violet frowned. "It feels real to me. I don't think I ever truly felt alive until that day I fell in the sea and nearly drowned." She kissed him again. "You saved my life in more ways than one." She reached out and touched the wooden pendant around his neck; her own pendant was tucked securely inside her t-shirt. Despite her certain words, she too, found it all a little difficult to believe at times.

Greg held her closer. "I'm just so glad that I saw you that morning, that I found you in the water. For a while, I thought that you were gone for sure."

Violet was silent for a while. "I think I was. I think I was given a second chance. I've dreamt of it since, of a conversation where I asked to come back."

"Really?" He kissed the top of her head. "I'm glad you did. I don't know what I would have done if you'd decided not to return."

Violet felt a tear welling in the corner of her eye, and it fell undetected onto Greg's thick fleece jumper.

"Let's not think about it. I can't wait to get this cast off so we can go a bit further away. What were your plans, travel-wise? Anywhere that you really wanted to see?"

Greg shook his head. "I had no plans. I just bought a camper van and got on the ferry. Met Leona on the ferry, and she's pretty much shaped our travelling. It was her that found the cottage we were staying at in La Rochelle. I wonder now if it was because of a vision; she was quite insistent that we stay there."

"Does she get many visions?"

"Not a lot, I don't think, but then she might just keep them to herself. She Saw you, and she knew we would meet, but she didn't See *how* we would meet. She's best when it comes to the weather."

Violet raised her eyebrows. "The weather?"

"Yep, she has an uncanny knack for forecasting the weather. Very handy at times, saved us in a few sticky spots."

Violet stared up at the stars again, looking for a shooting star to wish on.

"Are you getting cold?"

Violet shook her head. "No, let's just stay here a little while longer."

Greg held her closer still and rested his chin on her head.

"Okay, just a little while longer then."

CHAPTER FOURTEEN

"Hey, Linen. What's happening in the world?"

Linen looked up from the lake at Aria and shrugged. "Not much, Velvet and Laguz are still together. Her leg is better now so they've been travelling around a bit more. She told him a little about her past life memories, but not much. At least she seems to be writing it all down now though. It'll make the Awakening process a bit quicker if she happens to fall asleep again." He flew up to kiss Aria on the nose. "How about you, how was class?"

Aria flew to the edge of the lake and settled there, stealing the remains of Linen's triple chocolate cupcake. "It was okay."

Linen frowned and went to sit by her side. "Okay? What's wrong?"

"No, really, the class was fine. Though I do worry that the world will be full of people with amnesia by the time we've finished. It's just... I went to see the Rainbows after."

"And? Are they okay?"

"They're fine. They're little beams of light, how could they not be okay? Anyway, I asked them when they would be leaving for Earth, and well, they said they were waiting."

"Waiting? Did they say what for?"

"No. I asked them, but they wouldn't answer. I told them that Velvet and Laguz were together now, so the world would Awaken and enter the Golden Age, but they didn't comment. They just repeated that they were waiting."

"Huh." Linen looked back down at the lake where Velvet and Laguz were sat side by side in front of a roaring bonfire. "Maybe we'll find out soon what they're waiting for."

"Yeah, that's kind of what worries me." Aria flew up from the lake, licking her sticky, chocolatey fingers. "I have to go. I'm doing a class next on the environment. Lesson number one is why it's a really bad idea to cut grass."

"Why is it a bad idea?"

Aria put her hands on her hips and looked at Linen in disgust.

"Did you really just ask me that?"

* * *

Violet flicked through the pages in her diary, reading the odd sentence here and there about the last few months that she had spent with Greg. Once her cast had been removed, they had travelled further afield, and had even crossed over into Switzerland and then through Germany, staying with different hosts, meeting more travellers like themselves. Violet was getting pretty good at spotting Earth Angels and working out what realm they were from. Leona would usually confirm her thoughts. She and Leona realised the connection between them, and had since been working together to see if Violet could See anything. But so far, all she'd had was the odd dream that had come true.

Her finger touched a poem she had written in her diary. She'd written it after a night of stargazing on the beach with Greg. She still couldn't believe they were finally together.

And that they had the rest of their lives to be with each other. Violet sighed. The rest of their lives. She wasn't sure exactly what they would be doing. She very much wanted to set up a retreat like Esmeralda and Mike. But every time she'd tried to bring up the subject, Greg would distract her. Perhaps he was just afraid to return to England. After all, for all they knew, his wife may still be looking for him. She'd told him that she thought he should visit his family, at least to let them know he was okay, but he said that he didn't feel like they were really his family, and he didn't want to mess them around.

Violet wasn't overly keen to return to England either, especially in time for another cold winter, but she just didn't see an alternative. She needed to get a job; her travel fund was getting low, despite having done a few odd jobs for cash as they went along.

She closed her diary and put it back in her rucksack. She lay back on the small bed and closed her eyes. She thought about all the moments she had shared with Greg so far and smiled. Her heart was so full at times she thought it would burst. Every touch, every kiss, every whisper in her ear, made her heart skip a beat. Which is why she wanted to help other souls to find their Twin Flames. Love like this was most definitely the kind of love that could perform miracles.

"Vi? Are you in there?"

Without opening her eyes or sitting up, Violet answered for Amy to come in. She heard the door open and the van moved as Amy climbed the step into the tiny space.

"Sorry, were you asleep? Only, lunch is ready."

Violet opened her eyes to see her friend peering at her in concern. She laughed. "No, I wasn't asleep, I was just lost in thought." She slowly got up, stretched as much as the low ceiling allowed, then followed Amy out of the van.

"So do you think we'll stay here for long?"

Violet looked at Amy. "I'm not sure. Do you not want to?"

Amy shrugged. "It's nice here, but I'm just a little tired. Besides, I'm starting to run out of cash. If we do stay, I'm going to need to find some kind of employment."

Violet sighed. "Yeah, me too. I was just thinking earlier that it might be time to go home. To England. I was planning on talking to Greg about it. Though I get the feeling he's avoiding the subject."

"We've got to go sometime, can't just travel around forever. What about having a family? Do you want kids? Does he? Neither of you are getting any younger, you know."

"Thanks, Amy. That makes me feel so much better. I'm not sure what I want. I suppose I assumed I would be a mother at some point, but I have no idea what he wants. To be honest, we haven't even discussed it. We, er, don't talk much."

"Okay, okay, no need to make me jealous."

They reached the kitchen door and Violet laughed. "Sorry, Amy, I'm sure you'll get to be with your Nick at some point soon."

"I sure hope so. I know Danny was a nightmare, but being a nun isn't much fun either."

"Hey, Violet, Amy, come have lunch. Do you know where Greg is though?"

Violet smiled at their host. "I think he was outside chopping up wood, I'll go get him." She left the kitchen and went back outside into the bright sunshine and found Greg busily chopping up firewood, ready to be stored for the winter.

"Hey." She came up behind him and slid her arms around his waist. He put the axe down and turned to face her.

"Hey, yourself. Have you finished the painting already?"

he asked, tapping her green nose.

"Yeah, Amy got a little mad with the paint. We did quite a bit this morning then had a break. Lunch is ready now." She scratched at the dried smudge on her nose.

Greg smiled. "Okay, I might just finish this bit then I'll join you."

"Okay. I was just wondering, are you ready yet, to go home? To England? It's just that I need to start earning money as soon as possible if we're going to get a place together and start our own retreat."

Greg was silent for a while. "Have you asked Amy and Leona what they want to do?"

"They're ready to go back too, at least for a bit; I think Leona might set off again at some point. I'm not sure she's really the type to settle down."

Greg nodded. "Okay, well I guess we should head back then, get the ferry home, try and sort out somewhere to live before the winter sets in."

Violet smiled and reached up to kiss him. "I'll let the others know."

They kissed passionately for a few moments before Violet left, and walked back to the house. She didn't notice that when Greg started chopping the wood it was with more vigour than before.

* * *

"Leona?"

"What's wrong, Greg?"

Greg smiled at his friend. He settled next to her on the step leading into the barn, where she was sat watching the sunset.

"How did you know something was wrong?"

"You've been a bit quiet recently. Are you worried about going back to England? Because I'm sure it'll all be fine. I can't foresee a problem, anyway."

Greg shook his head. "No, that's not it. Have you actually Seen anything recently, about the future?"

Leona shook her head. "I get the odd flash every now and then, but it's jumbled, like the future keeps changing so rapidly that all of the possibilities are getting mixed together until they make no sense. It makes me feel like someone just keeps changing their mind."

Greg laughed, but there was no humour in it. "I know how they feel."

Leona frowned. "What do you keep changing your mind about?"

"Everything. I just can't decide what the right path is. What I should do."

Leona shrugged. "There is no such thing as the right path. There are many paths, you choose one and you see what happens. If you don't like where the path leads, then you follow a new one."

Greg nodded. "But what if you switch to a new path, then you realise the old one was the right one after all, but by then it's too late to switch back?"

"In that case, only God can help you."

* * *

Five days later, the four of them set off, heading for Calais. Velvet looked over at Greg, who seemed to be concentrating very hard on the boring country road they were driving down. Though he had agreed to return to England, he had been very quiet and hadn't joined in the discussion of where the best place to have a retreat would be. They arrived quite late at a small campsite where they were staying for the night. They were planning on catching the ferry the next morning.

After a restless night, Violet awoke with a start, having

dreamt that she was drowning. She sat up and breathed heavily in the silence for a few moments, feeling as though she couldn't get enough air.

"Hey, are you okay?" Greg whispered sleepily, reaching up for her. Violet nodded and calmed her breathing. She lay back down next to him and he pulled her close to his side.

"It was just a dream," Violet whispered back. "I was drowning."

Greg squeezed her tighter to him. "That's horrible. Though it's probably just a memory from your little dip in the sea."

Violet shook her head. "No, I've had the dream before, when I was still in England. It felt more like a warning than a premonition of drowning, though."

"A warning?"

"That something was going to happen."

"Like what?"

Violet shrugged. "Don't know."

Greg was quiet for a moment. "Violet, there's something I need to say."

"What?" For some reason Violet's heart thudded in her chest, and she fought to keep her breathing steady.

"I don't want to return to England."

Violet frowned. "Oh, okay, you'd rather live here?"

Greg shook his head. "No, I want to keep travelling; there are things I need to figure out."

"I suppose I could work something out money-wise, maybe try and write some travel articles or something."

There was a heavier silence.

"I don't think you should come with me. I think you should go back to England with Amy. And Leona, if she wants to go."

Violet blinked, then swallowed hard. "I don't understand; why don't you want me to come with you?"

"I'm sorry, Violet," Greg whispered. "I just don't think

you're the one."

Violet's heart stopped. She felt herself go cold as his words hit her like tiny sharp icicles all over her body.

"But I love you," she whispered, realising that this was the first time she had said the words, because they just hadn't seemed necessary before.

"I'm sorry, Violet, but I just don't love you."

Without warning Violet's throat closed and the tears fell, soaking into Greg's t-shirt. "I don't understand. The last few months, you've never said or done anything to suggest that you felt this way," Violet choked out. "Why now? We don't have to go back to England, we can travel some more, then see how it goes."

Her eyes tightly closed, Violet's heart thudded again when she felt Greg shake his head.

"I'm sorry, Violet, I just don't think we should be together anymore."

Biting her lip to stop herself from sobbing, Violet pulled away from his side and sat up. She slid off the tiny bed and started hastily pulling her clothes on.

"Where are you going? It's not even seven yet."

Not trusting herself to speak, Violet pulled her bag from underneath the bed and started throwing her things in it.

"Violet, please don't be like this. I'm sorry, I just don't feel the same way you do."

The tears spilled down Violet's cheeks. She couldn't bring herself to look back as she shoved her shoes on and stumbled out of the camper van. She staggered across the few steps to where Amy and Leona slept and hammered on the locked door.

Amy poked her head out a few seconds later. "What the hell?" She took in Violet's appearance and opened the door wider. Violet put her bag inside then turned away.

"Wait a minute, Violet, what's going on?"

"Greg's not coming back with us," Violet said, walking towards the toilet block.

Amy threw a jumper on over her pyjamas and slipped her shoes on before running after Violet. She caught up with her just outside the door.

"I don't understand. What do you mean, he's not coming with us?"

"I mean he doesn't love me. He doesn't want to be with me. He's not coming." Violet's face crumpled and she threw the door open and ran into the toilets, locking herself in a stall before Amy could collect herself.

"Violet," Amy called over the sobbing. "Violet, please, let me in."

After a few moments, Violet slid the catch across, and Amy opened the door. Violet was sat on the floor, doubled up, her shoulders heaving.

Amy sank to the filthy floor and put her arm around her. "Shhh, it's okay, you'll be okay."

Violet shook her head. "I love him so much. I had this whole picture in my head of how things would be, of us growing old together, finally getting to spend our lives together. And out of nowhere, for no good reason, he's just destroyed it." She clutched her stomach, feeling sick. "I can't lose him again, Amy." Her body shook. "I just couldn't bear it."

Amy was at a loss for words. She sat there with Violet until her stomach began to growl and Violet's sobs had subsided a little. "Come on, we should get some breakfast, we're getting the ferry at ten."

Violet allowed herself to be pulled to her feet. At the sink, she splashed some cold water on her face, barely glancing at her red face in the cracked mirror.

Amy led her out of the toilets and back to the camper van, which Leona had already left. Violet glanced over at Greg's van and saw Leona inside. Her stomach clenched.

She still couldn't believe it. How could everything change in such a small amount of time? Just the night before she'd fallen asleep, safe and loved in his arms. Though apparently he didn't love her at all. Violet doubled up again, sobs wracking her body. She felt sick.

"Come on, Violet," Amy tugged her gently into the camper, sitting her down on the unmade bed where Violet then curled up into a ball.

"What do you want to eat?"

The thought of food made Violet heave. "I don't want anything," she whispered.

"A drink?"

Violet shook her head, trying to control her sobs, but failing.

Amy gave up trying to get her to eat or drink and sat beside her, stroking her hair.

"Shh, it's okay. Everything's going to be okay."

At these words, Violet sobbed harder.

* * *

"I'm sorry, Violet."

Greg felt her tears soaking into his t-shirt and his heart clenched. He held her tight to him, breathing in the scent of her hair. "I wish I could feel the way you do, but I just don't," he whispered.

He felt Violet shaking as she pulled away from him. He bit his lip and a tear ran down his own cheek. Violet stopped a few feet away, then turned back. She came back to him, and kissed him one last time.

"I love you."

Greg couldn't respond. His throat closed up as she ran to the camper van and clumsily got in. He watched Amy and Violet drive away, tears streaming down his face.

"I didn't See this one coming," Leona said. "Is this what

you meant when you asked me if I'd Seen the future?" Without waiting for a reply, she continued. "Are you sure this is the right thing? It's not too late to catch them up. It's not too late to get her back."

Greg shook his head and wiped his face with the back of his hand.

"No, this is the right thing to do. I don't love her enough, she deserves better than that."

Leona looked at the van disappearing into the distance. "I was so sure you were meant to be together."

"Yeah, well, like you said, people are harder to predict. Maybe it would be better to stick to the weather." He took a deep breath and smiled slightly to show he was teasing. "So then, navigator, where to next?"

* * *

For the first time in a long while, Aria felt big sticky tears drip slowly down her cheeks. She turned to Linen as they watched the events unfold, their usual snacks forgotten.

"I don't understand, what is Laguz doing? Why is he sending her away? How could he say he doesn't love her? They're Twin Flames! He went back for her twice, now he has her right there, in his arms, in his life, loving him, and he's pushing her away!"

"Maybe he's scared," Linen said quietly, his tiny face grave.

"Scared?" Aria repeated in disbelief. "Of what? Of being happy?"

"Of being trapped maybe. I mean, look at the situation with the wife and two kids-"

"They weren't his kids! That was a totally different situation; they were Greg's kids, not Laguz's. Of course he felt trapped. But he's himself now, he's free, why on Earth would he not want to spend every single moment with Velvet? This could be their last lifetime on Earth together."

Linen shrugged. "I'm afraid I don't know. I don't have any of the answers. It doesn't make much sense to me either."

Aria stared at the lake where a broken-hearted Violet returned home to England, and went back to work in her old job.

"How is she going to Awaken the world now? Look at her, she can barely function."

Linen shook his head. "I don't know. I'm beginning to wonder if the Golden Age was just a dream after all."

Aria bit her lip. For once, she couldn't bring herself to tell him not to be so gloomy, because she had a sinking feeling in her stomach that he may be well be right.

* * *

Violet spent her time staring blankly at a computer screen by day and a TV screen by night. She had lost all connection with herself. Her dreams were jumbled nonsense; her thoughts were a mess. It was nearly too much just to eat, dress, wash and do all the normal, necessary things that came with living with other people. Amy's parents had happily offered her the spare room, but Violet knew she couldn't stay for too long. Being back in England, back in this town, made Violet feel like the six months with Greg had never happened. The day they'd returned, she'd taken the wooden pendant from around her neck and replaced it in the carved wooden box. She intended to return it to Maggie. She couldn't bear to look at it. Even now, a couple of months later, she couldn't understand what had happened. She was desperate to contact him but what little news she'd received from Leona through Amy suggested that he didn't want to know.

"Vi? Violet, are you okay?"

Violet looked up at her best friend and struggled to focus on her face. She blinked a few times and managed to nod. She looked down and was surprised to see a fork in her hand, hovering over her full plate of dinner. She set the fork down and sighed.

"Violet, you need to eat something." Amy put her hand on her friend's arm and squeezed it. "I wish I could do something to take away the hurt."

Violet managed to smile. "Of course you do, you're an Angel, that's what you're made to do." She shrugged her shoulders. "But I don't think that this is something you can fix."

Amy was silent for a while, her half-eaten meal going cold in front of her. "I've been thinking about what you said a few months ago, when we were staying at that pig farm." She took a breath and waited to see if Violet reacted in any way to her words. "You said that Greg was your Twin Flame." Violet closed her eyes and nodded slightly. Amy continued, her curiosity winning out over her need to be tactful. "Do you still think that?"

A single tear trailed its way down Violet's pale cheek. She shook her head. "No, no I don't think that anymore." She opened her eyes and looked at Amy. "I know it now. I know that he is my Twin Flame. Without a shadow of a doubt."

"How?" Amy breathed. "How do you know?"

"Because only the loss of a Twin Flame could hurt this much, Amy." She swallowed. "This feeling isn't new to me. I have lost him before. More than once. But this time," she shook her head. "This time may well be the last time I can bear it." She pushed her chair back and stood. "I'm sorry, I can't eat. I need to be alone right now." She left Amy sat at the dining table and went back to her room. She sat on her bed, and looked around at the impersonal cream walls. She ached to be in Greg's arms. She just couldn't believe that she had lost him again.

Her gaze fell on her diary, filled with all her beautiful memories of their time together. The things they'd done, things he'd said.

She picked up the diary and flicked through, until she found that night on the beach under the stars. Tears welled up and fell onto the page as she murmured the words.

"'Our love is like the stars shining above: infinite, everlasting, radiant; glowing brightly in the darkness, never fading away'." She ripped a piece of paper from the back of her diary and grabbed a pen. She rephrased the poem slightly, then folded the paper up, writing Greg's name on the outside.

She tucked it back inside the diary and closed it, setting it on the bedside table.

"I give up," she whispered. "I'm ready to go home now."

* * *

The sun was barely beginning to rise above the distant horizon when Violet pulled up at the beach. She got out of the camper van and tucked the keys under the wheel arch on the passenger's side. She hoped Amy would find the note she'd left for her. It seemed slightly crazy, driving such a long way just to do what what she was about to do, but Violet felt that this was the only way.

She walked towards the waves; the beach was deserted. When she reached the shoreline she stopped, the waves barely lapping her shoes. She thought she heard a voice in her mind, calling her name. She smiled as a vague memory surfaced, where a soul had once told her that he knew if he ignored the whispers of the Angels, he was sure to return home.

Violet sighed. Her heart feeling like lead, she began to walk into the sea. The first few steps were easy enough, but before long she was struggling to move against the icy waves, her now-healed leg aching with the effort. She closed her eyes and another memory surfaced of a song, long blond hair in the breeze, a rune pendant. She kept walking.

* * *

"Do you want to talk?"

Greg looked up at Leona and shook his head, then resumed gazing at the waves crashing onto the rocks. The rocks from which Violet had fallen on that early morning. Maybe it had been a mistake, returning to La Rochelle. He sensed his friend move closer then sit next to him, close enough to feel her warmth, but not close enough to touch.

Talking wasn't going to help him right now. Neither was thinking, but he didn't know how to switch it off. He should have known that Leona wouldn't be able to stay quiet for long.

"I'm not sure I really understand what happened. Was Violet not Velvet? I thought she was supposed to be your Twin Flame."

Greg sighed. Faeries were not known for their tact, apparently. "Yes, Violet was Velvet. And, yes, she was my Twin Flame."

"Okay, now I really don't understand. If you know that she's your Twin Flame, if you know that you've spent lifetimes with her and that you should be together, why is it that you sent her away?"

"I don't know. I know that I should love her, I know that I always have before, but this time, I don't know; I just don't feel it."

"That's so strange. What do you think is holding you

back from feeling it? Surely it must be there, hidden inside you."

Greg shrugged, never moving his gaze from the turbulent water.

CHAPTER FIFTEEN

"Velvet."

"Hey, Gold," Velvet responded quietly. "I know you're disappointed in me, and I'm sorry. I just couldn't do it anymore. The pain was just too much."

Velvet stepped into Gold's arms and he embraced her tightly.

"I understand. But do you understand that there's no going back this time?"

Velvet nodded into the heavy golden fabric of his robes.

"I know. I don't want to go back. I want to go forwards."

Gold stepped back from her. "You want to go home? For good?"

Velvet nodded. "I'm so tired, Gold. I waited for so long for a chance to be with Laguz on Earth again, I haven't the energy or the patience to wait another thousand or more lives for another chance. I can't spend another moment knowing he's out there and I cannot be with him."

Gold sighed. "My dear, Velvet, I can't say I envy you for all your human lives, but don't you see? You and Laguz were together in this lifetime. It may only have been for a short time, but you were together; you did have your final Twin Flame relationship on Earth. Those times you spent together, the love that you felt when in his arms, it was all real, I promise."

A tear escaped down Velvet's cheeks onto her purple robes. "I guess you're right, Gold. And perhaps I should have stayed, perhaps there was a chance for us yet. But I guess I'll never know. I really do think it's time for me to move on now."

Gold shook his head. "If you're quite sure."

Velvet nodded. "Before I go, could you just tell me one thing?"

"Of course, Velvet."

Velvet bit her lip, unsure as to whether she wanted to know the answer. "Will the humans make it? Or will the world end as the Seers predicted?"

Gold was silent for a moment, then he looked down at the mist swirling around their ankles.

"I see," Velvet whispered. "How long?"

Gold shook his head. "Not very."

Velvet closed her eyes and thought of all her beautiful friends and family, and all the amazing Earth Angels on Earth, all doing their best to Awaken the world, all hoping to see the ever-elusive Golden Age.

"Gold, may I ask just one more thing?"

"Of course, you can ask me anything, Velvet."

"Did I make any difference at all?" Velvet whispered, her eyes still closed. After a moment she felt a hand on her arm. She looked up at Gold to see him smiling.

"Velvet, I couldn't possibly begin to tell you all of the differences you made on Earth, or all of the differences that you will continue to make even though you are no longer there."

Velvet breathed in deeply. "Really?"

"Velvet, would I lie to you?" Gold's right eye twitched

just then, and Velvet stifled a laugh.

"Of course not, Gold. Thank you, I feel marginally better about my abrupt departure, knowing that I at least had some impact."

"Velvet, I honestly couldn't have asked any more of you than what you have achieved."

"Thank you, Gold." She took another deep breath, and felt a shift in the energy around her. "Is it time?"

Gold nodded, and stepped to the side. A circle of light appeared in the mist behind him. A figure stepped through it, hands outstretched towards Velvet.

Velvet smiled. "A beautiful Angel with wings studded with stars," she whispered.

"This is Starlight, she will guide the way home."

Velvet nodded. "Yes, she will." She turned to Gold. "Goodbye, Gold. Thank you again, for everything."

"You're welcome, my dear soul. Farewell now."

Velvet reached out and took Starlight's hand. Within a second they both disappeared, leaving behind a cloud of purple glitter and a swirl of white lights.

Gold watched the glitter and lights mingle then fall into the mist.

"Goodbye, Velvet. You truly were a beautiful soul."

* * *

"I can't believe it."

Aria stared at the lake as the events after Violet's death unfolded. "How could she do this? I know she was devastated but she should have carried on! What will happen to the world now?"

Linen shook his head, his face sad. "I really thought she could do it, but I guess the loss of a Twin Flame is just too much, and she's been through it several times." He reached over and took Aria's hand, she leant into him and a tear fell onto his lap.

"I guess I can understand that," she said quietly. "I couldn't lose you. I would follow you anywhere in the Universe rather than lose you." She sat up straight. "Which is why I don't understand how Velvet could give up so easily."

"Easily? Didn't you see how broken she was? I know it was hard to see from here, but I think Laguz was pretty convincing when he told her that he didn't love her. What was she supposed to do? She couldn't change the way he felt."

"I guess not, but I just don't understand it! He was Awakening, they'd found each other, they'd spent months together, how could he then suddenly just decide he didn't love her?"

"As I've said before, humans are funny creatures."

* * *

"Greg."

Greg looked up from where he sat on the sand to see Amy walking towards him. He looked back towards the sea, and wiped his face with his sleeve. A few seconds later he felt Amy sit next to him. They were silent for a while.

"Is it really true?" he whispered.

"Yes," Amy's voice cracked. "It's true."

Greg's heart thudded painfully. "I never meant to hurt her, I was trying to do what was best. I never meant for this to happen, I just couldn't feel, I couldn't feel what-" Greg held his head in his hands and his body shook.

"I know. I think she knew too, but she just couldn't do this without you." Amy put her hand on Greg's back, but made no attempt to try and soothe him; her own pain was just too raw. She retrieved a folded up piece of paper from her pocket, its ragged edge fluttered in the sea breeze.

"This is for you."

Greg looked up, his chest heaving. He took the paper from her, recognising Violet's scrawl. He smoothed his thumb over his name on the front. He opened the paper and read it silently, the tears continuing to stream down his cheeks.

I believed our love to be like the stars shining above: infinite, everlasting, radiant; glowing brightly in the darkness, never fading away. But I guess it was just a shooting star after all.

CHAPTER SIXTEEN

"Aria? Aria, my love, what is it? What's wrong?"

The tear-stained green Faerie looked at Linen, her lip quivering. "I've just been to see the Rainbows."

Linen put his arm around her. "What did they say?"

"They said that they won't be going to Earth now. They said that now Velvet is gone, there won't be any chance of a full-scale Awakening. The Golden Age isn't happening." More tears streamed down her cheeks. "It's over, Linen. It's all over."

EPILOGUE

Earth, twenty years later.

Greg looked out at the sea from his window, and sipped his scalding hot tea. Watching the waves never failed to make an impression on him. Though now instead of a sense of belonging, he felt a deep sadness. The sea held many memories; he wished they had all been good ones.

He took another sip, and allowed himself to sink into his memories for a moment. Though it had been such a long time, he could still smell her hair. He could still hear her laughter. He could still see her smile. He wished he could see her again. Talk to her. Apologise to her for not saving her. Hopefully he would be able to soon.

He missed her. And he knew he wasn't the only one. He had kept in touch with Amy and the Spiritual Sisters, as they did their best to make changes in the world. Amy had finally met her own Twin Flame, Nick, and had been happily married to him for fifteen years now. At the wedding, Greg had met Maggie, who was his sister in a previous lifetime. It had been a strange feeling, knowing her so well when he had only just met her. She gave him the carved wooden box that he'd apparently made. It had Violet's rune pendant in it, the leather cord worn from all the travelling.

Greg went over to his bedside table now and touched the carved figure on the top of the box. It did look like Violet. He sat heavily on the bed and opened the box, taking out the photograph he kept there. He'd taken it one morning while Violet still slept. Her face was peaceful. He wondered if she was at peace now. He replaced the photo in the box, closing it carefully. He picked up the book next to it, smoothing the printed name with his thumb. He'd received the copy with the new cover just the day before, and he was re-reading it. They were Violet's words. Or Velvet's words, rather. Everything that Violet had written in her diaries and had told him, he had recounted and shaped into a story. The story of an Old Soul who had come to Earth to Awaken it. To help Earth experience the most glorious time it had ever experienced. Her words had Awoken many souls. Her memories of the Earth Angel Training Academy had triggered the memories of the many Earth Angels who had been there, who had been taught by her; helping them to remember their true purpose in life.

But it hadn't been enough. The world had not Awakened in the way that Violet had envisioned. The world was still a deeply negative place, with war and poverty still thriving. The Earth Angels had all been doing their very best, but if the prophecies were to be believed, there wasn't long left before it would all be over.

Greg sighed. Though it seemed ridiculous, he felt responsible for the demise of the world. Perhaps if he had been able to feel the love he had for Violet, and if he had been able to keep her here, then things might have been different. The world might have Awakened, and be headed for the Golden Age. He ran his fingers over the illustration of a shooting star, and a tear fell on it, making it shimmer for a second.

He bit his lip and stood unsteadily, then made his

way downstairs to the kitchen. He set his mug down and grabbed a jacket from the hook behind the back door. He set off across the rocks, then over the grassy dunes, from the house where they'd stayed all those years ago. He had moved to La Rochelle several years before, hoping to keep Violet's memory alive in the place where he had first met her. He had thought about turning it into a retreat, but it just wouldn't have been the same without her. He and Leona had talked about doing it together, but then she'd met her Twin Flame and had moved to Australia to be with her. He hadn't seen her in many years, but she wrote to him every Christmas.

He reached the edge where the grass met the sand and sat heavily, his knees protesting. While his thoughts wandered, the sun set, and the sky went through all the colours of the rainbow before turning an inky blue. He lay back on the grass and watched as the stars started to shine.

When the shooting star he was waiting for streaked across the sky, Greg closed his eyes and smiled.

"I love you, Violet. I'll love you for eternity."

The End

"Velvet? What are you doing here?"

"Now, Gold, is that really the way to treat an old friend?"

Gold blinked, and remained frozen where he sat on the sand. Velvet sat down beside him, her purple robes rippling in the ocean breeze.

"I don't understand. You left for the stars over two decades ago, how have you come back?"

Velvet smiled and breathed in deeply. "Goddess, I've missed being by the sea." She looked at Gold and noticed the twitch in his right eye. "It's okay, Gold. I'm okay. I've just come to ask you a bit of a favour."

"A favour? First I would like to know how you've managed to return?"

"I thought you knew everything, Gold. Certainly nothing seemed to get past you when I ran the Academy."

"Apparently there are flaws in my awareness. Please, Velvet, enlighten me."

Velvet chuckled. "There's not much to it, my dear friend. Yes, I left for the stars twenty Earthly years ago. But although back then I felt I needed a clean slate, when it came to losing all my Earthly memories, I found I just couldn't let them go. So Starlight let me keep them."

Gold gestured impatiently for her to continue when her pause went on for more than a few seconds.

"I watched Earth, Gold. I watched what happened, I saw how the Earth Angels did their best, and I saw how it was all about to end. And I realised something."

"What?"

"That I should never have left."

Gold raised his eyebrows. "I thought that was blatantly obvious twenty years ago, my dear."

Velvet laughed. "To you, maybe. But to me, leaving seemed like the only option." She sighed, serious again. "I suppose I hoped that the world would still Awaken, that the Rainbows would still go to Earth, and the Golden Age would happen, finally."

"If you still hoped for all that, why did you want to leave? Why didn't you want to experience it?"

"Because none of it would have meant anything without Laguz. To be on the same planet as him, and not be with him, was the worst kind of torture I could possibly imagine."

"You have survived without him before. Surely you could have done it again."

"Actually, that's why I'm here."

Gold's eye began to twitch. "I thought you were here to ask me a favour?"

"I am. Gold, I have to go back."

Gold's eyebrows shot up, and he opened his mouth a few times but nothing came out. Finally he cleared his throat. "Go back to what? Weren't you watching? This is the end. Soon, there will be nothing left."

"Oh, I know that. I don't mean go back to the present day. I mean go back to the moment before I left the last time."

Had they not already been in the Fifth Dimension, Velvet would really have feared for her friend right now. He looked about ready to have a heart attack.

"You want to go back in time to before you drowned?"

"Yes. I do."

"This has never been done before."

"I don't see why not. After all, time is an illusion really, isn't it? Now, then, before, after. It's all just the same moment."

Gold frowned. "You have been spending far too much time with Starlight."

Velvet smiled. "You were right about her influence on me. She's the reason why I'm here. She made me realise that

I shouldn't have given up. That no matter how overcast the sky, the stars continue to shine. We just have to be patient enough to wait for the clouds to lift. And maybe I can help with the Awakening so that humans get to experience it properly before the end. If, of course, you still think that the Awakening is the best thing to do."

"Of course I think the Awakening is the best idea. It was my idea, after all. I'm just surprised that after everything you've said about the pain and loss, and the fact that you wilfully left Earth to escape it all, that you would want to go back. You do know that there is nothing you can do to stop the inevitable, don't you? That no matter how many humans Awaken, it is likely that the Earth will still end."

"Yes, I understand that, Gold. And I have also come to realise, that alive on Earth, or in spirit here, or among the stars – the pain of losing a Twin Flame never fades. Maybe I was lucky after Atlantis to have blocked it out, but this time, it's never going to leave me. And so I need to go back, Gold. I need to do what I can to help with the Awakening. I need to try and help the Earth Angels bring about the Golden Age."

Gold was silent as he watched the waves rolling onto the sand. "Are you not tempted to wait? To see him? He will be here soon."

"I know, but if I see him, I might not find the strength to leave him again. And I must do this, Gold. I cannot explain fully why, but I must."

Gold looked at Velvet. "The two of you could be together now, you know. There are no obstacles. If you go back in time to your life on Earth, then you are sentencing yourself to another couple of decades of living without him. Is that really what you want?"

Velvet smiled. "So it's certain that if I go back, we won't get back together?" She sighed and then shrugged. "It doesn't change anything," she continued, without waiting for an answer. "I need to go back, Gold. Can you help me?"

"How do you know that this is even possible?"

"Anything is possible, Gold. Anything. I learnt that from you."

Gold was silent for several moments before finally nodding. "You're right. But I need to go see someone first. Would you like to wait for me here?"

Velvet nodded. "Yes, I would."

"Very well. I shall be back as soon as I can."

"Take your time, Gold. I'm not going anywhere."

* * *

"Gold? Have you changed your mind? Have you come to join us?"

"No, Linen, I'm afraid not. I have just come to ask a favour, actually." Gold looked around the office. "I also would like to say that I think you are doing a magnificent job here. I am very impressed."

Linen's wings fluttered a little more rapidly and faint spots of red appeared on his cheeks.

"Aww, well, Gold, what could we do? The souls will all need somewhere to be. It seemed like the right thing to do. Besides, I know so many of them from their time here previously, it'll be like having one big family."

"Still, it truly is fantastic of you."

Linen raised an eyebrow. "I must say, Gold, all of this flattery is making me a little suspicious of this favour you need."

Gold chuckled. "No, no. The favour really isn't that bad, it's just a little, well, complex."

"Complex? Maybe you should start from the beginning."

Gold sighed and settled himself into the nearest chair.

"Velvet has returned."

* * *

"Oh, Gold! You scared me there." Velvet looked up at the Elder standing next to her. She stood up and brushed the sand from her robes. "Did you manage to see whoever it was you needed to? You were awfully quick."

"Yes, I found him, and he was able to do what I asked."

"Oh, well that's good, isn't it?" Velvet frowned. She couldn't quite make out the expression on Gold's face.

"Yes, it is. But I must ask again, Velvet," Gold turned to face her and looked deeply into her brown eyes. "Are you absolutely certain you wish to go back?"

Velvet smiled. "Yes, Gold. I appreciate that you are doing something quite spectacular for me. I realise that not everyone gets the opportunity for another chance like this, and I realise that I may not actually deserve it. But it's something that I believe, wholeheartedly, that I need to do."

"Very well. You will be returning to Earth the moment after you would have if you had chosen to go back after trying to drown yourself."

Velvet frowned. "What do you mean? I thought you said that there was no going back that time, that there was no one there to save me?"

"There wasn't. But there will be this time."

Velvet shook her head. "Though I understand a little more of it, this time-travel thing still kind of blows my mind."

Gold smiled. "It's supposed to. Now, are you ready?"

"I can go right now?"

"'*Now*' is all that exists, remember?"

Velvet laughed. "Touché. Okay, yes, I'm ready."

Gold raised his hand, but before he could click his fingers Velvet reached out and touched his arm. "Thank you, Gold. I'll see you in twenty years."

"You're welcome, Velvet. I do wish you well."

CHAPTER FIFTEEN

TAKE TWO

"Hello? Can you hear me? Can you open your eyes?"

Violet blinked rapidly then her body shook as she coughed up sea water onto the sand. She was only vaguely aware of the strong arm supporting her.

"That's it. You're okay now, just breathe. You're okay."

Once her lungs were empty of water, Violet looked up at the stranger and blinked. A strong sense of déjà vu washed over her as she stared into the bright orange eyes.

"Linen?" she whispered.

"Sorry? I didn't quite catch that." Her rescuer leaned in closer and Violet caught a glimpse of his red hair.

"Linen, I wondered if your name was Linen," she said a little louder, her voice hoarse from the salty water.

The stranger shook his head, and held out his hand. "No, my name is Freddy. Pleased to meet you..."

Violet shook his wet hand. "Velvet. No, I'm sorry, I mean Violet." Violet shook her head. "I'm sorry, I'm just feeling a bit strange."

"I'm not surprised. You know, it would be better to get a washing machine than to try and wash your clothes in the sea while you're still wearing them. In winter, no less." Freddy gestured at her waterlogged jeans and jumper, and for the first time, Violet became aware of her body. She shivered violently then, and Freddy wrapped his arms back around her.

"Come on, let's get you home. You'll catch pneumonia if you stay in those wet clothes too long."

Violet nodded and allowed him to pull her to her feet. Once she got her balance, he let her go for a second while he picked up his surfboard.

Violet noticed the design on it and frowned. "Are you sure your name isn't Linen?" she asked.

Freddy smiled. "No, 'fraid not."

Violet stared at the black board with orange flames painted on it, and fragments of memory flashed through her mind, causing her to stumble.

"Whoa. I'm not sure you're steady enough to walk. Would you like me to carry you?"

Violet shook her head. "No, I'm okay, really. I was just remembering something."

"Okay, well hold onto me, the sand may look like a soft landing, but it still hurts. Now where can I take you?"

Violet looked up at the car park beyond the sand dunes and spotted the camper van. She pointed to it. "That's my friend's. I borrowed it."

Freddy whistled. "That's a nice vehicle. I've always wanted a camper van, always wanted to go travelling, look for some decent waves. There never seem to be any around here."

Violet frowned, her mind still foggy. "If there are no decent waves, how come you're out here in winter, in the freezing cold, at the crack of dawn, surfing?"

Freddy shrugged. "Don't know really. I just woke up this morning with the strongest desire to surf. Though I didn't get too far. I'd only just got in the water when I saw you."

"Oh," Violet replied, unsure as to what to say.

Their progress across the beach was slow, but eventually they made it to the camper.

"Uh oh, I hope your keys weren't in your pocket, cos if they were, I'm not sure they still will be."

Violet shook her head. "No, they're on the front passenger's side wheel."

Freddy frowned, then left Violet leaning against the side of the van to go and check. He came back with the keyring on his finger.

"Look, it's really none of my business, but seeing as I just pulled you out of the water and gave you the kiss of life, I figure I get to ask: you didn't intend to come out did you? Not alive, anyway."

Violet blushed a little when he mentioned the CPR, then shook her head. "No, I didn't." She cleared her throat, wincing as it stung. "But I'm glad I did." She looked up into Freddy's orange eyes. "Thank you. I really do owe you."

Freddy grinned, and once again Violet thought of Linen.

"Any time. Now, do you want me to drive you home?"

Violet shook her head. "No, I couldn't possibly let you do that, it's a long drive. I'll be fine, thank you."

"Are you absolutely certain?"

Violet smiled at the words. "Yes, I am. But before you go, let me give you my number, if you ever need anything, and I can help, maybe one day I could repay you."

She opened the driver's door and reached into her bag, pulling out a pen and some paper. She wrote her phone number and name and handed it to him.

Freddy looked down at the paper and grinned again. "Sure, thanks, Violet. Drive safely now okay, I might not be around to save you a second time."

Violet smiled back. "I will. Bye, Freddy." She got into the camper van and closed the door. Freddy stood watching while she reversed and pulled out carefully onto the main road.

* * *

"Wow, Linen, it really worked! Well done!"

Aria reached into the giant popcorn bucket in front of her and stuffed a handful into her mouth.

"You seem surprised, Aria. Have you no faith in me at all?" Linen asked in mock hurt.

Aria swallowed her popcorn then giggled. "Oh, sweetheart. You know I have complete faith in you."

"Shh, we can't hear," a voice complained behind them.

Aria looked over her shoulder and whispered, "Sorry!" She turned back to Linen and giggled silently into his shoulder.

"Do you think Velvet has any idea that the entire world is watching her right now?" Linen whispered into her ear.

Aria shook her head and glanced around the massive theatre full of people. "I think she'd be horrified if she knew. She didn't even like teaching more than thirty people at a time. If she knew millions were watching her every move like this, she'd just die."

Linen smiled. "You know, though it's nice to be able to watch this on a big screen, I kind of miss the times when it was just you and me on the edge of the lake."

Aria grinned. "Do you know what? I was just thinking the same thing." She clicked her fingers and suddenly they were in their own private theatre.

Linen looked around, then more loudly than before, whispered, "Now why didn't I think of this?"

* * *

Violet stood in the doorway of her friend's room and watched her sleeping for a moment. She crept in and retrieved the note she'd left her on the bedside table, then slipped back out. After throwing all of her water-logged clothing into the washing machine and putting some dry, clean clothes on, Violet sat cross-legged on her bed and got her diary out. She closed her eyes for a moment, took a deep breath, then she opened her eyes and began to record all she could remember from the moment she walked into the sea. Though already fading and becoming hazy, a few sharp moments stood out, and Violet did her best to capture them in words, afraid that if she forgot it all again, she would never find her way.

Though she had left the house just that morning feeling as though she couldn't take another moment of living, something had shifted quite dramatically. Violet no longer felt a heaviness in her heart; she no longer felt trapped by her own longing and loneliness. Somehow, she felt as though she had been set free, and now her overwhelming desire was to do something with this new feeling of freedom.

Two hours later, her hand ached and her stomach was growling. She had just put her diary and pen aside when there was a light tap on the door.

"Come in," she called out, stretching her sore muscles.

"Hey," Amy said, poking her head in, "I wasn't sure you'd be up yet."

Violet smiled. "I've been awake for a little while. Sleep well?"

Amy nodded, rubbing the sleep from her eyes. "Yeah, I think so, had some very strange dreams though."

A memory flashed through Violet's mind of Gold, sat on the beach. "I know what you mean, mine were quite odd, too."

"So what do you feel like doing today?"

Violet thought for a moment then smiled. "I think it's time that the Spiritual Sisters went on a road trip, don't you?"

* * *

"Hey, Laguz! Glad you could join us!"

"Hey, Aria, Linen, it's good to see you guys."

Aria flew over to him and gave him a hug. "It's weird seeing you blond again, I'd got quite used to the tall, dark and handsome look."

Laguz chuckled. "Yeah, I had too, actually, it was a bit odd to come back here and look like this again. But it feels good."

"So what can we do for you?" Linen asked.

Laguz glanced around the cluttered office and his gaze came to rest on the gleaming white grand piano. "I was looking for Velvet, actually. You wouldn't know where she is would you?"

Aria and Linen glanced at each other and Laguz's heart sank as a strong feeling of déjà vu washed over him.

"What is it?"

"She's not here, Laguz. She's gone back to Earth," Aria said.

Laguz frowned. "What do you mean? There's no Earth left, there won't be another human civilisation there for centuries now."

"She hasn't returned to the present day Earth, she's returned to Earth as it was twenty years ago."

Laguz's eyebrows shot up. "You mean she's gone back in time?"

Aria nodded. "She returned to the moment after she drowned but before she died completely. Gold came here and asked Linen if he could get one of his friends to rescue her, so that this time she wouldn't die."

Laguz rubbed his eyes. "Whoa, now. Slow down, I don't understand. Velvet has gone back in time, and won't die this time, because Linen asked a friend to go back in time and save her."

"He was my brother, actually. A fire Faerie called Flame. He owed me a few favours."

"If they've gone back in time, then surely that means that everything will change? And if everything is going to change, then how come every other soul hasn't also gone back in time?"

Linen sighed. "To be honest, I don't understand the ins and outs of it all myself, but what Gold said was that though Velvet living until the end may well change things in small ways, in the grand scheme of things, even if the world completely Awakens, it will probably still end. Therefore there's no need for every soul to go back and experience the last twenty years again, because chances are, it won't be all that different."

"I think he should have more faith in Velvet, personally," Aria said. "I think she could make big changes."

"What if we want to? What if I want to go back?"

Aria frowned. "But why would you want to go back?"

"Because if Velvet's still alive, there's a chance that we could get back together! There's a chance that I could find her, and make it up to her."

Aria glanced at Linen. "Lin, didn't Gold say..."

Laguz looked at Linen. "What? What did Gold say?"

Linen sighed. "I asked him if Velvet going back meant that you two would be together again, and he said no, that it wasn't likely."

Laguz's shoulders slumped. An uncomfortable silence fell, and Aria flew over to Laguz and laid a tiny hand on his shoulder.

"I'm sorry, Laguz. But maybe it would be better to wait here until she comes back."

Laguz shook his head. "No, I've wasted too much time doing nothing. I need to take action. I've spent the last twenty years of my human life regretting pushing her away.

I'm not going to waste another minute. Any chance you could get Gold here for me?"

"I'm already here, Laguz. Welcome back."

Aria squeaked and jumped, her tiny wings fluttering nervously.

"Gold, how soon can I get back there?"

Gold sighed. "You know that it might not change things? That you might well just spend the next two decades alone again?"

"Yes, it doesn't matter. I need to try. I can't just wait around here."

"Very well, then. I can send you back to the moment before the news of Violet's death was given to you."

Laguz nodded, recalling that awful moment. "Yes, I would like to live having never experienced that."

"Good luck then, Laguz." Gold raised his hand to click his fingers, and with the whispers of good wishes from Aria and Linen, Laguz closed his eyes.

CHAPTER SIXTEEN

TAKE TWO

"Greg? Did you hear what I just said?"

Greg blinked and looked around. Leona was standing there, one hand on her hip, waiting for his reply.

"Leona!" He jumped up and pulled her into a hug, then spun her around.

"Jeez, Greg, what's got into you this morning?"

Greg set her down and stared into her small face. "It's just so good to see you again."

Leona frowned. "Okay, now you're worrying me. You just saw me five minutes ago, and you've seen me every day for the past eighteen months."

Greg laughed. "I know, I know. I'm sorry. I'll stop acting so strangely now." Suddenly, he became aware of his own body and he flexed his muscles, marvelling at how it felt to be young again. He looked up to see Leona still looking at him as though he had sprouted antennae. "Sorry, Lee, what was it you said to me?"

"I said... I said..." Leona paused, a confused look on her face. "Huh, I've completely forgotten what I said to you now."

"Now who's losing their mind?" Greg teased.

"That's really going to bug me now, what the hell did I

say?" Leona continued muttering to herself as she walked out of the room.

Greg shook his head in amusement and looked around the room. It took him a few moments to identify where they were. He looked up at the window, and though it was dark outside, he knew exactly what lay beyond. He closed his eyes and recalled the morning he had witnessed Violet fall into the sea, and of running out there to rescue her. Another hazy memory resurfaced then, of Leona bearing news that had torn his heart in two.

His heart thudded in his chest and he struggled to take a breath. Was it a memory, was she already gone? Or was it a premonition?

He staggered out of the dining room and up the narrow stone steps to the floor above. He reached the bedroom and knocked.

Leona opened the door, still looking a little annoyed with herself. She took in Greg's expression and frowned. "Are you okay?"

"Have you heard from Violet?"

Leona's eyebrows shot up. In the last few months, she hadn't dared mention Violet's name, despite still being in contact with Amy.

"I had an e-mail from Amy the other day, she said that Violet was, well, okay."

"Okay? She's still alive?"

"Alive? Of course she is, why?"

"I need her address. I need to see her."

Leona's mouth fell open in shock, but she quickly closed it and smiled. "Of course. She's staying with Amy at her parents' house. Do you want me to come with you?"

Greg shook his head. "No, you'd better stay here; after all, we're supposed to be looking after the place."

"Okay, hang on then." Leona went into her room and pulled out her diary. She copied down the address and handed the piece of paper to Greg.

"Can I ask what brought about this change of heart?"

Greg looked down at Leona's neat, tiny writing and shrugged. "I'm not sure exactly, but I'm hoping that I'll know when I get there."

Leona smiled and patted his arm. "Good luck. Say 'hi' from me."

Greg nodded and turned away. "Thanks, I will."

* * *

"Woohoo! Go, Laguz!" Aria shouted, her tiny voice echoing around the theatre.

"It's a good thing we're in our own theatre now," Linen remarked dryly, reaching for the chocolate-covered strawberries.

Aria giggled. "I don't care if everyone hears me! He's doing it! Laguz is going to find Violet and admit to her how much he loves her! Aren't you even just a tiny bit excited?"

Linen smiled at the over-excited Faerie. "Of course, but I'm just wondering how this fits into the scenario that Gold painted, where it was so improbable that they would ever be together again."

"Gold's not right all the time you know."

"Aria, don't you realise who Gold is?"

"Of course I do." Aria crossed her arms defensively, though she wasn't really sure who he was. "But even he must have some off-days."

Linen chuckled. "I guess so. Let's hope that the changes Laguz and Velvet make in this new reality benefit everyone before the end."

"You still think the world will end, no matter what they do?" Aria looked up at the screen, where she saw Laguz driving his camper van across France.

"Aria, you know that nothing could possibly change the

ultimate outcome," Linen said gently, laying his hand on her arm. "Not even Gold."

Aria sighed. "Oh well. I suppose we should just enjoy the show then."

"That's not a bad philosophy to have in life, Aria. Let's hope that Velvet and Laguz do the same."

* * *

"Violet! Welcome, my dear Old Soul!"

Violet opened her arms to receive a hug from Esmeralda. She smelled of spring flowers.

"Hey, Esmeralda, how are you?"

"I'm good. It's so good to see you again. And you, Amy." Esmeralda turned to Amy and gave her a hug. "Now then, who've we got here?"

"I'm Keeley, this is Fay, Maggie, Leila and Beattie."

Esmeralda hugged them each in turn. "It's wonderful to meet you all, I'm so glad you have come to join us here for the weekend. Mike is around somewhere; I'll introduce him to you later. Right now, I'll show you to your pods, and then I think we should all get together in the lounge for hot drinks and cake."

There were nods of agreement all round, and the group followed Esmeralda up the winding path to the pods.

Despite the wintry chill, Violet lingered for a moment and breathed in deeply. She took in the birdsong and distant thrumming of a plane overhead. Within seconds she felt calm, and a feeling of serenity enveloped her. This had definitely been the right thing to do. She had a feeling that everything was about to change for the better.

* * *

"I'm sorry, Amy and Violet aren't here. They've gone away

for a few days."

Greg's shoulders slumped. He rubbed his weary eyes. "Do you know where they went? It's really important that I see Violet."

Amy's mother bit her lip. "Who did you say you were again?"

Greg smiled. "I'm sorry, I should have introduced myself. I haven't had much sleep in the last couple of days. My name is Greg, I met Amy and Violet in France, we travelled around together for a few months."

Amy's mother's eyes widened slightly and Greg wondered just how much she knew about him and his relationship with Violet.

"They've gone to a retreat in the country. Do you want me to get the address?"

"Yes, please." Greg leaned against the front door frame while Amy's mother went inside. She reappeared a few minutes later.

"It's right out in the middle of nowhere, do you have a Sat Nav?"

Greg shook his head and took the paper. "No, but I have a map. I'm sure I'll be able to find it. Thanks."

"You're welcome. I hope you find them."

* * *

"Vi, may I join you?"

Violet looked up and smiled at Maggie. She was sat on a rock at the edge of the quarry where Esmeralda had taken her a lifetime before.

"Of course, pull up a rock."

Maggie sat beside her and looked at the expanse of jagged stone. "Lovely view."

Violet laughed. "Not really, but it is nice and peaceful."

"Vi, I don't know quite how to say this, but I had a

vision of you a few days ago. And it was worrying."

"What was it?" Violet asked, already knowing the answer.

"It was of you putting the rune necklace in the wooden box and saying goodbye to me."

A tear trickled down Violet's face, and Maggie's breath caught. "You wouldn't, I mean, you're not going to, this isn't a goodbye trip, is it? You're not going to do anything stupid, are you?"

More tears fell and Violet took a deep breath to try and calm herself. "I tried."

Maggie grabbed Violet's hand and squeezed it. "Oh, Vi, how? When?"

"A few days ago. I walked into the sea and kept going. I was hoping to drown, but a surfer came along and pulled me out."

Violet looked at Maggie, and her heart ached at the tears running down her friend's face. "It's just been so hard, Maggie. You have no idea what it was like for me to lose Greg. I couldn't breathe without him. I couldn't sleep or eat. Everything just hurt so much. And I know it seems crazy, it's not like we'd been together for long, but he was my other half. I just couldn't see the point in continuing without him."

"I wish you'd come to talk to me. I wish you hadn't let yourself get that far. What if you'd drowned?"

"That's the strange thing. I think I did. I think I died, but I chose to come back. Just like the time Greg saved me in La Rochelle. Do you think that's odd?"

Maggie shook her head and wiped her face with a pink floral handkerchief. "No, I think it was meant to be."

Violet wiped away her own tears with the back of her hand. "Ever since the surfer pulled me out, I feel like the weight has been lifted a little. The pain of losing Greg is easier to manage somehow. I know now that I need to carry on, regardless. I can't let losing him make me lose my life."

"Violet, I love you, you know that, don't you?"

Violet smiled at Maggie and put her arms around her. "I love you too, Maggie. And I'm sorry that I tried to leave. I should have come to you sooner. I should have got all the Sisters together. Because that's the whole point of our friendship isn't it? To help each other through all the crap that life throws at us."

Maggie laughed, then suddenly went quiet and stared off into the distance.

Violet watched her friend, used to this sudden change. When Maggie's eyes refocused and a smile came across her face, Violet spoke.

"What did you See?"

"That you might want to get that rune pendant out of the box again."

* * *

After several more hours of driving and asking four people for directions, Greg finally found the tiny lane that led to the Twin Flame Retreat. He parked the camper van and walked towards the main house, his tiredness suddenly vanishing in the anticipation of seeing Violet. He had no idea what he was going to say, or how she was going to react, but he was aching to see her face again. It felt as though he'd spent an entire lifetime without her, not just a few months.

As he passed a tent in the garden, he saw flickers of light and the sound of hushed voices inside. Not wanting to interrupt, he went up to the main house and tried the door. It was unlocked, so he let himself in to escape the chilly breeze.

After using the bathroom, Greg went to wait in the lounge, and saw an upright piano in the corner. It looked as though it had been gathering dust for some time.

He walked over to it and opened the lid. He pressed down an ivory key and the clear note rang out. He bit his lip and sat down on the bench. Though he had no memory of ever having done so, he somehow felt, instinctively, that he could play the piano.

He looked around, but there were no music books. So he closed his eyes, let his hands hover above the keys for a moment, then slowly, softly, began to play.

* * *

"Now, I want you to dig up the box, and look at it for a moment."

Violet saw the box she had dug up and setting aside the fork, gently pulled it out. It was not a battered metal box this time. It was the beautifully carved wooden box with Mermaids on the side and Velvet, her, on the top.

"Now I want you to open the box. Inside it is your answer."

Violet took a deep breath, remembering what Maggie had said earlier in the day about getting the rune pendant out again. She carefully undid the catch and opened the box.

There was nothing inside.

Violet's heart sank. But then she heard the most beautiful sound.

Her eyes snapped open and the visualisation of the box in the garden disappeared. Esmeralda was looking at her, confused.

"It sounds like someone is playing the piano," she whispered, not wanting to disturb the others, who were still deep in their meditation.

Violet nodded. Her heart was racing. She motioned to Esmeralda that she was going to leave the tent, and Esmeralda nodded. Slowly, she got up and slid out of the tent flap, hearing Esmeralda continue the meditation. She walked up the path to the front door, feeling as though she was going to faint. She reached the front door and slowly eased it open. The piano music became louder, and a cascade of memories washed over Violet.

She stood in the door of the lounge, afraid to look at who was playing in case she was disappointed. Finally, before the music reached the end, she wrenched her gaze from the floor and looked up. The sight of Greg sitting at the piano, lost in the music, was enough to make her heart stall.

When the last note hovered in the air between them, Violet moved towards him. When she was close enough to touch him, he looked up.

"That was our song, wasn't it?"

Violet nodded, unable to speak. She was in shock that he was there, and in awe that he had remembered a detail of their previous existence.

"You wrote it for me. I remember now."

Violet nodded again.

Greg reached out for her, then pulled his hand back, unsure.

He stood up and Violet stepped forwards, melting into his strong embrace.

"I'm sorry," he whispered into her hair as he gripped her tightly. "I'm so, so sorry. I should never have pushed you away like that."

Without warning, tears ran down Violet's cheeks, and all of the grief of losing him drained away with them.

"I love you, Violet. I hope you can forgive me."

Violet pulled back a little and looked into Greg's eyes. "I love you, too."

* * *

"Aria, you're making me dizzy." Linen shook his head at the crazy green Faerie flying in mad, haphazard circles around the theatre.

"I can't help it! I can't believe they got together! It's so incredible!" She came to a sudden stop less than a foot away from Linen, making him jump.

"I told you that Gold wasn't always right, didn't I? He must have been having a major off-day!"

"Actually, I knew this would happen, I just didn't want them to know."

Gold's sudden appearance made Aria squeak in shock and fly backwards into the big screen.

"Hello, Gold." Linen nodded at the Elder.

"Hello, Linen, Aria. I hope you've enjoyed watching the show."

Aria flew closer. "What do you mean you knew they would be together? Why would you lie to them?"

"For some reason, when some human beings are told that they shouldn't do something, or that something is not possible, it makes them all the more determined to make it happen."

Aria raised an eyebrow. "So by telling them it wasn't going to happen, you made it happen?"

"Something like that, yes."

"Wow, you really are quite clever."

Gold chuckled. "Thank you, my dear Faerie. I do try. Now, I was wondering if you could do me another favour, Linen."

Linen nodded. "Of course, what is it?"

Gold looked up at the screen and smiled. "I think our two dear friends are about to make some monumental changes to the last twenty years of Earth's existence. I think it would only be fair if we offered all the souls here the chance to go back and experience it, don't you?"

Linen smiled. "I think that would be fair. I will call a

meeting and put that to them."

"Excellent."

"Gold?" Aria said suddenly, her face serious.

"Yes, my dear?"

"Is there any chance that I could go too?"

Linen's mouth dropped open in shock. "What?"

Gold smiled. "Of course, Aria. If there is a soul that wishes not to return, then you are welcome to take their place. But I thought that you had no desire to experience a human life?"

"I've been thinking, it's only for a couple of decades, and well, I could be a Faerie again here afterwards, couldn't I?"

"Of course you can. Linen, you are also welcome to do the same." Gold looked at Linen's expression and stood. "I think I had better be going. If you both decide to go, I wish you well. Thank you for all that you have done here."

Before Linen could collect himself enough to respond, Gold was gone.

"Lin, sweetie, are you okay?" Aria hovered next to Linen, rubbing his arm.

"You want to go to Earth?" he whispered.

"Don't you? I mean, it's been fun, watching it from here, but don't you think it would be good to experience it first-hand?"

"Yes, I do. But I never dreamt that you would feel that way."

Aria shrugged. "Me neither, but watching Laguz and Velvet and Amethyst there makes me want to go and do my bit too. Besides, if we get to go as walk-ins, we've got a little more chance of remembering who we really are, haven't we?"

Linen nodded. "Yes, I suppose you're right. He flew to his feet and held out his hand. "I guess we should go and tell everyone. Ready?"

Aria clasped his hand and squeezed it. "Ready."

EPILOGUE

TAKE TWO

Earth, twenty years later

"I'd like to thank you all for joining us here today for this special gathering. I know that you all wish to be with your loved ones, so thank you for sparing this time. I'd also like to thank all of the Earth Angels who have stood here on this stage today, to give us their words of wisdom at this time of great transformation." Violet looked out at the audience of thousands, and looked into the camera, knowing that millions more people all across the world had tuned in to watch the final messages.

"I know that many of you are Earth Angels, who, like myself and the others who have spoken today, came to Earth to help with the Awakening; to help the world experience the Golden Age for the very first time. And I know that though you are keeping your energies at a high vibration, there will be a feeling of disappointment that it hasn't happened." Violet sighed. "I know that I feel that way." She looked at Greg who was sat in the front row, next to Amy and Nick. In the same row sat Beattie and her Twin Flame, Ryan; Leila and her daughter, Amber; Keeley and her Twin Flame, Karl; and Maggie and her Twin Flame, Steve.

Amy nodded encouragingly at her, and Violet smiled.

"Twenty years ago, I could never have imagined the world being the way it is now. The people on Earth are far more loving, tolerant, kind and generous than they were back then. There seems to be more happiness and laughter, less war and crime. And best of all, is that so many Flames have been reunited." Violet paused as a hand shot up in the audience. She nodded at the person to speak.

"What makes you think that we aren't in the Golden Age now? More happiness, less war, and the reunion of the Flames sounds pretty golden to me."

Violet frowned. "I'm sorry, do I know you?"

The girl smiled. "We met in another dimension. My name is-"

"Aria?" Violet asked, amazed.

Aria smiled. "You remember me!"

Violet laughed. "I don't think it's possible to forget you, Aria. And as for your question, the reason I know that we have not managed to experience the Golden Age, is because the Rainbow Children have not arrived. Not to mention the fact that every Seer in the world has been prophesising for years that the end of the world will happen at this point in time."

Aria frowned. "What if their prophecies are wrong? What if it's just a bad case of déjà vu?"

Violet shook her head. "I'm not sure I know what you mean?"

Aria bit her lip and looked at her companion for guidance. He nodded at her and whispered something. Aria turned back to Violet.

"The world has already ended."

The audience, who up until now had been watching the exchange with interest, gasped.

"What we are experiencing right now, well, it's a sort of do-over. You see, when you drowned in 2012, you really did die. And you didn't want to come back. So you moved on to the stars, and the world continued without you."

Violet's mouth opened and closed like a fish. She looked at Maggie in confusion. She had never told anyone but her about her suicide attempt. Maggie shook her head, just as confused.

"But without you, the world didn't Awaken. Without your books, your talks, and the Twin Flame retreats that you set up all over the world, Earth didn't really have a chance. And so twenty years later, tomorrow morning, in fact, the world ended."

Violet finally found her voice. "So what are you trying to say? How are we here now?"

"You came back from the stars and you asked Gold for another chance. So he sent you back to the moment when you drowned and we arranged to have someone save you. Anyway, it's all very long and boring, but the point is, by giving it another go, you changed the course of the world. You and Laguz got back together and you found your purpose in life and acted upon it. So here we are, Awakened, reunited with our Flames and living in alignment with our purposes. Because of you."

Violet blinked, and a tear fell down her cheek. "So the world isn't going to end?"

Aria shrugged. "I don't know, to be honest. Considering the massive changes that have happened, you never know, maybe it was enough to stop it. But even if it is the end of the world, it's not such a bad thing. When it happened before everyone just ended up at the Academy with Linen and me and it was like a big, mad but mostly happy, family."

Violet looked at her companion. "Linen?"

Linen smiled. "Hey, Velvet. I mean, Violet. Sorry to crash your party, but well, Aria has been dying to tell you all of that, and I couldn't stop her."

Aria mock punched Linen's shoulder. "Hey, you weren't

supposed to say that."

"Sorry."

Aria sat down and Violet noticed that sat next to Linen was another familiar face. She smiled at Freddy and he grinned back. Taking a deep breath, Violet tried to gather her thoughts, aware of the many eyes watching her at this very moment. In all her career as a spiritual author and speaker, and founder of the Spiritual Awakening Movement, she had never been truly speechless until now.

After several moments, she opened her mouth to speak without really knowing what she was about to say.

"My friends, it seems that maybe there are still some mysteries left in the world. And if civilisation still exists in the morning, I would implore you to explore those mysteries. I am so very glad that I was given a second chance. I am so incredibly grateful to all of you for giving my words some thought, for being open to believing in the truly fantastical." She looked down at Greg, tears streaming down her face.

"Thank you for loving so much, and so deeply. The reunion of the Flames was successful, even if the transition to the Golden Age was not. I'm glad that all of you who found your Flames got to spend this lifetime together." She took a deep breath and smiled.

"If my friend, Aria, here is right, then even if this is the end, it will all work out just fine. There is nothing to fear, no darkness to endure, nothing to lose. When we awake tomorrow morning, we will either be on the Other Side, or we will just have entered the Golden Age. Either way, I will see you again."

With applause surrounding her, Violet smiled at the audience, then left the stage for the last time.

* * *

"Violet?"

"Charlie, is that you?" Violet blinked in shock at the man stood in front of her.

He smiled. "Yeah, it's me. You gave a great speech. I'm glad I was able to make it."

"Thank you." Violet was too shocked to form a longer response.

"And I just wanted to apologise. For the way I behaved, for the way I treated you. It wasn't until I read your books that I realised who I was, and why our relationship had been like that."

Violet frowned, and shook her head. "I don't understand. Who are you?"

"Corduroy."

Violet gasped and her hand flew up to her face. Now that he had said it, it seemed so ridiculously obvious.

"I still love you, Violet. And I don't think that will ever change." Charlie looked up to see Greg approaching. "But I know that you and Laguz are Flames, and that you and I are friends. I was just hoping that maybe if we do all wake up tomorrow, you'd like to still be friends. Of course, that depends on whether or not you can forgive me."

Violet felt the familiar threat of tears. One fell as she stepped forwards to embrace the Old Soul

"There's nothing to forgive, my friend," she whispered into his ear. She felt him nod.

"Thank you."

* * *

The journey had been a long one, but Violet was determined to make it back to La Rochelle, to their cottage by the sea, by midnight. They had driven back from the gathering in London, seeing signs everywhere that people were taking the prophecies of the end of the world seriously. But there was no chaos. No rioting or looting. Instead they saw parties taking place in the streets, gatherings of people laughing and having fun. Violet watched them with a smile, thinking that perhaps this was a little of what the Golden Age would have felt like.

When they arrived at the dark cottage, they didn't bother to unpack the car, but instead went in, lit the fires and went straight up to the tiny front bedroom.

Violet was just dressing for bed when she felt Greg's arms encircle her from behind.

"Does it bother you?" Greg murmured into her ear.

She frowned, then realised that she had been unconsciously cradling her stomach. She dropped her hands to her sides and shook her head.

"Does it matter to me that we didn't manage to conceive a child, only for it to die a few years later at the end of the world? No, it doesn't bother me. Besides, the fact that it never happened throughout all these years together proves that it was never meant to be."

"You would have made an amazing mother."

Violet smiled, not trusting herself to speak. She turned to face Greg and kissed him. "I'm just so glad to have spent these last twenty years with you. Our relationship is the most important thing in my life. And I am so glad that we are still standing together at the end."

Greg kissed her back. "Me too. Though I can't help wishing that we had more time to be together. It seems to have flown by."

Violet smiled. "When I said it was the end, I meant of the current human age. Not us. We'll be together on the Other Side. You can be sure of that."

Greg pulled her close and hugged her tight.

* * *

It was just gone midnight, and they were lying in each other's arms in bed.

"I can't believe Aria came back," Violet whispered into the darkness. "She was so terrified of losing her wings."

Greg smiled and continued stroking her hair. "Maybe she learned how to defeat her fears. She seemed quite happy as a human."

Violet smiled, snuggling closer to Greg, breathing in the warmth of his skin. "Do you think she might be right? That this has all happened before?"

Greg swallowed hard. "I know she's right."

Violet looked up at his face, where a tear had slid down his cheek. She waited for him to elaborate.

"You did die. You did leave this Earth. And I lived for twenty years without you. I spent every minute in regret that I pushed you away. When the world ended and I found out that you had gone back in time, that you were alive on Earth again, I knew I had to come back too. I knew I had to find you, and be with you. It doesn't quite make up for my idiocy, but I'm so very glad that I got a second chance to be with you."

"Why didn't you tell me all of this before?"

Greg shook his head. "I don't know. I suppose I didn't really know for certain that those memories were real. Until Aria showed up today."

Violet closed her eyes and Greg held her closer.

"I suppose it doesn't really matter now. I'm glad you came to find me though."

"Me too." Greg sighed. "Do you want to stay up? See it happen?"

Violet shook her head. "No, let's just go to sleep. There's nowhere I want to be more than in your arms right now."

"I love you, Violet. I'll love you for eternity."

Violet's heart skipped. "Our love will outlast eternity itself."

"Starlight?" Violet awoke with a start, the images of her dream still floating in front of her eyes.

"Violet? Are you okay?"

Violet blinked in confusion. "Is it morning already?"

Greg looked over at the digital clock. "No, it's only three."

"How come the crystal is making rainbows then?"

Greg looked around the room. "I can't see them."

Violet threw the covers to one side and moved to the window. Greg joined her.

He followed her gaze to the skies. "Do you think this is it?" he whispered. "Because it feels similar to before."

Violet looked up at him and shook her head. "I don't know. How did it happen before?"

"It was a meteorite, I think."

Violet looked back out of the window. Her breath caught when she saw the streak of light cross the sky. On any other night, she would have made a wish. But she knew that she'd already had all of her wishes granted.

Greg slid his arms around her, and held her close. "It looks like a shooting star, doesn't it?" Greg said, his voice rough.

Violet looked up at him, remembering the poem she'd altered so long ago, the poem she had never given to him, and wondered if he remembered it from before. Greg leant down and kissed her, and Violet realised that it didn't matter anymore. She was here, in his arms, at the end, and that was the only thing that mattered. As the bright light lit up the sky and the beach below, Violet buried her face in his shoulder and wrapped her arms around him. She breathed in the scent of his t-shirt and closed her eyes.

"That's strange," Greg whispered.

Violet pulled away from him and looked back out of the window. Her breath caught at the sight of thousands of streaks of light streaming down from the sky.

"Those are too small to be meteorites. What is going on?" A clearer memory of the single star that had fallen came to him, and he frowned. "Something has changed; this isn't how it happened last time."

Before he could finish speaking, Violet had already put her dressing gown on and was moving to the door.

"Where are you going?"

"I need to be out there. I don't know why, but I do."

Greg grabbed his jumper and joined her.

They walked hand in hand to the beach, and Violet breathed in the still, salty air, her eyes fixed on the beams of light still streaking through the sky. A strange blanket of silence had fallen, and even the waves made no sound as they rolled in.

Once on the sand, Violet stopped, and lifted her face to the sky. As the light descended further, she gasped.

"They look like rainbows." Her hand tightened around Greg's, and a memory of a young girl came to her. Rose told her that at the beginning of the rainbows there would be gold.

Without understanding why, Violet lifted up her free hand, and as though drawn to her, a rainbow of light fell to her, and landed in the palm of her hand. She lowered her arm carefully and stared in amazement at it. She felt the warmth of it, the healing that it brought. She closed her fingers around it, and heard the same gentle voice that she had heard in another lifetime, in another dimension.

"Everything is going to be okay now. When you chose to come back, when you chose to try again, you changed the fate of the world, Velvet. This is no longer the end, but the beginning. The Golden Age is finally here."

Tears streamed down Violet's face and she looked up at Greg, whose face glimmered in the rainbow-light.

He moved closer and Velvet held the rainbow out to him, but when his hand touched the light and her hand, instead of it transferring, it grew brighter until it enveloped them both.

"Maybe just one last wish?"

Violet heard the voice in her ear, then felt a tingling in her stomach. She placed her hand there and felt the warmth. The light lasted another few seconds then faded away.

She stepped into Greg's arms and held him tightly.

"The Rainbows have arrived. Everything is going to be just fine now."

"I'm not sure I understand."

Violet smiled. "You will." She looked up at him. "I'll love you for eternity."

Greg leaned down to kiss her.

"Our love will outlast eternity itself."

The Beginning

"Linen?"

"Yes, Aria?"

"What just happened? Was I right? Is the world not going to end?"

"I think you may well have been right, yes."

"So Velvet's return really did save the world after all. Do you think Gold knew this would happen, or was he was having another off-day?"

"I think he probably knew."

"Oh. Linen?"

"Yes, Aria?"

"Does that mean we're stuck here now, as humans, until we die?"

"Yes, Aria, I'm afraid it does."

"Oh. Well, I guess it's not so bad. Being human doesn't suck as much as I thought it might. It would be good if technology advanced enough to give us wings though."

"Yes, that would be good."

"Linen?"

"Yes, Aria?"

"Have you got any chocolate?"

Here's the first chapter of the third book in the Earth Angel Series - The Other Side

CHAPTER ONE

"Mikey! It's dinner time! What are you doing out there?"

Mikey looked up when he heard his mother calling him and frowned. He looked back down at the tiny winged creature sat in the palm of his hand and sighed.

"I'm so sorry, I have to go now. Will you be here tomorrow?"

The Faerie nodded and smiled. "I will. I look forward to seeing you again, Mikey."

Mikey smiled back. "Good night, Faerie." He watched as the tiny being got up and with a wave of her dainty hand, flew into the rose bushes.

"Mikey! Where are you?"

With a sigh, Mikey waved at the rose bush and got up from the lawn. Brushing the bits of dirt and grass from his shorts, he picked up the forgotten wooden truck that he used as a prop, and slowly made his way back to the house. It was Thursday, which meant that dinner would be meatloaf. Again. What he wouldn't give for things to change. Routine was so dreary to him. Luckily, he had his Faerie friends to keep him company.

When he reached the back door, he pulled on the handle and stepped into the kitchen. The smell of the meatloaf hit him as he entered, and without being able to stop himself, he wrinkled his nose in disgust.

"I really wish you would come when I call you. Where have you been? You're filthy! Go wash your hands and set the table; your father will be home at any moment." His mother continued to get the meal ready, and Mikey nodded mutely, going straight to the bathroom to wash his hands. Once he was a little cleaner, he returned to the kitchen and mechanically got the cutlery, napkins and placemats out to set the table. He set three places, one each for his mother, himself and his father. He laid his father's place carefully. His hand lingered over the placemat, wishing, as he did every night that he laid the table, that just this once, his father would actually be there to eat with them. It seemed that all his father did was work. Most days, he would arrive home so late that Mikey would already be in bed asleep. But his mother held the hope every evening that he would be home in time for dinner, and so insisted that a place be set for him at the table.

A little while later, two steaming plates of food were on the table, and Mikey was sat beside his mother, as she kept up a stream of chatter. He nodded and smiled, but his heart felt heavy. He was still thinking of his conversation with the little Faerie in the garden. He didn't dare mention the conversation to his mother. He had tried to, two years before, but she and his father had been so upset that they had done everything in their power to convince him that there was no such thing as Faeries. They said he just had an overactive imagination, and he shouldn't tell his stories as if they were real.

But no matter what they said, he knew he wasn't making it up. He knew Faeries were real. He had tried to talk to his friends at School about it, thinking that they might believe him, but they just made fun of him instead. For several months, they called him 'Faerie boy' every day.

Mikey had told the Faeries about it, and they said to him that one day, people would realise that Faeries were real. And that they lived in the same world as them, just on a different vibrational level, which meant that only some people could see them and hear them.

"Mikey? Are you listening to me?"

Mikey blinked and snapped back to the present. He put the forgotten forkful of meatloaf into his mouth and nodded.

"Okay, we'll work on it tonight then. It would be good to be able to play the whole song, wouldn't it?"

Mikey smiled and chewed the meatloaf. He did enjoy playing the piano with his mother. Despite her impatience at times, she was a very good teacher.

Later, after he had washed the dishes, and his mother had dried them and put them away, they sat side by side on the piano bench, and he copied his mother's hand movements on the keys as she taught him a classical melody that she loved to play.

They played until it was truly dark outside, then with his eyelids drooping, Mikey was ushered to his bedroom by his mother. He changed for bed and brushed his teeth.

His mother tucked him in and kissed him on the forehead. "Goodnight, Mikey. Sleep well."

Mikey nodded, his eyes were already closed. He thought briefly of the tiny Faerie again, and then he fell into a deep slumber.

* * *

"Hello, Mikey."

Mikey's eyes widened in shock as he looked up at the giant Angel, with massive wings studded with what looked like stars.

"Hello," he whispered back. Despite his surprise, he felt

no fear. This Angel had such a beautiful and friendly smile. He trusted her immediately.

"Do you know why I am here, Mikey?"

Mikey shook his head.

"I think you do. The Faeries have been telling you about the changes that are about to happen, haven't they?"

Mikey nodded slowly. "They told me that things would be changing on Earth. That people will believe in Faeries again. They said that Faeries and Angels would be coming to Earth as humans to help with the changes, to help make people believe again, before it's too late."

The Angel smiled and nodded. "That's right. Do you remember what they said would happen on the Other Side?"

"About the Children?"

"Yes. There will be a School for them. To help them prepare to come to Earth as well."

"I remember."

"Mikey, do you think you could help them?"

Mikey frowned. "What do you mean? How could I help them? I try to tell people about the Faeries, but they don't believe me."

The Angel smiled gently. "I don't mean help the people on Earth. I mean help the Children on the Other Side."

"But how can I do that? In my dreams?"

The Angel shook her head. "No, Mikey. I'm afraid you wouldn't be able to stay here. You would have to return to the Other Side."

Mikey bit his lip. "You mean I would have to die?"

The Angel knelt down on one knee so that she was on the same level as Mikey, and she wrapped her arm around him. "Mikey, my dear, sweet Child. There is no such thing as death. You will simply be going home."

Mikey nodded, but wasn't sure. "Isn't there anyone already there who can help?"

The Angel shook her head. "No one as special as you."

Mikey took a deep breath. He looked the Angel in the eye. "Will it hurt?"

The Angel wrapped her other arm and both her wings around him and surrounded him in a beautiful white light. "No, it won't. I will make sure of it."

Mikey closed his eyes and breathed in the scent of the Angel, which he could only describe as being heavenly, and nodded into her shoulder.

"I will do it."

The Angel pulled back a little and kissed him on the forehead. "You will know it's time when you hear a voice telling you to do something. A voice very much like mine. When you hear this voice, do exactly the opposite of what she tells you to do."

Mikey nodded. "Will it be very soon?"

"In a few days, yes. We need to start the changes on the Other Side as soon as we can."

"Will I see you again?"

The Angel smiled. "Maybe in the end."

* * *

When Mikey opened his eyes, it was still dark outside, but he was wide awake. His dream had been so vivid, so beautiful, and yet so scary at the same time. The Faeries had been telling him of their plans for some time, a couple of years, in fact. But they had never told him that he would be needed on the Other Side to help with the changes.

At the thought of leaving his mother, of dying, of not existing, his heart started to thump painfully, and his breathing became irregular and shallow. The beautiful Angel had promised it would not hurt, but what if she was wrong? And how would it happen? What about his mother?

Without him, she would be so lonely.

His lip quivered and a tear fell down the side of his face, silently hitting his pillow. Suddenly a light outside his window caught his eye. He sat up and threw his covers aside, then got out of bed quietly and moved to the window. Unsure of what he would see, he pulled the curtains open and looked outside.

The sight made him catch his breath. He watched in amazement as shooting stars lit up the sky briefly with their light. His breathing slowed. He felt calm, and enveloped in love.

He smiled, and wiped away his tears. He knew then that he would be safe. Because the Angel with wings of stars had told him so. He also knew, in that moment, that he was ready to go home.

* * *

"So I won't be able to talk to you again, because I have to go and help on the Other Side."

The Faerie nodded her tiny head sadly. "I will miss you, Mikey, but I am so pleased that you are doing this for us. You will be helping not only the Faeries, but also the Angels, Mermaids, the Starpeople and the humans, of course."

Mikey smiled. "Thank you for being such a good friend. For listening to me, and for being here whenever I needed you."

"Thank you for being you, Mikey. I look forward to the new world that you will be creating for us."

Mikey sighed. "It seems like a lot of responsibility."

The Faerie giggled. "Now you sound like a Faerie."

"Nothing wrong with that!"

"Indeed."

"Mikey! Where are you?"

"I'm sorry, I-"

"You have to go. I know. It's okay. I understand." The Faerie flew up from Mikey's palm, and came closer to his face. She kissed him on the nose. "Goodbye, Mikey. I do hope we meet again one day."

Mikey's eyes widened. "Goodbye? Does that mean I am going to die very soon?"

The Faerie shook her head. "No, Mikey. It means that you will soon be going home."

* * *

The very next day, Mikey heard the voice.

"Stay inside today, Mikey."

At first he nodded and continued to play, thinking that his mother had called out to him. But after a moment, he looked up and saw that his mother was in the back garden. He frowned. The voice was too clear to have been hers.

Then the Angel's instructions came back to him. "When you hear a voice like mine, do the opposite of what it tells you to."

Mikey breathed in deeply. Just then, his mother came in through the back door.

"Mikey, could you go to the corner shop and get some milk? We haven't got enough to last until the milkman comes tomorrow."

Mikey nodded. He put his toy soldiers down, stood up, and made his way over to his mother. She got her purse out of her handbag and gave him some coins.

"That should be more than enough. You could get some sweets with the change if you want."

Mikey tried to smile, but found it too hard. Instead, he hugged his mother, catching her by surprise.

"'Bye, Mum."

She chuckled. "I'll see you in a little bit. Be careful on the road."

Mikey turned to the door, and felt as though he was being pushed back by an invisible force.

"Don't go out of the gate. Stay inside."

Mikey kept moving towards the door, even though every step was a struggle. Once outside, he glanced back at the door, took a deep breath, then headed towards the gate.

"Go back inside. Don't leave the garden. It's not safe."

Mikey swallowed. It was hard to disobey the voice. Everything inside him wanted to turn and run back inside, into the warm arms of his mother. But he remembered what the Faeries had told him, and he remembered the beautiful Angel, and the shower of shooting stars.

He reached the gate, and had difficulty opening the catch because his hands were shaking so much.

"Mikey! Could you get some bread too?"

He looked back towards the house, but didn't stop to respond to his mother's request. If he didn't go now, he would change his mind.

He finally got through the gate, and then heard the beautiful voice once more.

"Stop!"

He looked up at the sky, to where it sounded like the voice had come from, then ran out across the road, directly into the path of the green car.

* * *

"Welcome home, young Mikey."

Mikey blinked and looked around him. He was surrounded by a swirling mist, and stood in front of him was a very kind-looking old man in heavy golden robes.

He suddenly became aware of the fact that he had just left his Earthly life, willingly. And that he had come to the Other Side with a purpose. With this in mind, he was ready for the question, even though he didn't know it was coming.

"I have something very important to ask you, and I need you to consider it carefully."

Mikey nodded.

"Do you want to stay?"

Mikey nodded again. Perhaps a bit too quickly, because the old man frowned a little.

"It is not your time yet, young Mikey, you may choose to return to Earth if you wish."

"No, thank you. I don't want to go back."

"Very well. Would you like to move on to the next dimension?"

"No."

"Do you want to return to the Elemental Realm?"

Mikey suddenly became aware that he was hovering above the floor. He looked over his shoulder at his wings and realised that he was a Faerie. His memories of his life as a fire Faerie came flooding back to him, making him smile, but he shook his head.

"No, I don't want to go there either."

The old man frowned. "Well then, young Mikey, Where do you wish to go?"

"I would like to return to the Earth Angel Training Academy, please."

* * *

Starlight watched the exchange with a smile. She had kept her promise, and Mikey had made the transition between Earth and the Other Side without any pain whatsoever. She watched Mikey as he met Velvet, the Head of the Earth Angel Training Academy.

She was interested by the fact that Mikey gave nothing away of what was to come. Starlight could see that Velvet was struggling to see the meaning of why this fire Faerie had returned to the Academy to work with her.

She saw Velvet assign Mikey a new appearance, and a new name – Linen. He was to act as her assistant.

Starlight nodded. So far, everything was working out perfectly.

If everything else went according to plan, then Starlight needed to set the next phase in motion.

A visit to the Indigo World was needed.

About the Author

Michelle lives in the UK, when she's not flitting in and out of other realms. She believes in Faeries and Unicorns and thinks the world needs more magic and fun in it. She writes because she would go crazy if she didn't. She might already be a little crazy, so please buy more books so she can keep writing.

Please feel free to write a review of this book. Michelle loves to get direct feedback, so if you would like to contact her, please e-mail theamethystangel@hotmail.co.uk or keep up to date by following her blog – **TwinFlameBlog.com.** You can also follow her on Twitter **@themiraclemuse** or like her page on Facebook.

You can now become an Earth Angel Trainee:
earthangelacademy.co.uk

To sign up to her mailing list, visit:
michellegordon.co.uk

EARTH ANGEL SERIES:

The Earth Angel Training Academy (book 1)

There are humans on Earth, who are not, in fact, human.

They are **Earth Angels**.

Earth Angels are beings who have come from other realms, dimensions and planets, and are choosing to be born on Earth in human form for just **one** reason.

To **Awaken the world**.

Before they can carry out their perilous mission, they must first learn how to be human.

The best place they can do that, is at

The Earth Angel Training Academy

The Earth Angel Awakening (book 2)

After learning how to be human at the Earth Angel Training Academy, the Angels, Faeries, Merpeople and Starpeople are born into human bodies on Earth.

Their Mission? **Awaken the world**.

But even though they **chose** to go to Earth, and they chose to be human, it doesn't mean that it will be **easy** for them to Awaken themselves.

Only if they **reconnect** to their **origins**, and to other Earth Angels, will they will be able to **remember** who they really are.

Only then, will they experience

The Earth Angel Awakening

The Other Side (book 3)

There is an Angel who holds the world in her hands.

She is the **Angel of Destiny**.

Her actions will start the **ripples** that will **save humans** from their certain demise.

In order for her to initiate the necessary changes, she must travel to other **galaxies**, and call upon the most **enlightened** and **evolved** beings of the Universe.

To save **humankind**.

When they agree, she wishes to prepare them for Earth life, and so invites them to attend the Earth Angel Training Academy, on

The Other Side

The Twin Flame Reunion (book 4)

The Earth Angels' missions are clear: **Awaken** the world, and move humanity into the **Golden Age**.

But there is another reason many of the Earth Angels choose to come to Earth.

To **reunite** with their **Twin Flames**.

The Twin Flame connection is deep, everlasting and intense, and happens only at the **end of an age**. Many Flames have not been together for millennia, some have never met.

Once on Earth, every Earth Angel longs to meet their Flame. The one who will make them **feel at home**, who will make living on this planet bearable.

But no one knows if they will actually get to experience

The Twin Flame Reunion

The Twin Flame Retreat (book 5)

The question in the minds of many Earth Angels
on Earth right now is:
Where is my **Twin Flame?**
Though many Earth Angels are now meeting their Flames,
the circumstances around their reunion can have
life-altering consequences.
If meeting your Flame meant your life would never be the same again, would you still want to find them?
When in need of **support** and answers,
Earth Angels attend
The Twin Flame Retreat

The Twin Flame Resurrection (book 6)

Twin Flames are **destined** to meet. And when they are meant to be together, nothing can keep them apart.
Not even **death**.
When Earth Angels go home to the Fifth Dimension too soon, they have the **choice** to come back.
To be with their **Twin Flame**.
The connection can be so overwhelming, that some Earth Angels try to resist it, try to push it away.
But it is **undeniable**.
When things don't go according to plan, the universe steps in, and the Earth Angels experience
The Twin Flame Ressurrection

The Twin Flame Reality (book 7)

Being an Earth Angel on Earth can be difficult, especially when it doesn't feel like home, and when there's a deep longing for a realm or dimension where you feel you **belong**.

Finding a Twin Flame, is like **coming home**.

Losing one, can be **devastating**.

Adrift, lonely, isolated... an Earth Angel would be forgiven for preferring to go home, than to stay here **without their Flame**.

But if they can find the **strength** to stay, to follow their mission to **Awaken** the world, and fulfil their original purpose, they will find they can be **happy** here.

Even despite the sadness of

The Twin Flame Reality

The Twin Flame Rebellion (book 8)

The Angels on the Other Side have a **duty** to **help** their human charges, but **only** when they are **asked** for help.

They are not allowed to meddle with **Free Will**.

But a number of Angels are asked to break their **Golden Rule**, and start influencing the human lives of the Earth Angels.

Once the Angels start nudging, they find they can't stop, and when the Earth Angels find out they are being manipulated from the Other Side, they aren't happy.

Determined to **choose** their own **fate**, the Earth Angels embark on

The Twin Flame Rebellion

VISIONARY COLLECTION:

Heaven dot com

When Christina goes into hospital for the final time, and knows that she is about to lose her battle with cancer, she asks her boyfriend, James, to help her deliver messages to her family and friends after she has gone.

She also asks him to do something for her, but she dies before he can make it happen, and he finds it difficult to forgive himself.

After her death, her messages are received by her loved ones, and the impact her words have will change their lives forever.

The Doorway to PAM

Natalie is an ordinary girl who has lost her way. There is nothing particularly special about her or her life. She has no exceptional abilities. She hasn't achieved anything miraculous. Her life has very little meaning to it.

Evelyn is the caretaker at Pam's. The alternate dimension where souls at their lowest point find the answers they need to turn their lives around. The dimension dreamers visit, to help people while they sleep.

One ordinary girl, one extraordinary woman.
One fated meeting that will change lives.

The Elphite

Ellie's life is just one long, bad case of déjà vu. She has lived her life before - a hundred times before - and she remembers each and every lifetime.

Each time, she has changed things, but has never managed to change the ending.
This time, in this life, she hopes that it will be different.
So she makes the biggest change of all - she tries to avoid meeting him.

Her soulmate. The love of her life.
Because maybe if they don't meet, she can finally change her destiny.
But fate has other ideas...

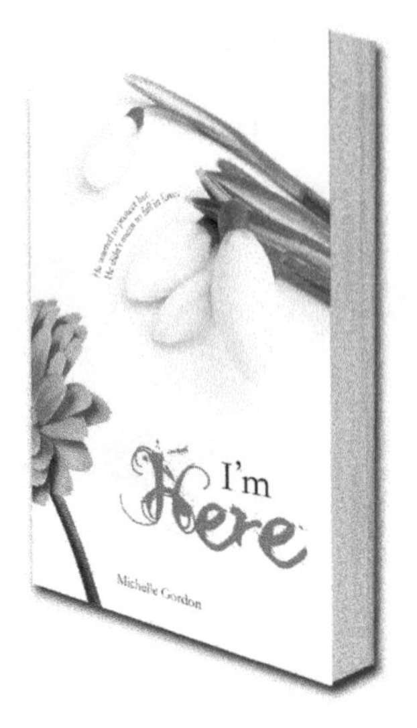

I'm Here

When Marielle finds out that a guy she had a crush on in school has passed away, the strange occurrences of the previous week begin to make sense. She suspects that he is trying to give her a message from the other side, and so opens up to communicate with him, She has no idea that by doing so, she will be forming a bond so strong, that life as she knows it will forever be changed.

Nathan assumed that when he died, he would move on, and continue his spiritual journey. But instead he finds himself drawn to a girl that he once knew. The more he watches her, and gets to know her, he realises that he was drawn to her for a reason, and that once he knows what that is, he will be able to change his destiny.

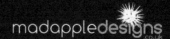

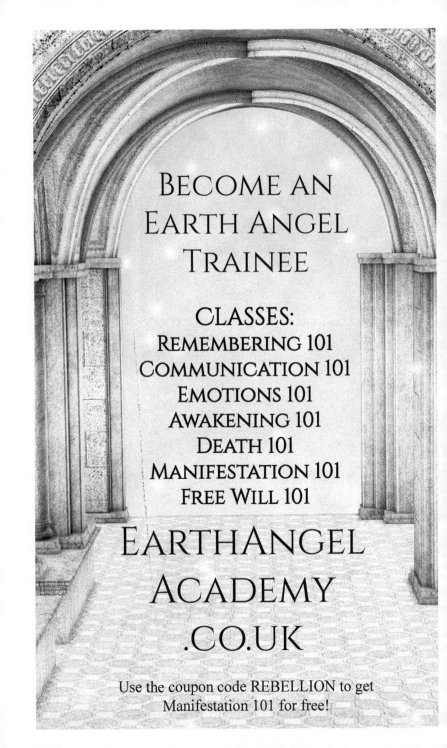

JOIN THE

EARTH ANGEL SERIES FAN CLUB!

And receive monthly letters, a selection of Earth Angel Series goodies, like limited edition prints, postcards, bookmarks or badges in the mail every month!

Visit

michellegordon.co.uk/fanclub

and sign up for just £5 (€6/$7) a month.

You'll also receive special offers and get inside information on the series before everyone else.

Full details and terms and conditions on my website. You can cancel at anytime, but I'm sure you will find that you will love the magickal packages!

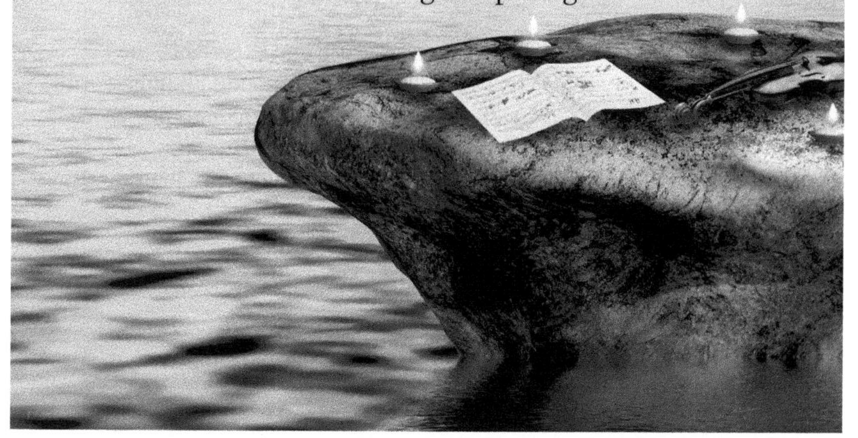

Lightning Source UK Ltd.
Milton Keynes UK
UKHW012352141218
334014UK00014B/1021/P